"YOU TASTE LIKE BLACKBERRIES," MICHAEL WHISPERED INTO HER MOUTH.

Shayna swallowed the comment, along with his desire. With their lips still locked, he ran his hand up and down her arm, stroking the skin, squeezing her hand in his. His lips left hers to trail kisses down to her neck and collarbone. He looked deep into her eyes. "I don't want to hurt you." She simply nodded, words blocked by a need, an urgency for her to throw caution to the wind. . . .

Praise for Zuri Day

"Day's sensuous African American romance offers new proof of the old saying, opposites attract."
—Booklist on *Lovin' Blue*

". . . sexy and entertaining . . . Day was able to weave a clever story of love, trust, acceptance and forgiveness."
—APOOO BookClub on *Love in Play*

Also by Zuri Day

Lies Lovers Tell

Body by Night

Lessons from a Younger Lover

What Love Tastes Like

Lovin' Blue

Love in Play

Heat Wave (with Donna Hill and Niobia Bryant)

Published by Dafina Books

Love
ON THE RUN
A Morgan Man Novel

ZURI DAY

Dafina
BOOKS

Kensington Publishing Corp.
http://www.kensingtonbooks.com

DAFINA BOOKS are published by

Kensington Publishing Corp.
119 West 40th Street
New York, NY 10018

All Kensington Titles, Imprints, and Distributed Lines are available at special quantity discounts for bulk purchases for sales promotions, premiums, fund-raising, and educational or institutional use. Special book excerpts or customized printings can also be created to fit specific needs. For details, write or phone the office of the Kensington special sales manager: Kensington Publishing Corp., 119 West 40th Street, New York, NY 10018, attn: Special Sales Department, Phone: 1-800-221-2647.

Dafina and the Dafina logo Reg. U.S. Pat. & TM Off.

First trade paperback printing: November 2012

ISBN-13: 978-0-7582-7511-0
ISBN-10: 0-7582-7511-0

10 9 8 7 6 5 4 3 2

Printed in the United States of America

For those running from, and running to . . .

ACKNOWLEDGMENTS

A huge hug to editor extraordinaire Selena James and Team Zuri at Kensington. More love than the heart can hold to all of the book clubs, readers, supporters, and fans whose ongoing support is why you're holding another Day in your hands! And a special shout out to my niece, Valencia Scott, whose 4 x 400 relay team took first place at the Kansas State Regional Track Meet, leading the Olathe East track team to a first place overall finish at state! Booyow!

1

On a warm, overcast day in late September, the
forever-grooving-always-moving female magnet Michael
Morgan found himself spending a rare day both off
from work and alone. After sexing her to within an
inch of her life, he'd sent his latest conquest—all long
hair (still tangled), long legs (still throbbing), and . . .
well . . . perpetual longing—on her melancholy yet
merry way. As usual when his mind had a spare moment,
his thoughts went to his business—Morgan Sports
Management Corporation—and the athletes he wanted
to add to this successful company's stable. At the top of
the list was former USC standout and recent Olympic
gold medalist Shayna Washington, a woman he'd been
aware of since her college days who he'd learned had just
lost the mediocre sponsor who'd approached her two
years prior. When it came to business, Michael was like
a bloodhound, and he smelled the piquant possibility of
this client oozing across the proverbial promotional
floor. Along with his other numerous talents, Michael
had the ability to see in people what others couldn't, that
indefinable something, that "it" factor, that star quality

that took some from obscure mediocrity to worldwide fame. He sensed that in Shayna Washington, felt there was something there he could work with, and he was excited about the possibility of making things happen.

The ringing phone forced Michael to put these thoughts on pause. "Morgan."

"Hey, baby."

Michael stifled a groan, wishing he'd let the call that had come in as unknown go to voice mail. For the past two months, he'd told Cheryl that it was over. Her parting gifts had been accompanying him on a business trip to Mexico checking out a local baseball star, a luxurious four days that included a five-star hotel suite, candlelight dinners cooked by a personal chef, premium tequila, and a sparkly good-bye gift that, if needed, could be pawned to pay mortage on LA's tony Westside. Why all of this extravagance? Partly because this was simply Michael's style and partly because he genuinely liked Cheryl and hadn't wanted to end their on-again off-again bedtime romps. But now, several years into their intimate acquaintance, she'd become clingy, and then suspicious, and then demanding . . . and then a pain in the butt.

Michael could never be accused of being a dog; he let women know up front—as in before they made love—what time it was. Michael Morgan played for fun, not for keeps. Fortunately for him, most women didn't mind. Most were thankful just to be near his . . . clock. He loved hard and fast, but rarely long, and while it hadn't been his desire to do so, he'd left a trail of broken hearts in his wake.

Broken, but not bitter. A little taste of Morgan pleasure was worth a bit of emotional pain.

But every once in a while he ran into a woman like Cheryl, a woman who didn't want to take no for an answer. So when entanglements reached this point, the solution he employed was simple and straightforward: goodbye. But sometimes the fallout was a bitch.

"Cheryl, you've got to quit calling."

"Michael, how can you just dump me like this?"

Heavy sigh. "I didn't 'just dump you,' Cheryl. I've been telling you for months to back off, that what you're wanting isn't what I'm offering. This has gotten way too complicated. You've got to let it go."

"So what did that mean when we began dating 'officially,' when I escorted you to the NFL honors?"

This is what I get for being soft and giving in. If there was one thing that Michael should have known by now, it was that mixing business with pleasure was like mixing hot sauce with baby formula. Don't do it. *Any minute she's going to start crying, and really work my nerves.* As if on cue, he heard the sniffles, her argument now delivered in part whine, part wistfulness. Michael correctly deduced that she was sad, and very pissed off at his making her that way. "You've been my only one for years, Michael—"

"I told you from the beginning that that wasn't a good idea—"

"And I told you that I didn't want anyone else. There is no one for me but you. I can't forget you"—Michael heard a finger snap—"just like that." Her voice dropped to a vulnerable-sounding whisper. "Can I please come over just for a little while, bring you some of your favorite Thai food, a few sex toys, give you a nice massage . . . ?"

Michael loved to play with Cheryl and her toys. And when it came to massages, he gave as good as he got. And then there was the sincerity he heard amid her tears. He almost relented. Almost. . .but not quite.

"Cheryl, every time you've asked, I've been honest.

Our relationship was never exclusive. I never thought of us as anything more than what it was—two people enjoying the moment and each other. I'll always think well of you, Cheryl. But please don't put us through this. You're a good woman, and there's a good man out there for you who wants what you want, the picket fence and all that. That man is not me. I'm sorry. I want the best for you. And I want you to move on with your life." He heard his other cell phone ringing and walked over to where it sat charging on the bar counter. *Valerie.* "Look, Cheryl, I have to go."

"But, Michael, I'm only five minutes from your house. I can—"

You can keep it moving, baby. I told you from the beginning this was for fun, not forever. Michael tapped the screen of his iPhone as he reached for his BlackBerry. "Hey, gorgeous," he said into the other phone.

"Hey yourself," a sultry voice replied.

"Michael!" *Oh, damn!* Michael looked down at the iPhone screen to see that the call from Cheryl was still connected. "Michael, who is that bit—" Michael pressed and held the End button, silently cursing himself for not being careful.

"Michael, are you there?"

"Yes, Valerie."

"Whose was that voice I heard?"

"A friend of mine. Do you have a problem with that?" Michael had never hidden the fact that when it came to women, he was a multitasker, especially among the women he juggled. But the situation with Cheryl had him very aware of the need to make that point perfectly clear, up front and often. If a woman couldn't understand that when it came to his love she was part of a team, then she'd have to get traded.

"Not at all," the sultry voice pouted. "Whatever she can do, I can do better."

That's how you play it, player! "No doubt," Michael replied as his iPhone rang again. *Unknown caller.* He ignored it. *Sheesh! Maybe I'm getting too old for this.* Just then, his house phone rang. "Hello?"

"Hey, sexy!"

Paia? Back from Europe already? "Hey, beautiful. Hold on a minute." And then into the BlackBerry, "Look, Valerie, I'll call you back."

"Okay, lover, but don't make me wait too long."

"Who's Valerie?"

The iPhone again. *Unknown caller.* Michael turned off the iPhone. *Cheryl, give it a rest!* "Look, Cheryl—"

"Ha! This is Paia, you adorable asshole. Get it straight!"

Michael inwardly groaned. How could he have forgotten his rule about keeping his women separate and him least confused? Rarely call them by their given name when talking on the phone. *Baby* was fine. *Darling* would do on any given day. *Honey* or *dear* based on the background. Even *pumpkin* or the generic yet acceptable *hey you* were all perfectly good substitutes. But using names, especially upon first taking a phone call, was a serious playboy no-no. *Yeah, man. You're slipping. You need to tighten up your game.* He'd just promoted this beauty to the Top Three Tier—those ladies who were in enviable possession of his home number. He and Paia were technically still in the courting stage— much too early for ruffled feathers or hurt feelings. At six feet tall in her stocking feet, Paia was a runway and high fashion model, an irresistibly sexy mix of African and Asian features. They'd only been dating two months and he wasn't ready to let her go. He even liked the way her name rolled off his tongue. *Pie-a.* No, he didn't want to release her quite yet. "Paia, baby, you know Mr. Big gets lonely when you're gone."

"Uh-huh. Because of that snafu you're going to owe me an uninterrupted weekend with you and that baseball bat you call a penis. You'd better be ready to give me overtime, too!"

"That can be arranged," Michael drawled. "Where are you?"

"I just landed in LA. But we have to move fast. I'm only here for a week and then it's back to Milan. So whatever plans you have tonight, cancel them."

"Ah, man! I can't do that—new client. But I'll call you later." Michael looked at the Caller ID as an incoming call indicator beeped in his ear. "Sweet thing," he said, proud that he was back to the terms of endearment delivered unconsciously. *That's right, Michael. Keep handling yours.* "This is my brother. I've got to go."

"Call me later, Michael."

"Hold on." Michael toggled between the two calls, firing back up his iPhone in the process. "Hey, bro. What's up?" Just four words in and said phone rang. *Jessica!* Unbidden, an image of the busty first-class flight attendant he'd met several months ago popped into his head. *Was it this weekend I was supposed to go with her to Vegas?* "Darling," he said, switching back to Paia, "we'll talk soon." He clicked over. "Gregory, two secs." He could hear his brother laughing as he fielded the other call. "Hey, baby. I'm on the other line. Let me call you back." He tossed down the cell phone. "All right, baby, I'm back."

"Baby?" Gregory queried, his voice full of humor. "I know you love me, fool, but I prefer *bro* or *Doctor* or *Your Highness*!" Michael snorted. "You need to hone your juggling skills, son. Or slow your player roll. Or both."

2

Michael smiled and nodded as he walked from his open-concept living space to the cozy theater down the hall. "What's up, Doc?"

"Man, how many times do I have to check you on that old-ass corny greeting?"

"As many times as you'd like. Doesn't mean I'm going to stop saying it, though. Plus I know it gets on your nerves and you know how much I love that," Michael confessed.

"If all of those skirts chasing you knew just how corny you truly are."

"A long way from those grade school days, huh?"

"For sure," Gregory agreed. "And girls like Robin . . . what was her last name?"

"Ha! Good old Robin Duncan. Broke this brother's fifth-grade heart. And that was after she took my Skittles and the Game Boy I bought her."

"Using that word *bought* rather loosely, don't you think?"

"Okay, I borrowed it from the store."

"And never took it back. Some might define that as stealing."

"Hey, I pay them back every year by donating, generously I might add, to their turkey giveaway. Not to mention my anonymous donation after that arson fire destroyed part of their storefront last year."

"Payback? That's what you call it? Ha! If Mr. Martinez was still alive I'd tell on you myself. But at least you're letting your conscience be your guide."

"No doubt. Say, how is it that you have time to bug me on a Friday night? You work the early shift?" Michael walked over to an oversized black leather theater seat, sat down, and opened up the chair arm console. A moment after he punched a series of buttons, a track meet video appeared on the screen.

Gregory, an emergency medical doctor, was rarely off on weekends, normally pulling twenty-four- to forty-eight-hour shifts between Friday and Monday and often unavailable for calls. "We're training a new intern. Believe it or not, brother, I've got the night off."

"You don't say. So who's going to enjoy the pleasure of your company?"

"I thought about calling the twins. You up for a double?"

The twins Gregory spoke of were longtime friends who'd grown up in the same Long Beach neighborhood as the Morgans. As childhood cohorts, they'd made pinky promises to marry each other. Unfortunately for Michael, one of them was trying to hold him to that bull.

"No, man, that's a code orange. I'm going to have to pass on that."

"Code orange? Lisa still bugging you to make her an honest woman?"

"We both know what Lisa's doing . . . trying to snag

a big bank account. I introduced her to Phalen Snordgrass, told her that he was going to be picked back up this year."

"Talented brother right there. I'm surprised she didn't go for it."

"Man, Lisa picks men more shrewdly than I pick clients. She's looking for someone who has more time left in the NFL than two, three years. I told her she was getting too old to go after the new drafts, that she should stop being so choosy before all of her choices were gone."

"You can handle Lisa's bugging. We haven't hung together for a while. Let's go out."

"No can do, bro."

"Why? What are you doing?"

"Right now I'm watching the female version of Usain Bolt," Michael replied. "And this country's next athletic superstar." He leaned forward, resting his elbows on his knees—as if he had to change positions to view his television screen. His latest electronic purchase was so large that someone manning the space station could see it.

"Is that so? Is she a new client?"

"Just signed her last week. She's coming over for an informal chitchat; we'll just kind of hang out and get a feel for each other."

"She's coming there, to your house?" Michael was sure that this tidbit got Gregory's attention. Michael was long known for not mixing business with pleasure, and bringing a potential client into his Hollywood Hills pleasure palace—revise that, a *female* client to where he lived—definitely sounded more like the latter.

"Yes." Gregory was quiet, and Michael imagined how his brother looked while digesting the story behind that one word. The two men could almost pass for twins themselves with their caramel skin, toned physiques, and megawatt smiles. But Gregory was actually eighteen months younger than Michael's thirty-one years, and two inches shorter than his sibling's six foot two. And while Michael sported a smooth, perfectly shaped bald head, Gregory's closely cropped cut gave him a distinguished look, one completely befitting a man in his profession.

"Shayna's special," Michael continued. "She has that 'it' factor, similar to a Michael Jordan, a Tiger Woods, or, in the world of track and field, a Carl Lewis. This country hasn't seen the likes of her since Flo-Jo."

Gregory knew that his brother spoke of the illustrious Florence Griffith-Joyner, a world-class track star who in the late eighties was known for her bright smile, long colored nails, and flowing mane. "Since when did you start focusing on track and field?"

"Come on, now. You know I never met a sport that I didn't like."

"You never met a woman you didn't like either."

"Aw, man. You wound me. I have very discriminating taste. But Shayna Washington is the real deal; on a good day she's the fastest running female in this country."

"Sounds like a winner, my brother. But I still don't understand why she's going to your home instead of meeting you at the office."

"I thought it might help to loosen her up, have a more casual meeting. When she signed, her lawyer did most of the talking. Other times we've met, she's answered my questions, but not much more than that. If I'm going to rep her, I need to get to know her; I need us to develop a camaraderie and trust. Plus, you know how the tabloids have been on me, ever since that last situation."

"All the more reason not to have her at your house!"

"That's just it. I spot them in or near the office almost every day and that's cool, because security is so on point. But so far my residence is still off their radar."

The downtown-LA skyscraper that housed the Morgan Sports Management offices boasted a very efficient and loyal security staff. And chances were that since it was Friday night, he could have suggested this penthouse spread with its 360-degree panoramic views and contemporary furnishings for their meeting. But he liked to play his cards close to his chest. The competition would know soon enough that he'd just landed the next track star sensation. This was what he told his brother.

"I guess I'll have to roll solo then," Gregory said.

"Look, if the meeting wraps up early I might join y'all for a drink. But if you have to take them both on, I'm sure that will be no problem for you."

"Ha! No, that's more Troy's style."

"Maybe," Michael retorted to the comment about their baby brother. "But it's probably been so long since you've had any that you need a double dose."

"Mind your business, brother. The freak days are long behind me, and believe it or not, I've been thinking more lately about meeting that special woman and settling down."

"Will you please tell Mama that so she'll get off *my* back?"

Gregory laughed. "Better you than me. Look, I probably should let you go. I'll take the twins to dinner, maybe even follow them to the latest Hollywood hot spot. I'll send you a text on where we're headed so you can maybe join us later. I've never known a woman who made you afraid."

"Please. You know better than that." A pause and then, "I'll join you."

"That sounds cool. Until then, have a good time with this new honey."

"Shayna is my newest client. Period. End of story." When the screaming silence transmitted his brother's skepticism, Michael continued. "You just told me I needed to hone my juggling skills. With that being so, do you think I'd be adding yet another player to the roster? Don't get me wrong, though. She is one fine specimen of a female."

"Speaking of fine females, remind me to tell you about Troy's latest situation. That boy's a trip." The youngest Morgan was a bigger playboy than Michael and Gregory combined: a fact on which all three brothers agreed.

"You met her?" Michael's eyes never left the big screen. He smiled as Shayna crossed the finish line a full two strides ahead of the second-place winner.

"Not exactly. Stopped at the Ritz for breakfast and saw them cross the lobby. They were on their way out of the hotel."

"How did she look?"

"Very happy," was Gregory's deadpan reply.

Michael laughed. "Sounds like young bro is doing his thing. And speaking of, I need to get back to doing mine." After again promising Gregory to meet him and the twins, Michael ended the call and got back down to work. Reaching for his beer before leaning back against his plush, custom-made, tan leather couch, he forwarded the Washington DVD to an interview she'd recently done on ESPN. While a bit timid for his liking, she was poised and well-spoken. Further, a certain kind of fire burned in her bright brown eyes tinged with hazel. For a split second, Michael wondered what it would be like to stoke her flame. He discarded the idea just as quickly. He would never again date a client. *Ever.* This lesson had been learned the hard way, when a determined baller with the LA Sparks had refused to accept that their passionate yet short-lived love affair was over. *Just like Cheryl.* He'd finally had to file a restraining order and she'd tried her best to sully his name. *Dang, is Cheryl going to make me have to do that again?* Thanks to his baby brother Troy's top-rate investigative skills, the near-smear campaign barely got off the ground before it was extinguished. Instead, the security firm owner had pulled in a couple favors and the former female phenomenon had been convinced—in an intellectual rather than forceful way—that damaging the Morgan name was not in her best interests. Last he heard, she'd moved to Denver and was dating a Bronco. *Ride on, b-baller, ride on.*

Michael leaned forward once again as images from Shayna attending last year's ESPY awards filled up the screen. She'd looked gorgeous that night: tight red dress on her stacked chocolate body, five-inch heels, and spiky short hair that highlighted her perfect facial features. Unlike many female track stars with strenuous workouts, Shayna's chest was not flat. She still had her girls and they were perched against the low-cut dress in a way that almost made Michael's mouth water. *Never again,* Michael thought, even as his mind conjured up his mouth and Shayna's breasts in an up-close and personal get-to-know. *This meeting is strictly business.* He placed his legs apart and adjusted a rapidly hardening Mr. Big, repeating the words aloud this time. "Strictly business." And then he worked very hard to believe them.

Yeah, right. Good luck with that.

3

Shayna eased off the gas as she reached the light at the famous intersection of Hollywood and Vine. She focused on the crowd of people crossing the street: obvious and not so obvious tourists blending with the obvious and not so obvious homeless, skateboarding teens, and harried businessmen, and a sidewalk preacher holding up a sign reading: JOHN 3:16. Glad for the diversion, Shayna silently mouthed the crudely written words: FOR GOD SO LOVED THE WORLD THAT HE GAVE HIS ONLY BEGOTTEN SON, THAT WHOSOEVER BELIEVETH IN HIM SHALL——

The blaring horn from the car behind her propelled Shayna into action. Switching from brake to gas pedal, she looked into the rearview mirror and threw up an apologetic hand in the process.

What—or more specifically, who—she thought she saw behind the car that had blared the horn sidetracked her once again. Screeching brakes and another long horn blare, this one accompanied by curse words, filled the air as the SUV changed lanes to pass her, holding up the universal digital symbol to underscore his displeasure.

Yeah, buddy, I feel you. After everything Shayna had gone through in the past month, it was a wonder that her attitude wasn't eff it all! But having that outlook would have been shortsighted because Shayna had things to be thankful for. Yes, even though her ex-personal-trainer-slash-former-classmate-slash-former-best-friend had turned into a playa-playa-play-on-slash-harassing-fool-who'd-lost-his-mind and turned her world upside down. But on the flip side, life was calmer since she'd paid a personal visit to his mother and pleaded her case, and his mother had told him to leave her the hell alone. Thank God that saga was over. *Wasn't it?* Then why was her heart in her throat because of what she could have sworn she'd seen in her rearview mirror. A shiny black Beamer belonging to . . .

Calm down, Shayna. How would he know you're in Hollywood, and why would he follow you even if he did? Dude is many things, but a stalker isn't one of them. Girl, there are thousands of black Beamers in southern LA. Millions, no doubt. It was likely that a fair percentage of said black Beamers were driven by dark-skinned black men with squinty eyes and short hair. And what was that about everyone having a twin? Yeah, that's it. Her crazy ex's worldwide twin just happened to be on Hollywood Boulevard, just behind the impatient SUV whose driver had performed a flip-the-bird drive-by.

Then again, she could have been hallucinating because now, despite glances into the mirror every nanosecond or so, not only did she not see a black Beamer, she seemed not to be able to find any Beamer of any color anywhere. She was tripping, plain and simple. What other explanation could there be?

The GPS instructed Shayna to make a left at the next corner. She switched lanes and also changed thoughts, from exes who might stalk her to the saint who would save her: Michael Morgan, the hotshot sports manager for whom she had just two words.

Day-yum!

She fought the thoughts that assailed her as she expertly navigated the curved, narrow streets leading to his place in the Hollywood Hills. Not too far from the Hollywood sign, he'd told her. Better to think of the house than the man inside it. It would do her no good to let her imagination run wild, as she had from time to time since being approached by Michael's assistant and having the "my people will call your people" convo before the first face to face meeting. Having done her homework, she was totally prepared for his confident presentation and astute knowledge of her storied career. Googling his image had even steadied her for his classic good looks. What had thrown her when she'd actually met him was the raw masculinity, the steaming sexuality that fairly radiated from his body and, more importantly, her body's reaction to it. Her attorney had handled the bulk of the conversation during that and subsequent meetings. She'd played it cool and calm when she was actually hot and bothered. Her mind had been focused on simply remembering to breathe and trying to appear unaffected when she was anything but. Thank goodness that was all behind her. According to her roommate-slash-busybody-slash-good friend Talisha, Michael Morgan and his brothers were notorious womanizers who fancied exotically beautiful women with long hair and even longer pedigrees. Now that she knew this truth, there was nothing for her to worry about. He wouldn't come on to her and she most definitely was not going to flirt with him. Just thinking of the last tidbit her roommate had shared, about Michael and his brother Gregory having famously dated twins at one time or another, maybe even swapping and/or sharing them, made her stomach roil. This information nipped all romantic attraction and fanciful imaginings in the bud. Granted, adults were free to do what they wanted but from Shayna's point of view, some things were just plain nasty!

Then why is your kundalini still tingling when you think about him? Because in spite of what she'd heard about him, there was something about Michael that she liked. He'd not only been the perfect gentleman during their meeting, but a very astute and intelligent one as well. She'd been more than a little impressed.

But she'd give Halle Berry, Whoopi Goldberg, Hattie McDaniel, and Octavia Spencer a run for their Academy Award–winning money before Michael would ever know how she really felt.

As if on cue her cell phone vibrated, reminding her of why she'd never cross the line when it came to her relationship with Michael Morgan. It was hard enough to end a strictly romantic liaison, let alone the kind she'd had with her ex, one with history and professional career and other strings attached. She reached over and silenced the phone. Within seconds, the vibration returned.

Looks like my mama-reprieve is over. Her ex was back to blowing up her cell.

Shayna almost grimaced as she ignored yet another call. *Please get a life and leave mine alone.* Talking with *his* mother now seems to have only been a temporary deterrent, and calling *her* mother was absolutely useless. Not only did Shayna's mother, Beverly Powell, view Shayna's ex as a son, but Shayna's ex was now also her brother-in-law. Confused much? Then you know how Shayna felt when she received the mind-altering and life-changing news: that her forty-three-year-old mother had married her ex's thirty-two-year-old brother. By this time, Shayna's relationship with her off-and-on boyfriend of ten years was more off than on, and when she'd ended things for good a few months back, her mother's situation had thrown a serious hitch in the breakup giddyup. Shayna realized she was frowning and tried to relax. Hard to do when her mother was such a trip. *Why'd she have to go and make things so complicated?*

"Your destination is on the right."

Shayna gave a silent thank you to her GPS genie. If not for the advanced technological device, she'd have had no idea that this was in fact her destination or even that a house lay beyond what looked like a tropical jungle. She pulled into the driveway where more of the yard was visible. Large palm trees anchored an ivy-covered fence and just beyond that was a water feature and a profusion of exotic flowers, though bird of paradise was the only one that Shayna recognized. A curved, cobblestone walkway could be seen beyond the wrought-iron gate with steps hinting that more beauty lay beyond what her eye could presently see.

Impressive.

For the first time since the celebratory toast with her attorney, Shayna allowed herself to get just a little bit excited. Until now, she'd held on to her glee. Why? Because for Shayna Washington, life had had a way of showing her that not only was all that glittered not gold, but that what often held the dazzle of a ten-carat diamond was actually some cubic zirconium madness. How excited had she been when her former best-friend-slash-PT-slash-boyfriend had told her about an iron-clad, no-risk, pinky-promise-really-I-mean-it investment where she could double the twenty-five thousand dollars—her life savings—in six months and they could move in to the condo she wanted.

Very excited.

So much so that when the money disappeared two months later she still moved her now penniless but still credit-score-strong foolish self into a rental apartment with the man who'd squandered her life savings. "More money's coming, baby," was his mantra for months, as the bills mounted and the rent, when paid, was usually late. Then came the wake up call: returning from a track meet to see a yellow-noted greeting from the sheriff's department. Congratulations on your gold medal. You've got forty-eight hours to get the bump out. Okay, she'd imagined the congratulations part, but the eviction notice had been all too real. Thank God for her USC college buds, track mates, and good friends Talisha and Brittney. They'd moved her into their place without one I-told-you-so. Though both of them had. Many times. And when their lease was up shortly thereafter they'd suggested getting a place large enough for the three of them. That was the Culver City apartment where Shayna now lived. Their friendship and unwavering support had given her the courage to finally kick her first love to the curb for good, and to put up a permanent roadblock to her heart.

Like now, as she ignored the phone that vibrated for the third time in less than three minutes. She'd known her ex for more than half her life and while he'd acted crazy before, it had never been like this. *What's up with dude?*

Determined to focus on her future instead of her past, Shayna took a deep breath, a last look in the mirror, and stepped out of her pride and joy, the top of the line Hyundai that was a part of her last winner's package. It was one of the few "luxuries" that remained of the past two years' modest yet ever-increasing success. *Okay. Admit it. You are excited about this partnership with that manly mass of muscles masquerading as Michael Morgan.* As she unlatched the gate and walked through the Garden of Eden that was her newly acquired sports manager's front yard, Shayna reminded herself to keep this shred of excitement under wraps. She rang the doorbell at the same time her phone vibrated. Again. No problem with dialing down her thrill meter. Her ex was making sure that she ix-nay the green light that beckoned her to a fling with Michael Morgan, and keep her eyes firmly on the caution light that was flashing *business only.*

4

"Shayna the Sprintress!" Michael smiled broadly as he stepped outside his door.

"Ha! Sprint what?" Michael's wacky-sounding comment dissipated the churning sensation that returned full force as soon as Shayna saw him—the sensation she'd relaxed on her slow walk to the door, when she'd felt nerves similar to those experienced before a race. She'd pulled in a deep breath through her nose and released it through her mouth. She'd felt better, even as she noticed and appreciated the beauty and quiet sanctity of the front yard garden, the Buddha statue welcoming those who followed the cobblestone walkway to the side of the house, and the water feature that spilled into a koi-filled pond. Now just seconds into seeing him again and that sexy smile was stirring up nerves once more. And not just in her stomach either. No, action or rather the desire for action was working on a whole other set of nerves in a whole other area. *Later for that, Shayna. Focus!*

"Sprintress," Michael repeated, after giving Shayna a brief hug. He casually took her hand and guided her inside his perfectly appointed home. "The next California Angels Track Team Superstar."

One of those touchy-feely affectionate kind, Shayna thought, forcing herself not to jerk her hand from his. He'd been this way during their other two meetings—too ready to touch her with an innocent enough hand on her arm or around her shoulder as she'd left his office the last time. "What's does that mean?" she asked, determined to keep her mind on what she was there for, and remembering that she wasn't there for him to touch this or feel that.

"You know, like countess or highness. You're going to be part of track world royalty, so hey . . . I'm thinking sprintress is a cool moniker."

Shayna's expression was dubious as she looked around. "I don't know about that." She was pleasantly surprised to see that Michael's home was not the stereotypical bachelor pad; no black leather, fur rugs, or stacked dirty dishes anywhere. Instead there were manly yet muted tones of browns and blues, navy mostly, contrasted with silver (or was it platinum?) fixtures, light bamboo flooring, and splashes of color courtesy of pricey art hung in strategic places. But the hands-down showstopper was the view of the backyard just beyond the floor-to-ceiling glass that made up the entire back wall, where the most luxuriously styled pool that she'd ever seen in real life commanded center stage. There was foliage, furniture, and a sunken fire pit that looked warm and inviting, and the typical sterile-looking concrete that surrounded most backyard pools was nowhere in sight. A large fountain sprayed water between the pool and the spa, and the turquoise-colored water made her want to jump in. The man beside her reeking of sex appeal made her want to jump in there with him. Naked.

Shayna, this isn't like you. You don't fawn over men. You are focused and disciplined. Now, act like it! Her chin rose just a tad as she discreetly continued taking calming breaths while seeming to eye his place. For the first few seconds, however, girlfriend hadn't really seen a thing!

Michael smiled as he watched Shayna check out his place. He'd purchased the fifties-style home two years ago and had it totally updated and renovated to suit the newest interior design trends and his particular tastes. Then he'd hired one of the country's preeminent designers to lay it out. He'd made sure that it didn't look like a man cave, but it definitely was a love lair. The women who'd been captured by his spell by the pool, in the pool, and just after coming out of the pool were too numerous to count. Looking at his newest client brought seduction to mind once again. "Like what you see?" he finally asked her.

Shayna pulled her eyes away from the stunning pool setting and back to Michael. "Very much," she said, then blushed at the double entendre before quickly turning away.

Me, too. "Please, let's have a seat in the living room. I'm going to have some orange juice. Would you like that, or something else to drink?"

"Orange juice sounds good."

"Cool. Be right back."

Michael left the room. Shayna resisted the urge for a closer examination of all the fine furnishings and instead checked her clothing—a beautifully tailored off-white pantsuit that complemented her curvy frame and dark chocolate skin—before adopting a ladylike position as she sat on the couch. No small feat since she was much more comfortable in a tee and track shorts, but she hoped she looked properly professional. The well-known (and roommate-drilled) fact that the Morgan brothers were playboys had Shayna fully prepared to let him know that her interest in him was about money, not manhood.

A fact that was easier said than done as Mr. Manhood came around the corner bearing two large glasses of fresh-squeezed juice, and Shayna's preparation was replaced with punanny pulsations. She'd purposely kept her eyes firmly on his during their greeting, before turning her attention to his place to further tamp down the blatant attraction she tried to ignore. But there was no getting around how fine her new manager looked in his casual attire of jeans and stark-white button-down shirt. He was built like a man who was no stranger to a gym. And tall, over six feet, Shayna figured. But in her seated position he seemed even taller. His presence fairly dominated the room.

"It's all about branding," Michael began, handing Shayna her orange juice and setting a stone coaster within reach before taking a seat on the couch. "Highlighting those unique qualities that make you stand out, and developing the position, situation, or product that when people see or hear about it, they automatically think of you." He took a sip of orange juice, placed it on his coaster, and continued.

"You remind me of Flo-Jo." Shayna's brows rose, knowing she looked nothing like Florence Griffith-Joyner. "Not in looks—y'all are opposites in that regard. But like her, you have that spark, that special thing, that indefinable something that makes people notice when you walk in a room, that makes people smile for no reason." Michael grinned. Shayna pulsated. "When I say her name, what do you think of?"

Shayna answered without hesitation. "Long hair and nails, stepping on the track looking like a fashion model."

"The one-legged long pant outfits."

Shayna nodded. "Those outfits were off the charts."

"Not to mention her record-breaking sprinting ability."

"No doubt." Though she'd only been two years old in 1988 when Flo-Jo set records at the Summer Olympics in Seoul, South Korea, Shayna had idolized the former track star since grade school, when a physical education teacher said Shayna reminded him of her. "Who's that?" Shayna had asked him. The teacher not only told her, but showed her. Turns out he'd been a huge fan and had photo albums filled with pictures and newspaper clippings of the running phenom. Sixth grade, that's when Shayna decided she wanted to be a track star. Like Flo-Jo.

"It's the same with all great athletes. They all have a trademark something. Michael Johnson had the trademark gold shoes; Michael Jordan, the trademark three-pointers and hook shots with his tongue hanging out. Venus and Serena changed what women wear and how women play on the tennis court; Phelps made swimming cool. They—" He was interrupted by the sound of a vibrating phone. Shayna immediately tensed up. Michael, who didn't miss much, didn't miss this. "You need to get that?"

"No," Shayna quickly replied, reaching for her phone. "I should have turned it off." She did so, her frown fleeting as she recognized the number of the texted message before dropping the phone back down into her bag.

Fleeting though it was, Michael noticed the flash of concern on Shayna's face. "You sure everything's all right?" Shayna nodded. "Because as your manager, I need to be able to trust that you're keeping it one hundred, and vice versa. I know that trust and respect are earned, and I plan to do that. But anything happening in your life that might affect you publicly, quite simply, I need to know about it."

"Okay," Shayna replied, wishing her voice sounded more confident. She cleared her throat. "Of course."

"So where were we? Ah, yes. Talking about 'the Sprintress.'"

Shayna rolled her eyes.

"Okay, maybe not, but you see where I'm headed."

"Away from that crazy nickname, I hope."

"Ha!"

A young black man sat parked on the side of the road in his black Beamer, silently fuming, creased brows and narrowed lips marring his otherwise handsome face. Suddenly, he jerked up the phone that he'd earlier tossed on the passenger seat and angrily punched the face next to the name on his Android, ready to punch her for real if she didn't answer. The call went straight to voice mail.

"Dammit, Shayna, answer the phone!" He threw down the phone again and slammed his fist against the soft, leather seat. "I can't believe that you're dogging me like this! We've been through too much for you to keep ignoring me!" He picked up the phone and then, knowing how all of the other attempts had ended, calmly placed it beside him and reached for his keys. "I've had it with this bullshit. You may not talk to me over the phone," he mumbled, bicep muscles rippling as his hand squeezed the wheel, "but I bet you'll talk to me before the day is over."

5

While anger was simmering elsewhere, a level of comfort was being found in Hollywood Hills.

"Anyway," Michael finished, "the world will never know that their oh-so-macho running back would rather dance with a tight end, if you know what I'm saying." Michael's eyes twinkled as he watched Shayna react with neck-thrown-back laughter.

"We didn't want to believe it," Shayna replied, speaking of the former classmate she knew who'd turned pro publicly and was gay privately. "When we were in school, he'd be the first one to call out some dude for acting feminine and all the time he was the one in the closet."

"Boisterous commenting is sometimes a red flag, with the loudest critic being the biggest hypocrite."

"But how did you find out? I mean, I know because he and I have been friends since high school. But you can count on one hand those who know his secret. And here you not only have the information, but in this day of no privacy for professionals, you've managed to keep it under wraps. How do you do it?"

Michael's response was deadpan, all matter of fact, no cockiness. "I'm good at my job."

Shayna's response was equally sincere. "I believe you."

They looked into each other's eyes and for a moment, a brief, unchecked moment, something passed between them. Something both recognized, but neither acknowledged. The atmosphere changed in the room. Heat that had nothing to do with the weather. The afternoon meeting lasted into the evening, their brand brainstorming punctuated by snippets of personal information and tiny windows into each other's lives. For Shayna, the discomfort of being around Michael dissipated and for Michael, the options for making Shayna a one-name star grew with each moment spent in her presence.

"Are you hungry?" Michael asked after checking his watch, surprised that so much time had passed.

"A little." Had she dared been honest with herself she would have added that what she desired was sitting in front of her, not in the kitchen.

"Then please excuse me for a moment." Michael left the room.

Okay, is this brothah getting ready to cook for me? The thought of those sexy biceps rippling as they stirred a sauce or flipped a burger made Shayna's mouth water more than the thought of food. *Naw, he's probably calling a restaurant to have something delivered.*

He was doing neither. After locating and having a brief conversation with Orlando, the chef who worked for him three to four days a week depending on his travel schedule, Michael sent Gregory a quick text: Meeting running long. Will call when done.

An hour later Michael and Shayna sat on the patio, having enjoyed the Thai food that Orlando had prepared, sipped bubbly that either rarely imbibed, and now relaxed in the beauty of a warm, autumn evening. And still the heat, pulsating and vibrant, like a third guest. Felt yet ignored. For both, there was a running inner dialogue that this was strictly business. A lie, but it sounded good in their minds.

The chef removed the dinner plates and set down dessert. As soon as he'd retreated into the house, Shayna picked up her spoon and dug into the creamy gelato creation. "Is this you every night?"

"What?" Michael didn't reach for his dessert. He was too busy enjoying the chocolate sweetness on the other side of the patio table, and wishing that he could have a lick of her instead of the ice cream in his bowl.

"This," Shayna said with a sweep of her arm across the table. "Chef-prepared dinners, moonlight dips in the pool, champagne wishes, and caviar dreams . . ."

Michael shrugged. "You could say that, but then again . . ." Another shrug. "It's not something that I think about. As I told you earlier, my growing up in Long Beach was fairly typical, pretty solidly middle class. Guess you could say this is my new normal."

"It's a pretty nice normal." For a brief moment, Shayna closed her eyes and focused on the ambrosia of flavors on her tongue. The deepest, darkest of chocolates, but she could detect other flavors, cinnamon and vanilla among them. "Wow, this is heaven right here, heaven in a bowl."

"Yeah, Orlando is the real deal. He can do it all: cook, bake, and make desserts like this. I stole him from one of my favorite eateries on the Strip, haven't been able to set foot back into that restaurant since!"

"I can see why; his food is amazing." Another couple bites and then Shayna continued. "How did you get into this, managing athletes?"

"I always loved sports, especially tennis. But by the time I'd graduated college, I'd learned that the best way to secure a long-term career in this arena was not to play a game, but rather to manage those who played each of them best. I started managing my college classmates' careers, securing promotional opportunities and endorsement deals. Some turned pro: football, basketball, a few tennis buddies, and a couple baseball stars. Before you know it I had a reputation and my own company."

"How old were you when you formed your company?"

"Twenty-three."

"Wow. A bit young for such mature decisions."

"I'm pretty sure of myself when I know what I want."

A frozen moment. Looks exchanged. And again. The heat.

"You were lucky to know your path so early." Aside from being successful in track, Shayna had no idea what she wanted her life to look like.

"I didn't always know," Michael explained, finally reaching for his spoon and scooping up a bite of the decadent gelato. "During college, my goal was to become a tennis star. I'm a huge fan of all sports, but tennis is still my favorite."

"You went to that other school, right?"

Michael chuckled at Shayna's reference to USC's rival, UCLA. "You mean the better school?"

"Here we go," Shayna intoned with a roll of the eyes. "Looks like I'm going to have to *school* you on some things."

"You know what they say. Don't start none, won't be none." He took another bite of the dessert. "Yeah, Big O did it again." After swallowing the substance that melted in his mouth, he agreed with Shayna. "This stuff is righteous."

"So if you were so focused on playing, how did you go from wanting to be a tennis star to managing people like me?"

"Injury in my junior year, at the same time a high-powered agent was talking to me about financial opportunities once I turned pro. He used to represent all the greats in basketball, football, baseball, you name it. The more he talked, the more I began thinking about a career doing what he did instead of what had me limping. At that time he'd already been in the business twenty years, much longer than I'd be able to reign on the court."

This was news to Shayna. Michael struck her as an invincible god who hadn't a care in the world and always got what he wanted. Unlike her, for whom "life had been no crystal stair." She'd read up on his background and didn't remember seeing anything about an injury. "I don't think I've ever read anything about your being hurt."

"That was by the design of that high-powered agent I mentioned. He made sure that everything was kept under wraps."

"Why?"

Again, that one-shoulder shrug that Shayna was quickly learning was a Michael Morgan reflex action. "Why highlight a weakness?"

Good question, one that in the coming months would serve Shayna well.

When she looked at her watch, Shayna was shocked to see it was just past nine p.m. The time had gone by faster than a 4 x 400 relay. She was pleased with the progress they'd made, and convinced that as much as she enjoyed her privacy and was slow to take people into her inner circle, she knew that signing on with Morgan Sports Management was a good thing. Michael looked at his watch as well. It dawned on Shayna that this was

Friday night, and she'd probably worn out her welcome by about, oh, three, four hours or so. Had she really been at his house for six hours? The time had flown by so quickly!

"It's getting late," she said, taking time to stretch before she stood. "Thanks for dinner."

"No worries at all." Michael stood as well, trying to ignore the feeling of discomfort at the thought of her leaving. "I'm excited about our partnership, and will contact you next week to set up a tentative PR schedule for the next three to six months."

They reached the door. Shayna held out her hand. "Thanks for everything, Michael." Again she mentally denied that there was any attraction. But her rapidly beating heart told a different story.

"I was born here, but my roots are southern; grandparents were born and raised in the red dirt of Georgia," Michael said, bypassing her hand for a quick embrace. "We prefer hugs over handshakes."

Minutes later, Shayna zipped down the circular road and turned onto Sunset Strip. She pondered the feelings surrounding her meeting with Michael and was surprised at the label she put on her mood—hopeful. Yes, that was it. Shayna laughed out loud. She hadn't felt this happy since, well, in a very long time. Even when tackling sticky subjects, like Shayna's fear of being exploited, Michael was open and straightforward. She smiled, feeling particularly proud of standing up for herself by reiterating words her attorney had spoken during the signing. "I don't plan on being the athlete so caught up in the game that they forget the business," she'd told Michael earlier, her eyes unblinking. "Leaving the sports world with nothing to show for all the hard work I've put in." Smiling, she remembered Michael's answer. "When it comes to business and my clients, I believe in being totally transparent. That's why I insist on independent accounting, as well as your right to view the books twice a year. I didn't come after you to hustle you," he'd continued, his dark eyes framed by long curly lashes looking totally sincere. "I came after you because I believe in you."

The frenzied Friday night traffic slowed, allowing Shayna the chance to take in her surroundings. Traipsing through Hollywood was a rare occurrence, and she marveled at the facelift this iconic city had been given. On a whim, Shayna spotted a novelty shop and pulled over. She and Michael had brainstormed on what could be her trademark. They'd tossed around a variety of ideas, but none of them fit. She pulled into a parking space, hoping to go inside the shop and get inspired.

She was so fixated on the display in the window that she paid no attention to who watched her from across the street, whose eyes narrowed and fists clenched as he began walking toward her.

6

"Hey man, where are you?" Gregory's raised voice cut through the din of the noise in the private club.

"On my way," Michael replied.

"You said you'd be here an hour ago."

"Didn't you get my text? The meeting ran late."

"Did it run into the bedroom?"

"Ha! My rule about not mixing business with pleasure has not been broken. They still there?"

"Yes, but your girl is being seriously hit on by one of my colleagues. You might want to add some urgency to your stroll."

"Trust me, her having a distraction is a good thing," Michael replied, walking into his dressing room and pulling out black slacks to replace his casual jeans. "Have you already forgotten what I told you earlier? That she's been asking about moving into marital territory?"

A bit of silence, and then, "Y'all have been messing around off and on since high school. I'd say that's a fair question."

"Really? Did I miss your and Lori's wedding announcement?"

"Come on, bro. That's a totally different story."

"Why, because it stars you instead of me?"

"Because Lori isn't interested in marriage and motherhood; she's all about being Miss Hollywood, which suits me just fine."

"Yeah, whatever, man." Michael looked at his screen as a beep signaled an incoming call. "Gregory, I've got to go. This is the call I've been waiting for."

"Please don't tell me it's another client."

"Okay, I won't. I'll text you when I'm on my way."

Michael clicked over to take the call from China, and the superstar basketball player who'd soon be playing for the Nevada Nighthawks. "*Nǐ hǎo,* Huang Chen," he answered in his best broken Mandarin Chinese. *"Zěnmeyàng?"* All thoughts of partying left as Michael listened to this potentially lucrative client tell him exactly what was up.

Browsing the store's interestingly stuffed aisles, Shayna pulled out her phone. She could just imagine her roommates with their heads together, trying to guess what had happened during her meeting with Michael. A smile reached her lips as she turned on the phone and looked at the screen. Missed calls from both Talisha and Britt. And messages, too! Without scrolling any farther, she accessed her voice mail, clicked her hands-free device, and listened as she browsed.

The automated recording announced that she had fifteen new messages. Shayna stifled a huff, remembering the calls she'd ignored on the way to the appointment with Michael.

"New message."

"Baby, it's—" Shayna quickly pushed the Delete button.

"New message."

"Shayna, why aren't you—" *Delete.*

"New message."

"You're pissing me off—" *Delete.*

More calls from *him,* Tee, Britt, Coach, until she got to the fourteenth message.

"Shayna—Michael Morgan." Why at the mere sound of his voice did her hot spot just do a happy dance? "Just called to let you know how much I enjoyed our meeting, sharing dinner, and getting to know you a little better. By this time next year, everyone will know you by one name—Shayna. Although I still like Shayna the Sprintress. Ha! Have a great weekend. We'll talk next week."

Still smiling, Shayna reached the back wall of the store. It was filled with masks. She picked one up, walked the short distance to the mirror, and lifted the mask to her face as she listened to the next message.

"Shay, it's Britt."

"And Tee," Talisha chimed in. "Yes, we're calling again—"

"—and together this time. We know you have a story," Brittney continued, "since you've had your phone turned off for the last two hours."

"Three," Talisha corrected. "And since you've been with that fine-ass Michael Morgan. Girl, you know you'd better call us back and—"

Laughing, Shayna hit the Call-back key. Talisha answered on the first ring. "Ha! Dang, girl. Were you just sitting there staring at the phone, waiting for me to call?"

"Please," Talisha responded. "It's not even that deep. I just got off the phone with Cameron. He's on his way to pick me up."

"Cool that."

A beat and then, "So?"

"So what?"

"Shay, quit playing." Shayna laughed. Talisha was quiet, and Shayna thought it was probably because she hadn't sounded this carefree in quite some time.

"You must have got some."

"Some what?" Shayna asked coyly.

"Whoa! Did you bang the baton, girl? You didn't!" Silence. "Did you?"

Shayna swallowed her laughter. She loved teasing her roommates, especially nosy, gossipy Talisha, almost as much as she loved running track. "The meeting went very well."

Talisha squealed. Her voice dropped low. "Is he big, girl?"

Shayna pictured Michael's broad shoulders, big hands and feet. *"Very."*

"Are you still at his house?"

She was sorely tempted to keep up the ruse, but figured enough for now. "We're getting together next week." And then, because she couldn't resist, "His lips are amazing." She didn't lie. Every time his eloquently delivered words had spilled out of that mouth, she'd imagined what other feats those thick, cushy lips could perform.

"I'm so mad at you. Okay, I'm jealous. But you did say that there was no way you'd ever get involved with someone you worked with again. I don't blame you, though. . . ."

Shayna's headset beeped. She continued listening to Talisha while pulling out her phone, trying to still her heart even as she hoped it was Michael. *Why? He didn't need to be calling her. She wasn't interested in him like that!* Yeah, right. And if anybody believed that, then they also believed that Biggie, Tupac, and Michael were alive. Shayna's hopes fell as she looked at the screen. Him. Again. She opened the message, intending to delete without reading. But the succinctly worded sentence caught her attention. And momentarily stopped her breath.

> I'm not going to keep being ignored. One way or another ... we're going to talk.

An image of the black beamer she thought she'd seen earlier popped into her mind. Shayna's head whipped around to the front of the store, eyes scanning the aisles. *That couldn't have been him, could it? Shayna stop tripping; that was hours ago. Besides, he's not like that.* Still, she placed the mask back on the shelf and walked to the next aisle. There were wigs and colorful hats with dreadlocks hanging from the rims, and a couple customers . . . but no one familiar. She knew her ex-boyfriend almost as well as she knew herself, and he wasn't normally prone to violence or other uncool acts, like stalking. But ever since the Olympics and the subsequent media coverage she'd received, he'd started acting like a full-fledged fool. But there was no way he'd try and force her to meet with him if she didn't want to. Would he? *Then just what did his 'one way or another' message mean?*

". . . crying if he breaks your heart because, baby, I'm not going to be the one who helps you. . . .Shayna, are you listening?"

"Tee, I've got to go."

Shayna could tell that Talisha had instantly picked up

the mood change. "What's wrong?" All humor was gone from her voice.

"Nothing, I just . . ." She quickly searched every aisle in the store. He wasn't there. *Of course not.*

"What is it, Shay?"

Shayna had no intention of answering that question. Her friends had already dealt with too much of this particular drama. Those last few days before they'd moved to the new place, when her ex showed up on their doorstep at all times of day and night, the roommates' lives had been madness. Had it not been for Talisha's boyfriend, Cameron, one incident in particular may have gotten way out of hand. And when Shayna had finally gathered the courage to break up with him, to tell him that she was leaving him for good, that it was over and she meant it, she vowed they'd never again go through something like that because of her. Summoning up her bravest voice, she responded, "It's nothing, Talisha. Is that the doorbell I hear? Go on out with Cameron and have a good time—but wait. Is Britt at home? I'm too excited about my meeting to go to bed early," she continued in a rush, before Talisha could once again think that something was amiss. "Maybe she'll want to find something to get into." Shayna refused to acknowledge any form of fear where her ex was concerned, but she did admit his message had left her rattled. Hanging out with Brittney would help put his nonstop calling and crazy texting out of her mind.

Shayna heard Talisha greet Cameron before she replied, "No, she went over to her mother's house to see her sister's new baby."

Right, Brittney's an aunt for the second time. Shayna quickly told herself that she was wearing her big girl panties and had no problem being home alone. *He doesn't know where you live, Shay,* she silently reminded herself, even as she finally acknowledged a tinge of fear she had for the man with whom she'd grown up. He'd never been violent. Had never given her reason to be afraid of him. But that was before she'd scored at the Olympics, before her status had increased worldwide, before, she imagined, he saw visions of money bags dancing in his head. In his mind, she'd left him because with her gold medals she suddenly felt as though she was too good for him, as if his possessive domineering behavior, and the woman's panties she'd found on her first night back home after deciding to change the sheets, hadn't played a role at all. That's when the phone calls had ratcheted up to harassment levels, and when she'd cut off all contact as a result.

"Shay, you sure you're all right?"

"I'm fine. Go on, have fun. Tell Cameron I said hi."

Shayna hung up the phone and, as casually as one could be while looking for someone suddenly acting like Charles Manson's stepchild, she moseyed to the front of the store and pretended to look at the postcards, magnets, and shot glasses displayed near the front. Her intent gaze, however, was on the sidewalk just beyond the window. Darkness covered the shadows, but a bright light in front of the building, plus the neon signs across the street, gave her a fairly good view of the area around her. She didn't see him. *And why would I? That man is just trying to get under my skin . . . jealous of my happiness and wanting to bring me down to his ignoramus level.* Shayna refused to let that happen. So after taking another turn around the store, she retrieved the mask she'd earlier admired, purchased it, and waved a cheery good-bye to the cashier as she stepped out the door. Looking to her right, left, and across the street, and determining that the coast was clear, she quickly walked the short distance to her car. She used the remote to unlock the door, and was just two steps away when a strong, determined hand wrapped around her upper arm.

Oh. My. God.

"Make a scene and I'll cut you," the voice hissed into her ear. "Now, come on."

"Let me go!" Pure instinct took over as she tried to loosen the vise-like grip the man had on her arm. *Jarrell?* No, couldn't be. The man's voice was deep, raspy, nothing like that of her ex.

What is he trying to do? Rob me? Or worse? Panic flowed over Shayna like water. Her heart slammed against her chest; her body slammed against the assailant's chest. She realized he was walking them toward a narrow opening in the side of the building. In that moment, a line from an old *Oprah* episode flashed into her head: *Never let your assailant take you to a second location.* No matter what type of weapon this man might have, she had no intention of finding out what was on the other side of the concrete wall. *Arrgh!* Using all her strength, she jerked away from his death grip. Or rather she tried. For an nth of a second, it seemed that freedom was possible. If only her arm wasn't attached to the rest of her body, and if only the attacker hadn't chosen the very moment that she stepped left to go right. The pain that shot through her side and up her shoulder was excruciating, surpassed only by the feeling of air leaving her lungs as the man wrapped his other arm around her waist, lifting her off the ground and trying to carry her—much like a running back would a football—through the narrow opening. The second location.

"Help! Somebody, help!" She was vaguely aware of

people around her, but no one directly came to her aid. With legs flailing and time running out as they both neared the doorway, Shayna summoned superhuman strength and bit down on the arm that held her captive.

"Damn!"

The man's hold loosened for a second, just long enough for Shayna to wriggle out of his grasp. Her left side felt as if it were on fire. No time to think of that now. She headed to her car, but after hearing heavy footsteps hot on her heels, and seeing someone trying to tape the event with a camera phone, she knew that she had to leave the scene as quickly as possible, like yesterday even. So she did the next best thing, that which she did best: run.

But not before she looked back, and locked eyes with her ex-slash-PT-slash-former-childhood-best-friend-slash-man-gone-crazy—Jarrell "Jay" Powell.

7

Michael whistled a tune as he splashed on cologne. His hand stopped midway between his jaw and the bottle, as he thought of Project Shayna—upping the profile of his latest client by first establishing and then expanding her brand. Everybody and their kin was endorsing perfume these days. *What could I call it? Shayna's Secret? The Sprintress? Run Tell This?* "Ha, man, you're crazy." Continuing to look himself in the mirror as he thought about a perfume for the up-and-coming track star, he asked, "Why not?" He made a mental note to add this to the list of possibilities he'd formulated since she'd left his home, along with the cereal commercials, talk show appearances, and maybe even some TV or movie options. *Hmm, maybe we'll even do some type of collaboration between her and Huang Chen, him running and her shooting hoops.* Michael smiled at the thought, his mind racing as he straightened his tie, gave himself one last glance in the mirror, and headed out of the room. He paused in his bedroom just long enough to put on his jewelry— diamond stud, platinum cross, and an understated

Rolex—and grab his suit jacket. He was headed to the garage when the gate bell rang. When expecting guests his gate remained open, but when he headed out of town or out for the evening, he always locked the security gate and activated the alarm.

Looking at his watch, he decided not to answer. *Man, Gregory is going to curse you out as it is.* He slid into the buttery smooth seat of his Jaguar XK, pushed the garage door opener, and eased down the drive. It was a beautiful evening in September, so he decided to drive with the top down. He stopped at the edge of the drive and as the top was making its soundless transition into the compartment at the rear of the car, he checked himself in the mirror before looking to his right, and then his left to back out into the—

WTH? "Shayna!"

The car was barely thrown into park before Michael was out the door and kneeling by his crumpled, heavily breathing new client. He scooped her up. "Aw!"

For the first time, he noticed how she clutched her side. "What happened?" he asked as long strides ate up the distance between the sidewalk and the still opened garage door.

Shayna shook her head, tears of relief now streaming down her cheek as she clutched Michael's shirt, holding on for dear life. Michael gave no thought to the still-running Jaguar as he walked through the kitchen, across the combined living/dining area, and down the hall to his bedroom. It didn't even register that he brought her here and not the guest suite. He gingerly laid her down, but when he tried to pull away, she held on to his shirt.

Her eyes were wild and searching, her voice barely audible. "No."

"Shh, baby, it's okay. My car is still running, and in

the street. I'm just going to pull it into the garage. I'll be right back." He raced down the hall to the front door, pulling out his phone as he did so.

"Gregory."

"Man, where are you?"

"I'm still at home, and need you to get here. Quick." In his urgency, Michael's voice took on a demanding, forceful tone.

"What's up, Michael?"

"I don't know yet. Just hurry. The front door will be unlocked. And bring your medical bag."

"Michael, are you okay?"

There was no answer because Michael had already hung up the phone. He hurried back into his room and found Shayna huddled in a fetal position. His heart clenched at how helpless she looked, how different from the somewhat shy yet laughing woman who'd left his house less than an hour ago. *What in the hell happened?*

Easing down on the bed, he placed a hand on her arm. It must have scared her because she jerked away, and then moaned at the pain the sudden move caused.

"Shayna," Michael tried again, his voice soothing, coaxing. "What happened? Were you in an accident?"

"Attacked," she whispered, so softly that Michael was sure he hadn't heard correctly. Surely he hadn't. He watched her wince as she moved again, and decided to hold off the questions until his brother arrived and examined her. "My brother's a doctor; he's on his way." Feeling as helpless as she looked, he again reached out to stroke her arm. He wanted to ease her pain the way he'd once tried to do with the family dog, a German shepherd named Lucky. Poor canine's luck almost ran out when he chased a ball across the street and was hit by a car. A then seven-year-old Michael was first on the scene. His initial reaction was to run up and put his hands on the dog. Almost got it bitten off. His brother's gift, on the other hand, was already apparent as Gregory joined him seconds later and softly rubbed the dog's nose, and Lucky calmed down almost instantly. Gregory then commanded his brother to run and get a sheet so he could tie off the wound, something he'd seen done on the eighties TV show *St. Elsewhere*. Gregory's ministrations had helped save the dog's life. Lucky lived another five years. Remembering the story about Lucky calmed Michael, and his urgent hand strokes became soft and reassuring. Gregory was on his way. Shayna would be all right.

"Orlando!" Michael called for his chef and then remembered he'd released him for the night. "I'll be right back; I'm just going to get you a glass of water." Upon returning, he turned on the lamp next to the bed. That's when he saw them: scratches, bruises, skin discoloration around her neck. He bristled, the hair on his arms almost standing on end as a thought entered his mind, one that he could barely contemplate, let alone believe. "Shayna," his voice was now low, restrained. "What happened?" So much for waiting for his brother's examination. "Who did this to you?" Fresh tears rolled down Shayna's face. "Baby, I need to know."

Shayna shook her head, as if the mere thought of the person responsible for her injuries caused more pain.

He started to push and then, again, decided to wait for his brother. Gregory's demeanor was less forceful than Michael's; over the years he'd honed and perfected the bedside manner necessary to deal with people in peril. His brother would be able to find out what had gone down. He was sure of it. Once again, he began to ease off the bed and once again, her hand reached out for him. "Please don't . . . leave me," she whispered. "Please."

A rush of something flooded into his heart at this very moment. It would be another several months before he realized that it had even happened, and even more so . . . what that something was.

"I'm right here," Michael answered, his mind filled with possible scenarios of what could have happened and why Shayna was frightened. He remembered how out of breath she was as he lifted her up, as if she'd just run a marathon. His brow creased as he tried to recall if he'd seen her car outside—the cherry red Hyundai that he'd teased her about outside her lawyer's office. He didn't remember seeing it, but then again he'd been busy. Still, it was a car that was hard to miss, even in waning daylight. Had she been carjacked? Robbed? Assaulted? And if so, for what reason? And where? Frustration filled Michael's chest as he took in the reddening scratches and deepening bruises, felt her skin growing cold to the touch. "You're cold. Let me get you a blanket."

He walked to the edge of the bed and opened the chest that had been custom made, along with his bureau and armoire. Pulling out a quilt that had been hand sewn by his maternal grandmother, he started as he heard the front door slam, before remembering that he'd told Gregory to come directly inside.

"Michael!"

"Back here, bro." Knowing that his brother would need to examine her wounds, he placed the quilt over her legs and feet.

Gregory came around the corner and into the room, his steps purposeful, his eyes scrutinizing. "What happened?" he asked, as he placed his satchel on the night-stand and opened it up.

"I don't know," Michael said, rising from the bed as his brother approached. He turned and looked at the woman who just an hour or so ago had left his home with a smile on her face. "Shayna." He adjusted the quilt that he'd placed on her, waited until she opened her eyes. "This is my brother, Gregory. He works at UCLA, and is one of the best doctors in the country. He'll take care of you now, okay?" Shayna nodded, but didn't turn her body to face the men. "Gregory, this is Shayna Washington."

Hearing the name, Gregory's brow rose in surprise. A quick look passed between the brothers. Michael subtly shook his head and Gregory nodded in understanding. They'd talk later. His tone softened as he addressed his charge. "Shayna, like Michael said, I'm Dr. Morgan." Taking off his suit jacket and rolling up his sleeves, he continued. "I just need to ask a few questions so that I can determine what's wrong. Can you lie on your back for me?" Shayna slowly uncoiled from her fetal position, wincing as she did so. "Where does it hurt?"

"Side," she croaked.

"Here, Shayna," Michael said, reaching for the glass. "Drink some water."

Gregory stayed his hand. "Not yet, Michael. Let me first determine what's happening internally. I need to raise you up and remove your jacket," he informed Shayna. "Michael, help me out." Michael held Shayna as motionless as possible while Gregory removed the now torn and soiled off-white creation. After Michael laid her down, Gregory softly placed his hand on Shayna's midsection. "I'm going to apply slight pressure," he said, his voice calm, almost melodic in its delivery. "It may hurt just a bit, but I need to determine if anything's broken. Okay?" Shayna nodded. Gregory placed a hand just underneath her breast and slowly, methodically worked his way down one side and up the other. "Feels like we've got a couple cracked ribs here," he said, moving his hands from her midsection down to her pelvic area, then across to the bruising on her arm. He squeezed the area around her bicep. "Pretty good bruise here, but no fractures or breaks." He noted the bruising around her neck and again, the brothers exchanged glances. "Some pretty nasty scratches, too, but those should heal quickly." He finished his examination and stood. "We'll need to get you to the hospital to get x-rayed," he said, pulling down his shirt sleeves and buttoning the cuffs.

"I'd rather not," Michael quickly interjected. "At least not until we find out what happened. I don't want this turning into negative press."

Gregory nodded. This wasn't the first time he'd had to get creative when it came to his brother's clients. "Very well, then. I'll call a doctor friend of mine and we'll take you over to his private practice. Get you checked out, taped up, and let the healing begin. But first, Shayna, we need to know what happened and who did this."

"My ex-boyfriend," Shayna whispered, her eyes fluttering shut with the pain of his memory. "I stopped . . . on Sunset and he must . . . he must have been following me. Tried to make me . . . go with him."

Michael gritted his teeth as an instant and all-consuming anger arose. There was nothing worse than a man who'd attack a woman, for any reason. "What's his name?" he asked, trying to sound nonchalant when in fact, his hand was already on his phone to call his brother.

"Jarrell," Shayna said. "Jarrell Powell."

"Excuse me a second," Michael said, and left the

room. He walked out of earshot of Shayna and punched a number on speed dial. "Troy."

"What up, big bro?"

Michael ignored the sound of multiple females in the background. "I need you to get the four-one-one on somebody for me."

"Who and why?"

"A man named Jarrell Powell. He just beat up my newest client."

"Damn." A beat and then, "I'm on it, brother."

Michael nodded at the indignation he heard in Troy's voice. "Don't go after him or anything, yet," he warned his hotheaded younger brother. "For right now, I just want to know exactly who I'm dealing with."

This Jarrell Powell dude was about to find out that when you messed with one of Michael Morgan's clients, especially one who made his heart beat the way Shayna Washington did, you'd just pissed off a whole posse better known as the Morgan men.

8

The next day, Shayna and Michael sat talking in the living room. At first she'd been evasive, but after several attempts by Michael to get a bead on Jarrell from Shayna's point of view, along with his assurance that everything she shared would remain confidential between them, she opened up.

"We grew up together, for years lived in the same complex. His mother and my mother were friends, and at one point, he spent as much time at my grandmother's house as I did. When we reached high school, he was the one who really encouraged me to run track. He became my personal trainer. One thing led to another and when I was sixteen . . . we started dating."

"What did your father have to say about that?"

"He's dead."

"I'm sorry."

"It's okay. I never knew him."

Interesting. Michael remembered watching a show about the effect on women who didn't have a father in the home while growing up, how they were much more likely to start dating young, and were more likely to choose the wrong man for the wrong reason. Had that been the case with Shayna? "So Jarrell Powell is your boyfriend." The background check hadn't been extensive, but as with all his clients, he'd had Troy run a profile on her. There had been no arrests, no record of drug use, and no mention of this best friend turned boyfriend who'd played a major role in her life. Obviously, a major piece of information had been overlooked.

"At one time, Jay was my best friend." Shayna looked at Michael, her eyes filled with confusion. "That's why his actions are such a shock. We shared everything, dating steadily through high school and my first two years of college. Then we started having problems, him feeling like he was taking a backseat to track, which he was, and starting to go out with other girls. We were on-again off-again for almost four years until I broke up with him for good right before the Olympics. Needless to say, that decision isn't going over well."

"Yeah, I'm sure he wanted to share your limelight."

"He felt that he deserved it, feels that he's responsible for me being where I am. It's true that he encouraged me back in the day, but I'm the one who's been putting in the work on the track day in and day out. Anything I owed Jarrell I feel I paid back a long time ago."

She sat on the same couch she'd occupied the day before, this time wrapped up in one of Michael's shirts (several sizes too big) and a pair of his shorts (several inches too long). Her ribs were wrapped as well, tightly and expertly. They had gone to Gregory's doctor friend's office last night, where his diagnosis of cracked ribs was confirmed. Two, on her right side. A blood vessel in her throat had been broken, causing a nasty looking purplish splotch, but the other scratches and bruises were superficial. After learning that her car was still on

Sunset, and that last night she'd run from there all the way to his house, Michael had insisted she stay, at least for the night, so that they could decide the best course of action. Shayna didn't want to, felt she'd already been enough of an imposition and should go home. Gregory advised against it while Michael simply informed her that leaving his house in her condition without her roommates there to take care of her and a fool still on the loose was not an option. Period. Having taken the sleep-inducing pain pill that Gregory had offered, there was nothing Shayna could do but leave a message on the phones that neither Talisha nor Brittney were answering to let them know that she was all right and would see them later. Then she'd enjoyed an incredible night's sleep in Michael's room (he'd insisted), and a scrumptious all-American breakfast that Orlando had prepared. And now, here she sat, feeling somewhat surreal, as she shared with Michael the details of her first and only love. Not at all what this twenty-five-year-old had planned for this particular Saturday. But here she was.

Michael reared back in the oversized chair that was positioned across from the couch. His emotions had been turned upside down since seeing Shayna huddled next to his wrought-iron gate. The line between professional and personal was not only blurred, but quickly becoming obliterated. Michael felt an indescribable need to protect Shayna, to take care of her, in a way he'd not only never felt about a client, but had never felt about anyone. He wasn't comfortable with that. Not at all. Still, he continued questioning this very personal part of her life by telling himself that as her manager and the shaper of her public image . . . he needed to know.

And for some inexplicable reason, Shayna felt a need to tell.

"Jay is basically a good person. He's got enough game for his own arcade, but he's smart and focused and at one time, I really cared about him. He always seemed so knowledgeable about everything. I thought he was sophisticated, going places. He wore suits to class, even in high school, and was a business major in college. He's good people."

"He's also the man who attacked you on a public street."

Shayna glanced up at Michael as her eyes became glassy. "I know. And I know I should hate him right about now. As it is, I'm pretty pissed off. But the man who tried to grab me isn't the Jay that I know. Plus, part of this is my fault."

"What?" Michael looked at her as though she'd lost a major part of her mind, if not all of it.

"No, Michael, you don't know the whole story. He's been calling and I keep ignoring him. Whatever has happened between us, he was my friend for many, many years." She continued, looking out the patio doors into a yesterday when Jay had been the sun in the sky otherwise known as her life. "If I'd just talked to him, maybe none of this would have happened."

"So you'll keep talking to him for the rest of your life, then he won't beat you up. Is that the logic that we're working with here?"

"I know it sounds crazy, and no, I'm not going to get back with him. But I've known him practically all my life and dated him almost ten years, since we were sixteen. You can't just turn off those feelings overnight, even if that's the right thing to do. He's now turned into somebody I no longer know, but at one time, we were happy. . . ."

Michael observed the sad yet dreamy expression on

her face and ignored the stab of pain that came with her acknowledgment of her love for another man. Growing soft in his old age, he'd later reflect, though some might have argued thirty-one wasn't all that old. "And then shift happened, when he was too immature to understand what obtaining dreams cost, what I needed to do to get to where I am now."

She clasped her hands together; twirled her thumbs. "It was so subtle I didn't even recognize it." After a moment, she continued. "He was always kind of possessive, I guess, but since we were so often together anyway I didn't recognize it. He basically ran our personal lives, my athletic career, everything. Then, during my second year at USC, which has its own workout and training regimen, I stopped working with Jay, stopped listening to his recommendations for my training schedule. That's when things started . . . going downhill."

"You fired him as your PT?"

"Technically, though he'd never been official in the first place. Plus, he still worked with me on weekends and came to all of my events. I basically had two coaches until my senior year. But when they brought in John Joyner, everything changed."

"What happened then?"

"Coach and Jay mixed like oil and vinegar. He, and I'm talking about Coach, set me up on an intense new regimen that cut into the time I spent with Jay. But Jay, being the self-centered guy that he is, saw my new schedule as Coach's attempt to separate us and accused him of liking me even though Coach is married and they'd just had a child at the time. It got to the point that I couldn't go anywhere without Jay knowing time of departure and estimated return. Later I realized that he was accusing me of cheating because of the women crowding his bed.

He kept apologizing and I kept taking him back, always on the strength of what once was. I should have ended the relationship a long time ago."

"What made you finally do it? I mean, for good?"

"Training for the Olympics was intense and by then Jay and I were fighting all the time. It was too much pressure. I just couldn't take it anymore."

Michael nodded in understanding. "And then once you came back with the gold, the accolades, the status . . . he realized what he'd lost and wanted to make amends."

"Jay was furious at not being a part of it all. And I did try and include him a little. He was the one who encouraged me in the beginning. But I didn't want to be his girl anymore and he didn't want to just be friends. He wanted everything; at one point he was demanding to be my manager even though he has no experience doing that at all! I told him in no uncertain terms that I wanted whoever managed me to have experience and that when it came to a relationship . . . that part of our lives is over."

Her voice sounded sure; her eyes . . . not so much.

"You should know that as my client, your protection and reputation is a high priority. We'll make sure that you're not harassed by him, or anyone else."

"I appreciate that, Michael, but my personal life really isn't any of your concern."

"I'm making it mine."

Both Michael and Shayna looked toward the sound of a side door closing. Seconds later one of Michael's assistants, Keith Byers, rounded the corner with Shayna's freshly cleaned suit in one hand and her car keys in the other.

Glad for the diversion, Shayna stood as quickly as her injury allowed and walked over to Keith. "Thanks for picking up my car and bringing these from the cleaners," she said, taking the car keys and cleaners bag from Keith's outstretched hand. She turned to Michael. "Thank you. I think I'll go change." Resisting the urge to flee from the room, she instead walked calmly out of the living area and down the hall to the guest bathroom. Taking a shallow bath here, as Michael's brother Gregory had suggested, was out of the question. It didn't matter that the thought of Michael's hands on her body had made her wet. She'd just gotten out of a crazy relationship. She was trying to establish her career. Hadn't she learned what could happen when things went sour with someone you worked with? No, better to keep the line of demarcation clearly drawn. So instead of following doctor's orders, she took a quick sponge bath at the sink, hurriedly slipped into the suit, retrieved her shoes from Michael's bedside, and, after closing her eyes to inhale the woodsy cologne scent that lingered in the room, she turned and left.

"You sure you're okay to drive?" Michael had stood and walked toward the hallway when he heard Shayna approach.

"I'll be fine."

"You're welcome to stay another night if you're not up to traveling."

Shayna shook her head. "The bandages help, and I'll stop and get the ibuprofen that Gregory recommended, but otherwise, I'm fine. Plus, my roommates are home and have been blowing up my phone. I've texted them that I'm on my way and if I don't show up they'll surely report me missing."

"Okay. I'll walk you outside."

They reached the red Hyundai where the two stood in awkward silence, not meaning to stare at each other but not able to look away. Michael wanted to hug her, but the whole cracked rib situation made that gesture unwise. Actually, he wanted to kiss her, to bury his tongue deep inside her mouth . . . and other places. But their business relationship made that unwise as well. He reached for her door handle and after she'd carefully sat down, reached over for the seat belt to buckle her in.

Was it his imagination, or had the whisper of a kiss touched his cheek as he stood back up? As he watched Shayna's car until he could no longer see it, the question remained.

9

She couldn't resist and yet still couldn't believe she'd done it. Touched her lips to Michael's temple before she could even think about it, let alone stop it. It had been a natural act, a reflex really. Or at least that's what she'd told herself all the way home, and even now, as she stood at her front door, her fingers pressed to where Michael's head had been. *He didn't feel it.* Something else she chose to believe. No more time to ponder the consequences now, however, because Shayna had barely opened the door when her roommates bum-rushed her and the comments started.

"It's about time you got here!" The loud voice bounced down the hallway and hit Shayna in the face.

That's Brittney's dramatic behind. If not for the pain and the tightness of the bandages, Shayna would have laughed out loud.

"Uh-huh, heifah," Talisha added. "You know your butt has some explaining—" They rounded the corner. Talisha stepped back, straight into Brittney, who'd been on her heels. Both women noticed the scratches on her face and the bruise mark on her neck. The color purple, and we're not talking about the kind that Nettie and Celie enjoyed in the lilac field. "Shay! What happened?"

The two women stepped aside so that Shayna could get past them and into the living room. "Don't tell me Michael did this," Talisha said, her voice low and threatening.

"Do we need to call the police on his ass?" Brittney asked. She was already reaching for her phone.

"Wait, guys," Shayna said, her raised hands a plea for silence. "I'll tell you everything, but first let me get out of these clothes and get some water. I need to take a pill."

Talisha's eyes narrowed as she noted the careful way Shayna took off her heels before starting down the hall. "Do you need any help?"

Shayna realized that it would be useless to try and keep her roommates out of her bedroom or her business so she didn't even try. "Come on in, y'all." She unbuttoned the jacket and winced trying to remove it.

Brittney gasped, noting that a tightly bound bandage had replaced the top Shayna wore when she'd left the house yesterday.

"Wait, Shay, let me help you out of it," Talisha said. "Put your arms down. Brittney, go get Shayna a glass of water." The mother hen of the trio, she carefully slid the jacket down Shayna's arm. Shayna unbuttoned her slacks while Talisha went into her closet for a loose-fitting pair of sweatpants and matching lightweight jacket that zipped up the front. Brittney returned with the glass of water. Two sets of intent eyes watched Shayna remove the painkillers from her purse, take one, and drink the entire glass of water.

"Sit," Talisha demanded, pointing to the bed.

"Spill it," Brittney added, as both she and Talisha sat on the bed as well.

Shayna took a deep breath. Suddenly she felt tired, drained, wanting nothing more than sleep to help her escape the reality of her last twenty-four hours. But these were her sister-girls, and the concerned looks on their faces prodded her on. "It was Jay."

Brittney's mouth fell open. "Jay did this? He beat you up?" Brittney knew the old Jay, the one who used to cook dinner when Brittney came over, then sit and watch comedies all night long. That Jay would never have done this.

Shayna nodded.

"What the hell?" Talisha shouted, with a frown that suggested she was about ready to take off her earrings and smear her face with Vaseline.

"How'd he find you?" Brittney asked.

Talisha didn't wait for an answer before firing another question of her own. "Did he follow you to Michael's place?"

"I don't know," Shayna responded, just realizing that Jarrell may very well have followed her to Michael's place and now knew where her manager lived. This thought did not sit well with her and she made a mental note to call Michael before going to sleep. "Y'all know he's been calling and texting me off the hook since Mom gave him my new number." Shayna was so mad at her mother for doing so that she hadn't called her yet. She needed more time before she could do so without cursing her out. "He called me at least a dozen times yesterday, texting, too. Finally, when I got to Michael's house, I turned off the phone.

"The meeting lasted for hours, and no"—she fixed her roommates with a pointed look—"nothing happened.

The meeting was totally professional, although I'd be lying if I said Michael didn't look good enough to eat. The only meal I had, however, was a Thai dinner that his chef cooked."

"Wow, he has a chef?" Brittney's expression turned dreamy.

"Forget about the food." Talisha fluffed up Shayna's pillows, motioning for Brittney to help her place Shayna back up against them. "I want to know how you got from charismatic Michael to crazy Jay!"

Shayna slowly shook her head, trying to recall the feelings of happiness and hopefulness she'd had upon entering the novelty shop. "I'm still trying to figure that out myself. Among other things, Michael and I discussed how to develop my brand, maybe have a signature look or piece of clothing like Flo-Jo, with her nails and one-legged outfits, or Michael and his gold shoes. I was thinking about that when I turned on Sunset and saw this store. I stopped, hoping that maybe I'd see something in there and get inspired. That's when I remembered that I'd turned off my phone. As soon as I turned it back on, I got a text message. It was from Jay."

"What did that asshole say?"

Shayna closed her eyes and took a breath to calm the fear rising up from inside her. She swallowed and answered, "That he was tired of being ignored and that we were going to talk, one way or another."

"Oh my God, Shay." Brittney placed a reassuring hand on Shayna's arm.

"I knew something was wrong when we were on the phone earlier." Talisha stood and began pacing. "Why didn't you tell me about the text? You know me and Cameron would have came and got you, followed you back home or whatever we needed to do."

"Because I didn't expect Jay to be hiding in the shadows waiting to attack me. That's why!"

"I'm sorry for yelling at you, girl. I'm just so mad! I can't believe he actually did this." Talisha sat back down, lowered her voice "You must have been scared to death."

"I was petrified. When Jay grabbed me, he disguised his voice so I thought it was a stranger trying to rob me or rape me or . . . I don't know what. I couldn't even think . . . just started fighting and yelling and trying to get away."

"Weren't there people around?" Brittney asked. "Somebody to call the police . . . or something!"

"There were, but these days, no one wants to get involved. Plus, it happened so fast. He grabbed my arm and I felt something pressed against my back. I don't know what it was, a knife, a gun . . . hell, maybe even a flashlight or something else less deadly. But he said that if I yelled that he would, you know, really mess me up. All I could think about was him doing something to me physically that would end my career. I believed him and at first I had planned to do what he said." Shayna became silent, inwardly reliving the terror of that moment.

"Then what happened?" Brittney asked, plopping down on the bed.

"Ow!"

"Oh, sorry!" Brittney placed her hand on top of the hand now clutching Shayna's side. "So sorry, Shay."

Shayna took deep breaths before replying, "That's okay. I think the pill is starting to take effect now."

Talisha crawled on the bed from the other side. "Shayna, you don't have to tell us if you don't want to. It's probably upsetting."

"No, it's okay, really. I'd rather get it over with tonight or you beatches will bug me forever!"

"You're right!" Brittney said, checking her perfectly manicured nails before offering a side glance in Shayna's direction.

"So . . ." Shayna sighed heavily before continuing. "We were by this door that led to the back of a business on Sunset, a private, totally hidden area between the store and the alley. The attacker, Jay, picked me up and tried to force me through that doorway. I had a feeling that if he got me back there, things might really get ugly. That's when the adrenaline kicked in and I fought for my life, and that's when my ribs got broken. Well, cracked technically, but I can't imagine that broken would feel any worse than this!"

"So when you were fighting, that's when you realized it was Jay?" Talisha asked.

"No, that wasn't until I broke away and started to run. I looked back, just for a second, and our eyes met." Shayna's brows creased as she relived the scene. "Now that I think about it, maybe that's why he was holding me so tight, he didn't want me to see who it was until he got me away from the public, in a more secluded spot. I should have just answered his stupid calls. Then this wouldn't have happened."

"I know you're not sitting there saying it's your fault that your ribs are cracked. And I know you're not going to let him get away with this!" So much for Talisha maintaining a calm demeanor. Hard to do when one's blood boiled. She looked at Shayna through narrowed eyes. "Did you file a report with the police?"

Shayna shook her head. "Michael, umm, he said he'd take care of it."

Brittney crossed her arms. "What does that mean, that he'll take care of it? Michael isn't law enforcement. You need to file a police report, Shayna! You need to have a record of what Jay did in case he tries again! Did you have time to get the names of any of the people around you, anyone who could corroborate your story?"

Shayna shook her head. "I didn't wait around to take names, wasn't even thinking about that. All I could think of was getting away. I tried to get to my car, but he was right behind me so I just started running. I had just come from Michael's and I instinctively started running back in that direction. I was so scared, y'all. When I got to his house, I just collapsed. He was leaving and almost didn't see me. I don't know what would have happened if . . ." She put her head in her hands, and the tears that she'd kept at bay most of the day came pouring out.

"Shh, it's okay, Shay," Talisha cooed, going from kick-ass anger to calmed-down compassion in the blink of an eye. "We can talk about it later."

"But wait, Tee. What about—"

"Let's let her get some rest," Talisha insisted, reaching for Brittney's arm to lead her out of the room. She stopped at the door. "Are you hungry, Shayna?" Shayna shook her head, and lay down on the bed. "Well, there's water on the table beside you. If you need anything, just let me know."

Shayna listened as her roommates' voices receded down the hallway. She smiled into the darkness, imagining their conversation and their suggestions on what should be done to her ex. Then she thought of Michael and his vow to "take care of it." *What did that mean?* Yes, Jarrell had hurt her, but did she want him hurt in return? And what about her mother, who'd given him her new number in the first place? Talisha had suggested that Shayna get some rest, and put the incident behind her. But Shayna worried whether the worst was truly over. Or had it only begun?

10

Michael pulled up to his mother's condominium complex and waved at the guard. She'd been here for three years, but every time he visited there was still a sense of pride. Michael and his two brothers had purchased the three-bedroom condo in a luxury high-rise near the ocean, and then talked their mother into leaving the home she'd shared with their dad and moving there. At one time, they thought she'd never consider leaving the Long Beach community she'd called home for three decades, that had seen various levels of gentrification over the years. "So many memories of Sam," she'd always say. But the changing face and cultural climate of the neighborhood where the boys had grown up, combined with the panoramic ocean view that could be seen from their mother's floor-to-ceiling windows on the twentieth floor, had sealed the deal.

"Hello there, Mr. Morgan," the guard said, handing him the required guest pass sticker to be displayed on his dashboard. "Beautiful day today, huh?"

"It sure is," Michael replied. He gave a final wave as he went past the raised arm, then looked in his rearview mirror just as his younger brother, Troy, steered his prized possession—a Maserati GranCabrio—into the complex. Michael shook his head even as he waved at his brother. Everyone had told Troy he was crazy for parking a luxury car in a crime-ridden neighborhood, but the youngest Morgan loved the Leimert Park community as well as his toys. "Who are the kids going to look up to if all of us leave?" he'd challenged his brothers. Neither Michael nor Gregory had had the answer to that question, so after that they'd left him alone.

Moments later, Michael noted the smell of something amazing and the sounds of something jazzy as he knocked on his mother's door.

Gregory answered. "Hey, man." He glanced over his shoulder and then continued in a lowered voice. "You all right?"

Michael nodded, stepping inside the room and giving his brother a shoulder bump greeting. "I'm good."

"And your client?"

Michael's brow furrowed. Aside from a text relaying her fears that Jarrell Powell might know where he lived and what type of car he drove, he'd not heard from Shayna, nor had he been able to reach her. "She's okay, I guess."

"Was Troy able to find out anything?"

"I don't know. We've been playing phone tag since last night." Michael walked over to the fireplace and nodded at the image in a large picture hanging above the mantel, as if in greeting, rubbing the frame with his fingers. He continued to stare at the picture of his father, the one the sons greeted at every visit. As strange as it may seem, he gathered strength every time he was near this work of art, sensed his father's presence, heard his father's voice answering the questions in his head. But before he could get to the most important query, the one about Shayna, his mother entered the room.

"Hello, son!" Jackie Morgan came around the corner with arms outstretched. A tall, slender woman with thick black hair and smooth brown skin, she was often mistaken for a much younger lady, sometimes a decade younger than her fifty-five years. Today, her shoulder-length hair was pulled back into a simple ponytail, her face was devoid of makeup save for a hint of gloss on her lips, and the scent of vanilla and lilacs clung to her as loosely as did the ankle-length flowery dress that draped her frame. "You look worried, son," she said after hugging Michael and then pulling back. "Everything all right?"

"Everything's fine, Mom." *Dang! Pull it together, Michael.* Of the three boys, Michael had always been the one who wore his emotions on his sleeve, or in today's case, on his face. Yet he was determined to keep his worries to himself. At least for now. "Something smells good. What is that . . . roast beef?"

Jackie and Gregory exchanged glances before she followed her son into the dining room. "It's rump roast, son," she answered. "Gregory, why don't you choose a nice bottle of red, a burgundy perhaps, or a smooth cabernet? Food's almost ready. Have either of you heard from Troy?"

As if on cue, the doorbell rang.

"What's up, my peoples, my peoples!" Without a doubt the most gregarious of the three, the youngest Morgan man made an entrance of swagger and noise, walking over and giving a quick nod to Sam's portrait before exchanging fist pounds with his brothers. He then went over to Jackie and lifted her off the ground.

"Put me down, boy!" Jackie's pummeling of Troy's

back was halfhearted; she squealed like a schoolgirl when he spun her around. As she landed, she turned to see Michael standing by the window, texting. His expression suggested that something was going on with him, but she was close enough with her son to know that she'd find out nothing that he didn't want to tell her. She only hoped she could lighten whatever load he carried while he was here. "Michael, I need you to set the table. Gregory," she continued, heading to the kitchen, "let's put those surgeon skills to work and have you carve the roast. Dinner is ready."

For the first few minutes after sitting down, the most prominent sound in the room was silverware clattering against china. "As always, this is great, Ma," Troy said, around a forkful of roasted potatoes, carrots, and Brussels sprouts.

"Stop talking with your mouth full, boy!" Gregory admonished.

"That's right," Jackie said. "A matter you'd get reminded of more often if you had a missus in the house, if there were any more women in this family besides me." She pointedly looked around the table before taking a ladylike bite of beef and then patting her mouth with a napkin. "I think y'all three should have sown enough oats to feed a starving country. Now I know you don't like my meddling and I'm not. Just giving my opinion is all and, for the record, I think it's time to move on to the next phase of your lives."

Groans. Moans. The rolling of eyes.

"And the sermon begins." Michael speared a healthy bite of roast beef and chewed.

"There are women in the family," Troy offered. "They're called cousins."

Gregory wisely kept silent.

Jackie went on, totally undeterred by the lack of enthusiasm. "Michael, Mary and I had lunch the other day. She told me that her daughter is now divorced and is moving back to Los Angeles." Mary was a former neighbor and one of Jackie's best friends.

"Hmm," was his noncommittal answer.

"I always liked Alison, and never did think she loved that guy from college." A beat and then, "She's always loved you, Michael. You two made such a good-looking couple. I think she married that guy simply because she couldn't have you."

"You think so?" Michael responded, ready to take the glare of the singlehood spotlight off himself. "I always believed her eyes were really on Gregory."

Gregory held up his hands in a sign of surrender, even though he had no intention of doing so. "Don't get me into it, big brother. You're the one who dated her for a year."

"And then broke her heart," Troy added, loving that it was Michael on the hot seat and not him. For a change.

"Let's not start talking about broken hearts, baby brother," Michael warned. "Because word on the street is that"—Troy coughed loudly—"somebody was seen at the Ritz." Troy coughed again and this time, added a kick under the table to Michael's shin.

"Who was at the Ritz, Michael?" Jackie asked.

"I, uh, had dinner there, Mom," Troy replied.

"Oh, yeah?" Gregory's eyes twinkled over his glass of tea. "I thought it was breakfast."

Troy fixed Gregory with a frown.

Michael delivered the knockout. "Perhaps it was both."

"I don't know why you boys think you can pull one over on your mother. I might have been born at night, but it wasn't last night!" She turned to Troy. "So you took some hootchie to the Ritz-Carlton? Really, son, you must mind your reputation."

"Mom, it wasn't like that."

"I agree," Gregory said, reaching for more vegetables. "She didn't look like a hootchie at all, Mom. In fact, she looked quite highbrow."

"Do they even say 'hootchie' anymore?" Michael queried. "And do you really think we'd want their company? Mom, your sons may spread their share of love around, but we do so with class."

Jackie crossed her arms as she fixed Michael with a look. "Whether you're screwing these women in the hood or in the Hyatt, a ho is a ho."

The response was threefold and simultaneous. "Mom!"

"That's no way to speak about another woman, Mom," Gregory gently admonished.

"I'm not talking about them, fool. I'm talking about you!"

Everyone laughed at this before Gregory continued. "How did I get in the hot seat? We were talking about Troy. He was the one coming from the bank of elevators and across the lobby. I was there to have breakfast!"

"Troy," Jackie said, drawing out his name. "Is what your brother saying true? Was it like that?"

"Well," he admitted, a bit sheepishly, "not *exactly* like that."

"How was it exactly?" Gregory asked.

Troy saw his opening and didn't hesitate. "Probably about how it was with you and the two women I saw on your arm last night!"

"Two?" Jackie exclaimed.

"Twins," Troy added, ignoring Gregory's warning scowl.

"What, we're into threesomes now?" Jackie asked, her brow raised in mock indignation.

"Mom!" The more conservative of the three, Gregory's skin warmed at the very thought of his mother's suggestion. Not that he'd be beyond participating in such an act, but he'd surely not want to discuss it afterward with one Ms. Jackie Morgan. "It was Lori and Lisa. We met for dinner."

"Oh, the Wilhoite children. I haven't seen those girls in ages, except for Lori in that movie they showed on TV One. Neither one of them are married yet?" Gregory shook his head. "Lori would probably be very understanding of a doctor's schedule," Jackie went on, remembering how nice the girls always looked at Easter and Christmastime. "She's probably quite busy herself, with her own acting career and all. She was always very respectable, a debutante. We've known her family for decades. Seems to me she'd make a suitable partner."

"Funny you should say that, Mama," Michael teased. "Lori and the M word came up in a conversation just the other day. Didn't it, Gregory?"

"Don't start," Gregory warned. "Or else I'll have to tell Mom about the chocolate cutie I found in your bed Friday night."

This led to a rebuttal from Michael, laughter from Troy, clarifications from Gregory—basically three grown men all talking at once.

Jackie listened to the ruckus for a moment, secretly glad for the cacophony of sound that filled the home that was sometimes all too quiet. She looked at her boys-turned-men and marveled at how fast the time had gone by. She thought of her late husband and their father, Sam, and how proud he'd be of them. Insisting that they break bread together once a month was her way of maintaining the closeness they'd shared growing up and keeping the family intact. What a legacy he'd left. *One that won't continue if these boys of mine don't stop their whorish ways!*

"All right, boys, that's enough. Now, listen. I know that you all are grown, and that what you do in your private lives is really none of my business. But none of us are getting any younger. Michael, soon you'll be thirty-two years old. Gregory, you're already twenty-nine, and Troy, you're just a year behind him. By the time your dad and I were your ages, our family was complete." Her voice softened as she looked around the table. "I loved being married to your father. Being single is great, but it is nothing compared to life with the right partner beside you. You don't want to be too old to play catch with your sons or swing your daughters in the air. And once they reach high school age, you don't want their friends asking if you're the grandfather. I'm tired of being the only female in this family. It's time for some in-laws and grandchildren. So, Michael . . . you need to get on it!"

"Whoa, why me?"

"'Cause you're the oldest," Gregory and Troy replied simultaneously.

"What about you, Mom?" Troy asked, wiping his mouth with a napkin as he leaned back in his chair. "Did you use those digits I slipped you and call Robert?"

Jackie gave Troy a playful slap on the arm. "I'm not like these forward girls these days. What would it look like for me to be calling up your superior?"

"Not superior, Ma. When his type of expertise is needed, he works for me. As I told you before, Robert retired from the police force after thirty-five years of service. He's a good man, respectable, and when I told him about you, he sounded interested." Jackie tsked, but her eyes showed a bit of a sparkle. "You're too young to be spending so much time in this house, watching those beautiful sunsets alone."

"I tell you what. You all gather dates to invite to our dinner next month, and I'll *think* about having a date of my own."

After that, the dinner conversation turned to what was happening in their professional lives, a topic that continued when Gregory and Michael later walked to their cars.

"I'm a bit curious as to how Shayna is doing," Gregory said to Michael. "Still no word?"

"Not directly. She texted me a message earlier that she was okay, but I haven't talked to her. I'll call her now." Michael retrieved his phone from his pocket and dialed Shayna's number. He was surprised when a male voice answered, so much so that he checked the face of his phone to make sure he'd dialed correctly. He had. "Uh, yes. I'm trying to reach Shayna Washington."

"Who's calling?" the gruff voice demanded.

"A business partner," was Michael's somewhat noncommittal reply, delivered in a voice that was especially calm considering the way his mind raced. *Who is this guy? Why is he answering Shayna's phone?* And the most important question. *What business is it of mine as to either who or why?*

"Shayna's, uh, a little busy with her man right now." A pause and then, "Is there a message?"

Michael frowned. *Jarrell? Naw, couldn't be.* "No, no message." He hung up the phone, his mind in a whirlwind. Surely Shayna wouldn't be with the very man who'd attacked her on Friday. Two days ago. But if not that knucklehead, who was answering her phone? And what was this distinctly uncomfortable feeling in the pit of his stomach? He called Shayna's phone again. When it went straight to voice mail, his concern increased.

"What's the matter?" Gregory asked.

"A man just answered Shayna's phone."

Gregory raised a brow. "Is that a problem?"

Michael was already heading to his car. "I don't know, but I'm going to find out."

"Michael!"

Too late. Michael had already reached his car and had started it up. As Michael accelerated out of the parking structure, Gregory hurried to his car, pulling out his phone and calling his headstrong older brother as he walked.

11

Shayna hurried from the bathroom to the living room, sure she'd heard her phone ring. She walked in to find it in Jarrell's hand. "Who was that?" she asked, rushing over to take her phone.

"Wrong number," Jarrell easily lied, holding the phone just out of Shayna's reach.

"Give me the phone, Jay!"

A sound from the other side of the living room wall reminded both Jarrell and Shayna that they were not alone. Shayna guessed that that was the point. Talisha hadn't been at all happy with the idea of Jarrell coming over, but neither she nor Cameron would hear of Shayna going anywhere to meet him. It was enough that Shayna had given in to her mother's pleading and saw him at all. Let it be said that Beverly Powell was nothing if not persuasive. By the time she'd talked to Shayna, Jarrell had already given her and his brother, Larsen, his side of the story. He'd only wanted to talk to her. He loved her, and just wanted them to be the family they'd always talked about since being sixteen years old. *Please,* Shayna thought indignantly, *tell that to someone who doesn't have cracked ribs.* A point that she hadn't even bothered divulging to her mother. Given the history, Beverly would have undoubtedly found a way for even that to be Shayna's fault.

She snatched the phone from Jarrell. The last call displayed was her mother's, from a half hour ago, the call that had landed Shayna in the predicament that she was in now. What kind of mother did that? What kind of mother tried to talk her daughter back into seeing a man who cheated on her? *One who was married to the ex-boyfriend's brother maybe, who'd always tried to be less of a mother and more like a friend—even the competition on occasion.* She eyed Jarrell before crossing over to the bar counter separating the kitchen from the living/dining area. After leaning against it and crossing her arms, she spoke. "You put my mother in the middle of this, knowing she'd bug me even more than you. That is the only reason that you're over here, so I can try and keep peace in the family. So I'm asking for the last time. What. Do. You. Want?"

"I told you," Jarrell said, as he began to cross the room. When he saw her tense up, he threw his hands up in an exasperated gesture and sat on the couch instead. "I came over to apologize. I can't believe I put my hands on you, Shayna. You know the last thing I would ever want to do is hurt you. I was just so frustrated the other night that I saw you and, I don't know . . . I just snapped."

"You may not have meant to hurt me, Jay. But you have, more than once."

"What? I've never before laid a hand on you."

"There's more than one type of pain, Jay."

"I know, because you've hurt me too. But I'm not

trying to make excuses, Shayna. I'm so sorry for grabbing you the other night."

"You've already said that, Jay, on Friday night; left a few messages, remember?"

"I didn't know if you'd gotten them."

"I got them."

Jarrell smiled, revealing a dimple that used to melt her heart. "Do you forgive me, baby?"

Instead of answering, Shayna stood straight and crossed her arms, glaring at Jarrell through narrowed eyes. Her roommate was right. No matter how much her own mother had encouraged it, Shayna had been crazy to agree to see Jarrell, to "hear him out" as her mother had suggested. She wasn't afraid of him, just done with him. As it was, Talisha had refused to leave the condo as long as Jarrell was there. She and Cameron were holed up in her bedroom—ears to the door, fists at the ready, Shayna presumed—prepared to roll gangsta into the living room at the first sign of trouble. Talisha had even threatened to call Shayna's mother and give her a piece of her mind. Even though that was probably the right thing to do, Shayna had talked her best friend out of it. Nobody understood why Shayna protected the woman who seemed not to protect her, why she did whatever Beverly Powell asked in order to get what always seemed lacking: acceptance.

"What you really want to know, and why you enlisted my mother's help in listening to you, is if I called the cops. The answer is no—not yet."

"Why would you call the cops?"

"Look at me!" Shayna hadn't told Jarrell about her cracked ribs, but her face was enough to show that she'd been assaulted.

"I called your mother because I couldn't reach you,

because I'd combed the streets after you ran away and when I couldn't find you, had stayed near your car for another hour. I was going crazy with worry, Shayna."

"You were going crazy all right. I've got the bruises to prove it."

"You hurt yourself trying to get away from me, Shayna. I just wanted to talk."

"I've told you a hundred times already, Jay. There's nothing left for us to talk about. I told Mom that as well. Neither one of you are listening."

"Beverly knows how I feel about you. How much I love you, that's all. She wants all of us to stay a family. Her and my brother and—me and you."

Shayna knew that both Jarrell's and her mother's motives had nothing to do with her well-being, and everything to do with their own selfish agendas. Being known as an abuser might sully Jarrell's long-term aspirations, the ones he'd shared with her from the time they were children, while her mother . . . Shayna shook her head to break the thought. She didn't want to think about Beverly Powell's twisted motives right about now.

"Jay, I don't know any better way to say it. I need a break." *And not in my ribs.*

"Please tell me that you forgive me, Shayna. And that we can just, you know, put this behind us."

"Whether or not I forgive you isn't important, Jarrell. What I need you to do is to understand that right now what I want is space."

"How long have we known each other, Shayna? Can't we at least be friends?"

"You've said what you came to say, Jay. Now you need to leave. I have things to do."

"Okay, I'll leave. But you're sure you're all right?"

"I'm okay." *No thanks to you.* Shayna walked to the door and opened it. "Good-bye, Jarrell."

Jarrell took his time in rising from the couch. He walked over to the door, stopping directly in front of Shayna. "I'll always love you. Remember that."

Shayna stood back so she could open the door wider. Jarrell got the message. He left.

12

No sooner had she closed the door than Talisha came out of her bedroom. "Geez, I thought he'd never leave. Are you okay?" Shayna nodded, even though her insides were shaking. "That asshole has a lot of nerve," Talisha continued, walking into the kitchen. "If you want me and Cameron to stay here this evening, you know, in case he comes back, we'll do it." A flash of light from the bar counter caught her eye. "Your phone, Shay," she said, picking up the cell and walking into the living room.

"What?" Shayna reached for her phone. "Shoot, that was Michael." Checking, she found that the sound had been turned down. "I didn't turn the ringer off. I caught Jay with my phone. He must have turned it off." She cleared the missed call and realized there had been two others. *Michael.* She hit redial.

Michael answered on the first ring. "Shayna."

Shayna sensed a seriousness beneath Michael's one-word greeting. "Sorry I missed your call, Michael. My ringer was off."

"I heard you were busy."

"Who told you that?" She flinched as the reflexive question was asked. There was only one answer—Jarrell—and only one way Michael would know that—if Jarrell had answered her phone. Shayna thought of possible answers and they were all terrifying: that Jarrell had identified himself as a friend (the least terrifying of choices), that he had identified himself as a boyfriend (which would be okay if not for the unacknowledged feelings she had for Michael), that he not only identified himself as Jarrell but also as her boyfriend (which would make her look like what she was not—a fool), or that he identified himself as the abusive *ex*-boyfriend who'd still been invited into her home (which would make her look not only like a fool, but a crazy one at that!). She opened her mouth. Words refused to come out. But knowing that being as quiet as the proverbial church mouse made her sound guilty at worst and stupid at best, she dug into her bag of tricks and pulled out some confidence. Clearing her throat, she spoke into the silence. "Why are you calling, Michael?"

"I saw my brother earlier. He asked about you."

"Oh?"

"Yes, he wanted to know how you're feeling. I told him that other than the message you sent last night and the quick text today, I hadn't heard."

Shayna carefully sat on one of three swivel-styled, bar-high chairs encased in soft, cream-colored leather. Her hand went to the bandage tightly wound around her torso as she looked out the patio glass of their second-story condo and peered at the barely discernible stars beyond a hazy sky. She'd always felt their place cozy, with its neutral-colored furniture, tan carpeting, and splashes of color through vases and art. But now, hearing Michael's voice, she was reminded of his place and the understated yet obvious luxury of his paradise—the feel of the bamboo flooring beneath her bare feet, the way his high-count sheets had caressed her bare thighs. The memories were still so fresh it was as if she could smell his cologne. She subconsciously breathed in to try and catch the scent.

"Shayna."

"I'm sorry, Michael. I was distracted by something outside." *And something within.* "I still feel sore and honestly the binding is a bit uncomfortable. But I was afraid to unwrap it because I don't want to do further damage. I have to get back in shape as soon as possible, hopefully in time for our next meet."

"Didn't you say that was in three weeks?"

"Yes."

"I don't know about that, Shayna. Tell you what. Gregory is on his way over to my house. Why don't you meet us there so that he can take a look at your bandages and make adjustments if necessary."

"Sure, I can come over—oh, wait a minute." Shayna looked down at what she was wearing, the baggy sweats that her roommates had provided, and wondered if she could dress herself in something a little more presentable—translated: sexier—for her visit with the doctor. Unfortunately, there was nothing sexy about the sound that tore from her lips when she reached up to try and remove her loose-fitting top.

"Something the matter?"

"No," Shayna lied, trying to put her mask of bravery back into place. She bit down on her lip, taking a deep breath and standing still until the pain subsided. "I can be over there in about half an hour. Is that okay?"

"Let's make it an hour to be sure Gregory is here."

* * *

Michael ended his call with Shayna and immediately called his brother. "Please say you've got a free hour or two."

"Please tell me you haven't done anything stupid."

"Like what?"

"Like confronting the man who answered Shayna's phone. You tore out of the parking lot like a bat out of hell."

"No, man. After calling her twice more and getting voice mail, I calmed down. Figured that if she was in trouble, she'd call me. Then I heard from Jessica and then Felicia and . . ." Michael had heard from them; what he hadn't told Gregory is that he'd turned down the chance to be with both of them. He'd even put Paia on hold, told her she might have to fly back to Milan without their being able to meet. What he also hadn't told his brother was that he was suddenly in jeopardy of losing his player card. What he hadn't even yet admitted to himself was the reason.

"Never mind. I might be free for the next few hours. What's up?"

"I told Shayna you were on your way over to my house."

"Why did you do that?"

"Because I want to see her."

"A little old to require a chaperone, don't you think?"

"I don't need a chaperone. I need a reason." Now that he'd said the words out loud, they sounded lame to his own ears. But in for a penny, in for a pound. "Can you come over here or what?"

"Wow." Gregory drew out the word with a chuckle. "Sounds like somebody might be trying to stretch the professional boundaries, and copping a little attitude while doing it. But having taken the Hippocratic oath, I have a duty to the well-being of my patients."

Michael let out a breath of relief. "Thanks, man. I owe you one."

"No worries, bro. I knew you were digging her from the jump."

"I'm not 'digging' her, as you put it, just being protective of my business interests, that's all. You know I don't play where I eat. Been there, done that, got the restraining order to prove it."

"If that's the case, then why don't you have Shayna meet me at my office instead of your house? As you know, I'm totally capable of handling your clients without your being there."

"We've already been through this, bro. I'm just keeping this story under wraps. Troy is checking out Jarrell and the characters he hangs around. Things might get ugly. So for right now, the fewer people who know about this incident, the better."

"Let me get this straight. You have an Olympic gold medalist who was attacked by her boyfriend."

"Ex-boyfriend."

"You don't press charges."

"Right."

"There's no police report."

"I've already told you this."

"And no hospital or doctor report to document her injuries."

"Her roommates took pictures."

Michael heard Gregory's frustrated snort through the phone. "This doesn't make any sense, Michael."

"She doesn't want it out there either. Something

about her mother's husband and how negative publicity might affect his business."

"You would think a mother whose daughter had been attacked would care more about getting justice for her daughter, never mind what it would mean for anyone else."

"Tell me about it."

A pause and then, "What is she going to tell the coach?"

"Freak accident—ran into by someone riding a bicycle."

"Is withholding information like that wise?"

"It is for now." Michael ended the call, pondering his brother's remarks. There was no denying the feelings he had toward Shayna: to promote and protect. These he was able to excuse as being logical—he stood to make not only a bigger name for himself but a whole lot of money. But there were other feelings, deeper ones, that he didn't want to acknowledge, refused to acknowledge. When he needed sexual healing, there were several ladies on his speed dial who knew their liaison was pure hot fun. His self-assurance had bloomed large along with his physique, and after being rejected for much of his early years, when the great looks and greater confidence kicked in, he made up for lost time by keeping an address book of lovelies at the ready—a different type for each season, sport, and industry event. That's all he wanted, no strings attached. For some reason he dared not ponder, he didn't want any of them. Right now, he didn't have time for . . .anyone else.

As Michael turned onto the street where he lived, his cell phone rang. He glanced at the face of it, brows slightly knitting at the "unknown" announcement. "Morgan." Silence. "Hello?"

"Michael Morgan, right?" a male voice inquired.

He tensed at once, almost sure that he'd heard this voice before. "Yes, this is Michael. Who is this?"

A short pause and then, "This is Shayna's boyfriend."

Michael didn't even realize he was gripping the wheel. Surely this couldn't be the man who'd attacked his . . . investment. Either the man was very brave or very stupid. Given how he'd pretty much ambushed Shayna, Michael betted on the latter. "Does Shayna's boyfriend have a name?"

"Jarrell."

Michael steered into his driveway. He turned the car off, but didn't get out. "What can I do for you, Gerald?" he asked while thinking, *This is going to be good.* The pause that occurred let Michael know that his pseudo-friendly demeanor had caught Shayna's assailant off guard. He'd probably expected a surlier greeting, a nastier encounter. Michael had something in store for him, no doubt. When the time was right.

"I, uh, I just wanted to let you know that me and her are, you know, together, and anything that involves her involves me."

"Is that so?"

"Yeah."

"Well, I tell you what *Gerald*—"

"Jarrell, man! J-a-r-r-e-l-l."

"Right. Tell you what, Gerald. You handle your business with Shayna, and I'll handle mine. And as long as your business doesn't affect my affairs, we'll be fine. If that ends up not being the case, such as if you ever touch her again, it'll be a problem."

"Don't try and threaten me, man."

"I don't make threats, just promises. And since only

a bitch would put his hand on a woman, I'd suggest you take me at my word."

Michael disconnected the call and promptly blocked Jarrell's number. The plot had just thickened, and Michael had more questions than answers. What was up with the phone call he'd just received? Why had Jarrell been at Shayna's house, answering her phone and in the process getting his number? And perhaps the most important question, why was this fact affecting him the way it did? When it came to dealing with his clients, especially the multimillion-dollar celebrity athletes, he'd seen a little of everything. He'd dealt with drug users, baby mama drama, sexual harassment and assault lawsuits, blackmail, and more. When it came to Jarrell Powell, Michael wasn't exactly sure what he was dealing with. But he knew one thing. When the smoke cleared, he knew which man would be left standing and which one would find his face eating dirt.

13

Shayna pulled into Michael's driveway and parked behind the white Mercedes next to Michael's Jag. She assumed the car was Gregory's, the impressive lines of the sleek sedan befitting the image of a doctor. She wondered what it must be like to have grown up in Michael's family, full, she imagined, of life, laughter, and lots of love. How else could they all have turned out so successfully? As she eased out of the car and admired the lovely front garden on her way to the door, she wondered about the third brother Michael had mentioned, Troy. She wondered what he did for a living and whether he was as fine as Michael and Gregory. A pang of sadness washed over her as she thought about her own upbringing as the only child of a self-centered mother, a woman who even now placed her own wants and desires before that of her daughter. Then she thought of Friday night, how Michael had tended to her emotional wounds while his brother Gregory had bound her physical ones. Aside from her best friends, Britt and Tee, and her beloved grandmother, Big Mama, she hadn't much experience with people truly caring about her.

There had been moments when Jarrell made her feel good, but those had too often been followed by a taunt or a dig. Even though she'd known him almost all of her life, he'd never provided her the level of care she'd felt from the Morgan brothers. When it came to the relationship with her ex-boyfriend, life had been all about him.

Shayna reached the door and rang the doorbell. Michael answered. He was not smiling. "Shayna," he said, his face an unreadable mask. "Come on in."

What's up with him? Was it her or had a blast of cold from the Arctic blown into the room? She followed him down the hall into the open-concept living area that she loved so much. Expecting to see Gregory but finding the room empty, she asked, "Where's the doctor?"

"On his way." Michael had passed through the living room to the dining room and now sat with his back to Shayna, typing on an iPad.

Shayna stood near the couch, unsure of what to do. Was this the same warm, caring person whom she'd left less than forty-eight hours ago? What had happened to sour his mood? Shayna looked at the custom-made silk-covered couch, but instead of sitting, she walked over to the floor-to-ceiling sliding glass doors that opened up to the fabulously landscaped backyard. Again she was struck with the contrast between how he lived compared with her cozy but relatively simple abode. She looked at the comfy, navy-striped lounge chairs and imagined the pool parties that probably happened on the regular, with beautiful women, handsome men, tinkling glasses, and mindless chatter. *Who cares?* She tried to tell herself that Michael's life and how he lived it was of no concern to her, tried to convince herself that she had no desire to be a part of it. She turned, and was surprised to find him staring at her intently.

Startled, she asked, "What is it?" Michael looked at her, remained silent. Her heart began pounding, and she worked to keep her breathing calm. His silence reminded her of Beverly, how she'd stare at her then preteen daughter before lighting into her over some imagined wrong. "Michael?"

After another moment, Michael set the iPad on the table and leaned back in the chair. "Jarrell called me."

Shayna gave herself time to collect her thoughts by walking over to the dining room where Michael sat, pulling out one of the heavy wrought-iron and cashmere-tufted chairs, and joining him at the table. On the way, she once again remembered her phone in Jarrell's hand when she came out of the bathroom. After realizing that he'd intercepted Michael's call, she deduced that he'd then deleted the evidence. Obviously, that wasn't all he'd done. He'd also gotten Michael's number. "I'm sorry," she said at last.

Michael turned to face her. "You may believe this is not my concern, but I'm curious, Shayna. How is it that the man who attacked you two days ago was at your house today?"

"My mother, Beverly, is married to Jay's brother, Larsen." Michael didn't even try and hide his surprise. "I know, long story. But the short of it is that she had me when she was eighteen and even though she's in her forties, she looks much younger. Larsen is thirty-two, seven years older than Jay. So"—she shrugged—"they hooked up."

"Given your recent breakup, that has to be uncomfortable for you. But what does your mother being married to your ex's brother have to do with him being at your house?"

"She talked me into letting him come over."

"Why would she do that?"

"Trust me, she has her reasons."

"Reasons that she would want you to entertain a man who'd attacked you? How do you feel about that?"

"It doesn't matter how I feel." Michael didn't respond, just continued staring, waiting for answers. "I was raised mostly by my grandmother; Mom was more of a friend to me. She's beautiful, men flock after her, and she always has one around. *Always.* She indirectly used me and Jay hanging out as a way to snag his brother. I guess that since he and I are now broken up, she's getting nervous."

Given that he had a mother like Jackie, one who would go to the fire for any one of her sons, he couldn't imagine a mother putting some nucka before her own blood. He couldn't imagine that at all. "How long have they been married?"

"Almost three years. When my grandmother died, Mom got the insurance money. She used it to help Larsen expand his limo business. I guess he figured he owed her." Silence and then, "What did Jay say to you?"

"That y'all were still together and that your business was his."

Shayna rolled her eyes and sighed. "I've told Jay in no uncertain terms that it's over between us. He doesn't believe me."

"He doesn't want to believe you."

"Yes, well, I have a track record." When Michael remained silent, Shayna continued, her voice soft, reflective. "This isn't the first time we broke up. It's not the second. Or the third. As I've already told you, he and I have been a couple off and on ever since I was sixteen. We've known each other since we were kids. There's a

lot of history there, which is why he thinks he owns me."
Shayna looked Michael in the eye. "But he doesn't."

Michael nodded, seeming to let these words soak in
before responding. "As long as you're honest with me,
I can handle your ex. I just want to make sure that *you*
can, not only so that we don't have to deal with some
type of scandal, but also so that I can know that you're
safe. He sounded quite possessive over the phone and
I've already seen firsthand what he thinks about
women." A frown marred his face, but was gone so
quickly that Shayna wondered if she'd simply imagined
it. "I heard the explanation about your mother, but I still
don't get it. Why did you let him come to your house?"

Shayna reached out and outlined the silver center-
piece with her finger. She noted the exquisite workman-
ship on the casting made to resemble a bowl of fruit.
Her mind jumbled as she thought to explain herself.
How did one tell a secure, confident man who'd probably never doubted his worth a day in his life about someone like her? How did one explain what it felt like to
always come up short in the eyes of another, how someone like Jarrell had been her lesser of two evils? How
did one explain what it was like to grow up with someone like Beverly for a mother? Because if she could
adequately explain it, then Michael would know why
Jarrell had been in her home earlier that day.

As it was, she was saved by the bell.

Michael walked to the door and seconds later returned with Gregory just behind him. Today his brother
looked more like the doctor, dressed in an olive green
scrub top over faded jeans. He carried a black leather
duffel bag and while his smile was pleasant enough, his
mannerisms were all business.

He reached the table and set his bag down on it. "Hello, Shayna."

"Hi, Gregory."

"How are we feeling today?"

"I'm still pretty sore, and for some reason it feels like the bandages have gotten tighter somehow."

"Let me wash my hands real quick and we'll have a look at it."

Michael looked over at Shayna, slid his gaze over her body before asking, "Do you want me to leave the room while he examines you?"

Shayna shook her head. "No." And she meant it. Even as her body began to thrum of its own volition at the mere thought of him watching her, even as she reminded herself that she wasn't the modest type, and that it was just her midsection after all.

Gregory returned from the bathroom. "Okay, Shayna. Stand up, and let me have a look." She stood. "I'm just going to unwrap the bandages; let me know if I'm hurting you, though I'll try and be as gentle as I can."

As Gregory slowly unwound the bandage, Shayna kept her head down, her eyes on the deft fingers removing the gauzy cloth. But she felt Michael's eyes on her. As the material was unraveled purplish bruises became evident, and the area around the cracked and bruised ribs was puffy, a definite rise against her otherwise washboard stomach. Gregory's brow furrowed with concern, and though Shayna couldn't see him, Michael's whole body was taut.

"Okay, we've got a bit of swelling going on here," Gregory said, stating the obvious as he gingerly touched the area with the tips of his fingers. Come on into Michael's room. I want you to lie down." She followed him into the bedroom and heard Michael's footsteps just behind her. "Just sit down," Gregory said to her, and when she did, he took hold of her shoulders while instructing Michael to lift her feet. "Now lie back," he quietly commanded, holding her shoulders firmly in order to prevent undo movement of her rib cage. Gregory quietly conducted the examination, including the bruising and scratches on her jaw and neck. Michael watched as Shayna closed her eyes, giving him a chance to stare at her unabashedly. He longed to run his fingers across her flat stomach, could almost taste the chocolate of her skin. He watched the rise and fall of her breasts, felt his joystick twitch as he imagined his tongue encircling the nipple he imagined to be plump and juicy as a blackberry, but twice as sweet. One of the thoughts that he'd had regarding her came back to him and he quietly left the room.

"I'll write a prescription for some medicinal lotion to help with the swelling," Gregory said, as he touched Shayna's shoulder. When she opened her eyes, he gestured for her to put both of her hands in his while he placed his other hand on her upper back and helped her up. "You'll also want to take a long soak, every night, in water that's quite warm but not scalding. Do that and then apply the lotion, okay?" Shayna nodded. "Let's get you wrapped up. Is there someone to help you do this once you bathe?" Again, Shayna nodded, blocking out the image of Michael that flashed into her head. *I wish,* she silently admitted, then just as quickly dismissed the thought. She was fairly certain of one thing: the manager who'd not only had to deal with a battered client winding up on his front sidewalk but also had to handle her crazy-ass boyfriend would probably not put her on the short list when it came to dating possibilities. Gregory deftly rewrapped the bandage around Shayna's rib cage.

Michael was just ending a call as they reentered the living area.

"What are you doing tomorrow?" he asked, as soon as he'd placed down the phone.

"Going to the track," Shayna answered. "I know I can't work out, but I can still talk to the coach, get pointers, and maybe use the Jacuzzi."

"On your legs only," Gregory interjected. "Any pressure in your rib area will be too much."

"What time is practice over?" Michael asked. Shayna told him, and he replied, "Then why don't you join me for dinner tomorrow. There's someone I'd like you to meet."

14

The evening was balmy as Shayna pulled her cherry red ride up to the restaurant's valet stand. She smiled as the flirty Latino opened her car door, winking as he greeted her while looking appreciatively at her bare legs, long for someone who barely topped out at five foot four. After much debate about fashion choices, Brittney had helped Shayna into a tan-colored mini, a soft, shiny jersey number with dolman sleeves. Her strappy jeweled sandals that laced up the calf not only added height to her stature but highlighted her muscled legs. She'd taken a couple aspirin before leaving the condo and with her cracked ribs tightly bandaged felt relatively okay.

Stepping into the Japanese restaurant that Michael had recommended after finding out she loved sushi, Shayna was immediately enveloped in the warmth of the room: russet wood and black leather with subdued lighting throughout and an open kitchen boasting high flames. She approached the hostess station, attended by a sultry looking Asian woman with long black hair, kohl-rimmed eyes, deep red lipstick, and a genuine smile.

"Hello, and welcome to Katana," she said. "Table for one?"

Shayna smiled. "No, I'm meeting someone."

"Are you Ms. Washington?"

"Why . . . yes."

The hostess smiled. "Right this way, please." Shayna was led to an open-air patio area that overlooked the Strip. She spotted Michael right away, talking on his phone and looking fine as usual.

He stood as she and the hostess approached. "Hello," he said once the hostess had directed her to their obvious destination. He hugged her, shoulders only, pulled out her chair, and waited until she sat down to retake his seat. It was something that Jarrell would never do, and made Shayna feel shy and a bit of a princess at the same time. "I'll be off in a second," he said, placing his hand over a portion of the phone as he did so. Shayna took the opportunity to look around her and take in the bright lights of the big city, the beautiful people in their element with conversation and traffic noise providing a disjointed yet somehow melodious backdrop.

Michael soon ended his call. "Sorry about that," he said, placing the phone on the table. He eyed Shayna for a moment before adding, "I think this is the first time I've seen you in a dress. You look gorgeous."

"Thank you."

He signaled for the waiter. "What would you like to drink?"

"Sparkling water is fine."

Michael placed their order then, after acknowledging someone who'd spoken to him, continued. "Given your full workout schedule, it's understandable why you don't drink alcohol."

"I was never much of an imbiber, except for the occasional glass of champagne to celebrate a big win. The last glass I had was in London."

"No, the last glass you had was at my house."

"Oh." Shayna warmed at the memory. "Right."

"The Fly Four," Michael said, raising his water glass in reference to the 4 x 100 United States relay team who'd brought home the gold. Shayna had also brought home the gold in the 100-meter race and the silver in the 200. He knew that her coach had expected her to win every race she ran, and when the 2016 Olympic torch was lit in Brazil, Michael had the feeling that she would do just that. With his guidance and support, there would be a significant difference: the whole world would be watching her and would already know her name.

After the waiter came over, introduced himself, and took their drink orders, Shayna reached for her menu. "So," she asked while browsing the appetizers, "who am I meeting tonight?"

"Choice McKinley-Scott," Michael responded. "Owner and designer of Chai Fashions, out of New York." Shayna looked up from the menu, her face a question mark. "I met her last year during Fashion Week; we've been kicking around some ideas for sportswear. I think she'll be perfect to design a look for you, something original that"—*shows off that tight, sexy, chocolate body*—"will make you stand out on the track."

"As long as it's not something too crazy," Shayna said, looking down again at the menu and missing Michael's grin.

"Don't worry, baby," he drawled, "anything with my name on it is class all the way. Or should I say . . . your name."

"Me? I'm not a designer."

"No, but you have a sense of style and, more importantly, the body to show it off. Choice will sketch out some ideas but I want you to be an integral part of the design process, to put your personality, taste, and stamp on the collection that will bare you name."

"How did you know that I like fashion?"

"It's my job to know everything about you. And no, I haven't hired a private investigator—just read, watched, and procured every ounce of public information available. I read about your penchant for fashion in an interview for *LA Weekly*."

"Wow, you really do your homework."

"I look at every possible angle by which we can establish your brand. A clothing line for somebody like you is a given."

Shayna nodded, and continued to ponder this thought as she browsed the menu. The more she learned about Michael Morgan and his thought process, the surer she was of her decision to have him rep her. He was one of the best. "What should I order, Michael?"

"If you'll allow, I'll order for the table. We'll start with the robatayaki—"

"That's what comes on skewers, right?"

"Right. And then we'll enjoy some sushi, and finish up with a nice beef or seafood entrée. You don't even have to worry about liking whatever is set in front of you. I honestly don't think the chef could make a bad dish if he tried. He—" Michael's attention was captured by someone coming up behind Shayna. He smiled, stood, and soon welcomed a slim, attractive woman into his embrace. "Shayna," he said once they'd parted, "this is . . . uh . . . Chai."

"Hello." And then to Michael, "I thought we were meeting Choice."

"You are."

"Michael Morgan," Choice/Chai drawled.

"Dang, my bad."

"It's okay, man. I'm sure my secret is safe with you"—she turned to Shayna—"and my potential client. It's a pleasure to meet you, Shayna." Lowering her voice, she continued. "Most people don't know that Choice and Chai are the same person. Long story. Tell you later."

"So tonight you're . . . Chai?" Shayna didn't have to share that she thought the idea a crazy one. Her look said it all.

"Ha! Correct." As the woman bent down to hug her, Shayna was enveloped in a divinely unique fragrance, a little musk, citrus, and floral action that was somehow sophisticated and earthy at the same time. By the end of the evening, she'd conclude it a perfect choice for the designer who wore diamonds like cubic zirconium, and even though hers was an "out there" look—waist-length hair (whether a wig or weave Shayna could only speculate), large tinted glasses, and a garishly loud big top over pencil thin jeans—the comfort she displayed in her own skin gave her a sistah-girl-next-door charm. "Have you guys ordered?" she asked, hooking the strap of a large leather handbag over her chair before she sat down. "I'm starved!"

During an hour and a half of delicious dishes and great conversation, Chai showed how she'd taken the running attire ideas that she and Michael had discussed and brought them to life. The designs, though simple, were nothing like what was currently worn on the track. The material was similar to today's look, lightweight and supple, but the bottoms were in more of a boy short design while instead of a straightforward tank, the crisscrossed design of the top added a feminine flair. Shayna's eyes sparkled as she looked through the simple drawings and listened to Chai's ideas for color choices. "Something bright and sparkly," she said, taking in Shayna's dark brown skin as she did so. "Not disco-y, you understand, but understated pizzazz, an iridescent or rainbow tone."

"I like the idea of the flash," Michael said, eyeing Shayna with what surely could have passed for unabashed appreciation. He finished his sake, and then continued. "Like you said, nothing gaudy, but something that complements her . . . body and skin tone." He licked his lips, subtly, unconsciously, and caused Shayna to clench her thighs against the squiggle that went from tummy to punanny and did the happy dance. "What do you think, Shayna?"

"I think it's not going to be us who have the last word, but my coach. He'll want to make sure that the cut will not have any impact on my running abilities and he'll only allow this look for my individual races. For the relay, the girls and I have to roll with the same look."

"Well, that can certainly be arranged," Michael answered. "I'll give John a call and schedule a meeting. Maybe we can do something for the entire team, right, Chai?"

"Most definitely."

"Cool."

Chai's phone rang, and she left shortly afterward to join her husband, a big baller, shot caller in the world of architecture back east. When she parted, it was as if a barrier between Michael and Shayna had been removed. The shiver that ran down Shayna's back had nothing to do with the weather and everything to do with the way Michael now observed her.

"What?" she asked softly, becoming shy and unnerved under his intent perusal.

"You're beautiful, you know that?" He blinked his eyes slowly, near-black orbs framed by long, curly lashes.

"You've drank too much sake," Shayna replied.

"Maybe," Michael said, the warm, soothing Japanese alcohol having loosened his normally controlled tongue. "But that doesn't stop the fact that your skin is glowing in the moonlight. It looks so soft, so . . . " He reached across the table and ran a finger down Shayna's arm.

She pulled back. "That tickles!"

Michael's phone vibrated and broke the mood. He looked down at the face, then picked it up. "Hey, man. Y'all there already?" He continued to gaze at Shayna as he listened. "All right then. I'm just finishing dinner. Give me a half hour. That was my brother," he said, once he'd ended the call.

"Gregory?"

Michael shook his head. "My youngest brother, Troy. We're getting ready to shoot hoops for a minute."

"You?" Shayna inquired, her look both skeptical and laced with humor. "In your condition?"

Michael signaled for the check. "You're just not used to seeing me laid-back, relaxed. I'm not drunk, not even tipsy. And even if I were, I can still make all kinds of moves." His eyes raked over her body. "Believe that."

And she did. As he walked her to the valet, his firm, strong hand lightly touched the small of her back, as they engaged in casual banter while awaiting her car, and later, when she'd shed her clothes and crawled between the sheets. Especially then, Michael was the self-assured, consummate lover that she'd imagined.

15

"Hey, girl."

Shayna looked up and smiled at Kim, the first-leg runner in the 4 x 100 relay and the only married woman in the racing quartet. Her husband, Patrick, ran hurdles and did the long jump. In both events, he'd taken the silver medal at the 2012 Olympics held in London, England. Shayna, Brittney, and Talisha hoped they could find a love like that experienced by Kim and Patrick.

"Hey, girl," Shayna answered, once Kim had joined her on the grass.

"I've heard of trying to get out of practice before, but a bicycling accident? Seriously?" Her twinkling eyes belied the disbelief in her voice.

"I'd rather be running, trust me on that. I'd do hills, marathons, anything rather than deal with this discomfort."

"You're still in pain?"

"It's getting better."

"So, Shay. I've never heard of you riding bikes and even so, you know Coach doesn't like us doing anything that could compromise our health."

Shayna hated being dishonest with her friend, but dutifully did as Michael had asked and relayed the lie that he called "spin"—that she and a bicycle rider had performed a get-to-know without proper introductions. "It was a freak accident," she finished. "I'll be okay."

"How long will you be out?"

"Just a couple more weeks."

"That's good." They fell silent, watching the various team members working out in their respective sports: high jump, long jump, triple jump, shot put, pole vault, hurdles, and running. Shayna rested back on her elbows and lifted her face to the sun, enjoying the gorgeous Southern California weather with its bright blue sky, fluffy cumulous clouds, and soft breezes. The grass was springy beneath her hands and in this moment, Shayna caught a glimpse at what contentment looked like. "Shayna."

"Hmm?"

"What's this I hear about you being represented by Michael Morgan?"

"Where'd you hear that?"

"Patrick ran into Jarrell; he told him. Is it true?"

"Yes."

"Wow, sis, that's totally cool, girl! Athletes are doing flips to get with his agency. What'd you do for him to pick you?"

"Nothing. He came to me."

"Word?"

"Yep."

"Hmm. Jarrell said that's why you and him broke up, because you slept with Michael to get him to represent you."

"What?" Shayna sat up quickly, forgetting all about her tender ribs and ignoring the pain that came with the sudden movement.

"Yeah, girl, that's the rumor he's spreading. He told Patrick that you've been trying to get back with him, but that Michael Morgan could have his leftovers."

"He is such a liar."

"I figured as much," Kim said, offering a compassionate touch on Shayna's arm. "I told Patrick that Jay was lying, that I remembered you telling me about the breakup back in London. But if he said that to Patrick, there's no telling how many other people he's told, or what other kinds of rumors he's spreading." Kim continued, her voice soft with concern. "Maybe I shouldn't have said anything."

"No, I'm glad you told me. I need to let Michael know about this just in case Jay tries to take these lies public."

"Girl, tell me this. Is Michael as gorgeous in person as he is on TV?"

Shayna's face softened as she remembered the night before.

She'd heard a noise, and thought it was either Brittney or Talisha. Her door opened and then he was there, wearing the same black shirt, faded jeans, black loafers, and bright smile that he'd sported at the restaurant. She said nothing as he approached her, wide eyed and waiting, and when he joined her in the bed, she did not protest.

No words were said and the moment he pressed his thick, soft lips on her equally full ones, none were needed. "You taste like blackberries," he whispered into her mouth. She swallowed the comment, along with his desire. With lips still locked, he ran his hand up and down her arm, stroking the skin, squeezing her hand in his. His lips left hers to trail kisses down to her neck and collarbone. He looked deep into her eyes. "I don't want to hurt you." She simply nodded, words blocked by a need, an urgency for her to throw caution to the wind and not miss this chance at what she was sure to be love-making of the highest skill. He shifted his body in order to continue his oral salutation, down to her shoulder and across to her chest. His intent gaze dropped to her nipples and they hardened under his perusal. He bent down and took first one in his mouth, and then the other, flicking the hardened pebbles with his tongue and then blowing on the wetness. Bypassing her wrapped mid-section, he continued down her thighs, knees, calves, and back up again. Her stomach clenched when he paused, repositioned himself, and spread her thighs. "May I?" he asked, voice husky, eyes black with desire.

She nodded.

"I didn't hear you," he whispered, placing a soft kiss between her thigh, and another at the top of her bikini-waxed paradise.

"Yes," Shayna gushed, in a voice that was foreign to her own ears.

A soft chuckle and then those lips. On hers. Down there. The perfect kiss. She hissed and spread her legs farther apart, totally oblivious to any pain except the ex-quisite ache in her honey pot, the throbbing nub that begged to be licked, and her clenching muscles that begged something long, and thick, and pulsing to squeeze. He parted her slick wet folds with his tongue, lapped her honey with swordlike thrusts and a fencer's precision, taking her nub into his mouth and causing it to bloom like a flower. "You taste good," he said. And then went back for seconds. And thirds.

Shayna was beside herself with ecstasy. Her hands

gripped the sides of his head, as her fingers rubbed the ultralight stubble underneath them. He chuckled as she held him there, captive between her thighs, grinding her heat against his open mouth and searching tongue, short gasps of breath coming from her slack mouth. He parted her with his fingers, totally exposed, and then licked her long and thoroughly, slowly as if time was on their side. Shayna felt the lioness of passion being unleashed, felt the coils of her core loosen as her body started to shake. *Awww!* Before the shuddering could cease, he'd rolled them over as gently as if she were a piece of priceless porcelain, had placed her on top of him and guided himself inside her. She gasped at the combination of agony and ecstasy as she widened to accommodate his massive girth, and the length as well. He held her still for a moment, until her nature fully welcomed his gift. And then he truly began the greeting, raising her up and down his moistened shaft, thrusting himself inside her with a ferocity she'd not known existed, twisting himself to reach parts of her insides that had never been touched, slamming into her soul with a wild abandon. They came as one, their cries a symphony.

It was the sound of her voice that had awakened her, and Shayna's heart had plummeted when she realized that her rendezvous with Michael had been in her dreams. As the fingers of dawn had etched themselves across the morning sky, Shayna had placed her fingers where she longed to feel Michael's manhood, trying with limited success to assuage the ache in the valley that her dream had caused. In these early morning moments she was all too aware that it had been almost four months since she'd had sex, and probably years—if ever—since she'd made love. It was here, in solitude and silence, that she remembered how real had been the vision even as she acknowledged her love for Michael, albeit only in her dreams.

"Shayna!"

Shayna shook herself out of the reverie. How long had she been daydreaming? It felt like moments, but the flashback had occurred in mere seconds. "I'm sorry, Kim. Just remembered something that I, uh, needed to tell Michael."

"Well, if the look you had on your face just now is any indication, it will be a juicy tidbit you share."

"No," Shayna said, feeling a heat that had nothing to do with the sun overhead. "Michael doesn't date his clients and with my ongoing Jarrell drama, love is the last thing on my mind."

"Hmph, whatever," Kim replied, her voice disbelieving as she picked at a wildflower growing in the grass. "So is he?"

"Is he what?" *A great kisser? A phenomenal lover? Hung like a jury split at six and six?*

"Gorgeous! Shayna, did you even hear me?"

"He's nice looking," Shayna replied, trying to sound even toned as a flush rose from her neck to her cheeks. "With probably a list a mile long of females to remind him of this fact."

Kim looked up, shielding her eyes against the day's brightness. "Here comes Coach," she said, rising quickly. "Let me get going before he dreams up more exercises for me to do."

Personally, Shayna was glad for the diversion. Better to deal with the dreams her coach might be having . . . than her own.

16

A week went by without Shayna seeing or talking to Michael. But he was never far from her thoughts. Ever since that stupid dream, she'd not been able to get him out of her head. It didn't help that Jarrell was back to his old habits, blowing up her phone and sending crazy texts. Seems his promise to leave her alone had a time limit. On a positive note, her ribs were healing nicely. She now only wore the bandage at night. She'd also started performing light stretches, and walking three to four miles daily around the track. If all went well, she'd be able to run in the Platinum Card Classics.. Not only was it an important event in the USTAF Series, but the prize money would add much-needed cash to Shayna's dwindling bank account. It helped to split living expenses with her roommates, but one of the main reasons she'd hooked up with Michael's firm was for the possibility of sponsor dollars. Running was her passion, and a sport, but it was also business, her livelihood. Michael had told her that he was the man for the job, and now she hoped that he was a man of his word. These were just a few of the thoughts running through her head on a rare evening where she had the condo all to herself. Until now, there'd been little time to miss Jarrell's companionship and while Shayna meant what she'd told Kim about no time for love, she'd neglected to mention the times of loneliness.

Having finished putting away her laundry, Shayna paused in front of the floor-length mirror hanging on her closet door. She was wearing baggy shorts and a loose, torn T-shirt. Lifting the shirt, she ran a hand over her midsection, pressing the areas that a short time ago had been in such pain. The swelling had vanished, along with the bruising, and while areas of tenderness remained, Shayna was pleased to see that she could move fairly freely without hurting. She finished her impromptu medical exam, but continued her perusal. Turning sideways, she eyed her profile, dispassionately and somewhat critically viewing her compact body, adequate breasts, and round booty. She faced the mirror, brought her face up close. When out with her friends she garnered her fair share of attention, she guessed. But her mother, a tall caramel beauty who looked more like Shayna's older sister than a mom, often derided her chocolate tone, and called her generous backside a "ghetto butt." Jarrell was drawn to women with generous cleavage, even that which had been created with a surgeon's skill, and regularly stated—often while tousling her shoulder-length hair—how much he loved long flowing weaves. With a pang more real than her cracked ribs had produced, Shayna missed Big Mama, the one and only person on the planet who'd told her she was beautiful, and Shayna believed it.

"Don't matter who else loves you if you love yourself," Big Mama had admonished Shayna more than once.

"But what about Mom? Why doesn't she love me?"

"She loves you," Big Mama explained. "Just don't know how to show it, never did. And then something happened that made her shut off her feelings."

"What?"

Big Mama had shook her head. "That's something she'll have to tell you. But she loves you, Shayna. In her own way, she loves you."

"What about my father, Big Mama? Did you ever meet him?"

"No, never did."

Shayna was seven years old the first time she asked about her father. Beverly told her he'd been "claimed by the streets" when Shayna was just a baby. Throughout the years, Shayna had often tried to learn more about her dad, but Beverly wasn't forthcoming. "Didn't really know him," she'd told her. "We broke up before you were born," she'd add. Beverly may have loved Shayna "in her own way," but Big Mama had loved her in every way, and had given her the strength that at times Shayna forgot she had.

Tired of her own thoughts, Shayna trudged into the kitchen, fixed herself a simple salad, and plopped down on the couch in front of the TV. Her mind whirled again, this time with thoughts of Jarrell. As she surfed the channels, she remembered the events surrounding the fifty-five-inch flat screen, shortly after she'd won an event for a five-figure prize and Jarrell was more than happy to help her spend the money. He'd been as excited as a five-year-old when he'd purchased the big screen, had spent most of the night playing video games when he'd finished setting it up. Jarrell had changed over the years, become more aggressive and possessive. But there had been good times. Once.

Shayna was thankful when the phone rang, interrupting

the inner dialogue that otherwise refused to keep silent. "Hello?"

"Hey, Shay."

"Coach?"

"That's right."

Shayna sat up as she muted the television. While John was a dedicated coach, everyone knew that the weekends not spent at track meets were committed to his wife and daughter. That he was calling her on a Saturday night meant something was serious. Her heartbeat quickened as she ran through the possibilities for this call, including her deepest fear—that someone was replacing her on the relay team or another event. "What is it, Coach?"

"I'm calling about the Cape Cod Classics coming up. We're going over the roster on Monday and I want to know if you think you'll be ready for that event."

"I'll be ready," Shayna answered without hesitation. Since high school, track had been the one constant in her life that never let her down, her salvation when life threw fast pitches and curveballs. She didn't want to contemplate life without it, especially since these points counted toward the World Indoor Championship happening the following March.

"What is your doctor saying?"

Even though it had been almost two weeks since Gregory had seen her, again, Shayna answered without missing a beat. "He said I was healing perfectly and on schedule. You saw the lightweight jogging I've been doing and yesterday I incorporated a few leg weights."

"Nobody knows your body like you do, but I'd still feel more comfortable talking with your doctor. Coming back to work prematurely can result in permanent damage. As much as I'd love to have you participate, we have to make sure you're healthy. So if you'll give me your doctor's name and number, I'll call him first thing Monday morning."

"I don't have it handy, Coach. Can I get it and call you back?"

"The wife and I are heading out to dinner. Why don't you call me with it tomorrow?"

"Will do." Shayna ended the call and dialed Michael. She hadn't talked to him since he'd invaded her dreams earlier in the week, and felt a bit embarrassed at the prospect of speaking with him now. As if to do so would reveal her secret, that she'd enjoyed their nocturnal rendezvous and wished that it had been real.

After several rings, the sound of Michael's voice poured into her ear. "Morgan." It sounded as though he were at a club or party; his voice was raised loud above the music.

"Michael, it's Shayna." Her voice rose as well, to be heard above the din.

"Hold on a minute." There was a rustling sound before his voice became muffled. Shayna's brow creased as she imagined him excusing himself from a foxy-looking female. "Hey, Shayna," he said from a quieter location. "What's going on?"

"Sorry to bother you, Michael," she said, though she felt not at all bad about taking him away from his date. "But I need your brother's number."

"Why? Is something wrong?"

"No." She told him about her coach's request.

"Oh, okay." Michael gave her the number. "If you get his voice mail, leave a message. He got a rare weekend off and went to Vegas, so he might not answer his phone." A pause and then, "So tell me . . . are you home alone on a Saturday night?"

Put like that, her reality sounded pitiful. She was at home and quite alone. Again, the dream flashed before her eyes and for a moment, more like a split second, she thought about inviting her manager over. "I'm taking it easy so my body can heal," she replied, quite proud of herself for coming up with such a legitimate-sounding answer on the spot. "We have a meet coming up soon and I've got to be ready."

"That reminds me. I need to see you this week. Choice will be heading back to New York soon and before leaving, she has a few samples she'd like you to try."

"We just met with her. She has samples all ready?"

"Yes. Choice is one of the most talented designers in the business, not to mention a workaholic; the reason Chai Fashions is such a success." A pause and then, "When's a good time for you to meet us?"

"Any day after six will be good. I'm at work until then."

"All right, I'll call you. Stay sweet, Shayna."

For moments, Shayna held the phone after the call had ended. His parting words had been delivered softly, almost whispered, like a caress. The gently spoken command stayed with her throughout the evening, as she watched a documentary on OWN and later, while soaking in a hot tub laced with healing salts. She thought of Michael. That night, again, she dreamed of him . . . fueled for sure by the last thought on her mind before slumber claimed her: *Stay sweet.*

17

Shayna squinted as her eyes adjusted from the bright outdoor sunlight to the subdued lighting of the downtown warehouse. When Michael told her where she'd be meeting Choice for the track suit fitting, Shayna had been a bit surprised at the location. After Googling Chai Fashions on the Web, she was sure they'd be meeting somewhere in Beverly Hills, possibly Rodeo Drive or some other street in the 90210 area. Instead she'd traveled down a familiar road near her alma mater, Olympic Boulevard, until she'd reached Santee Street, where she'd made a left, drove a few blocks, and parked her car in front of a nondescript corner building on the right side of the street.

Walking down a short hallway, Shayna turned into a fluorescent-lighted room filled with row after row of fabric bolts. Two long tables sat flush against the far wall, weighed down with various books, fabrics, and what Shayna guessed to be sewing accessories. Neo-soul flowed out of an iPod perched on the receptionist's desk. A voluptuous Latina with long thick black hair, sparkling black eyes, and a pleasant smile greeted her. "Hello. May I help you?"

"I'm here for a meeting with"—*Choice or Chai?*— "Chai Fashions."

"Sure." The receptionist nodded, reaching for the phone at the same time. "And you are?"

"Shayna Washington."

"Choice, Shayna's here." The receptionist pointed toward a hall. "All the way down that hall, last room on your left."

Shayna walked in the direction the receptionist had pointed, noting that the rooms on both sides of the hall were filled with sewing machines, sewing accessories such as thread, buttons, zippers, and the like, and mounds and mounds of fabric. As she neared the last door on the right, she heard the sound of Michael's laughter.

"Hey, guys," Shayna said upon entering the room. She was a bit taken aback at Chai otherwise known as Choice's markedly different appearance. Gone was the long hair (which Shayna now knew was a wig, not a weave), the oversized shirt, skinny pants, and clunky jewelry. Chai had obviously left the building. Today Choice wore a simple, formfitting jean dress with flat gladiator sandals. Her hair was short, natural, and dyed a shade of auburn that nicely complemented her skin. "Sorry to keep you waiting," she said, hoping that she'd successfully hid her shock at Choice's transformed appearance. "Traffic was crazy."

"No worries," Choice said, from behind a table where she was draping a shiny fabric over a dummy bust. "And yes, I'm the same woman you met the other night. Well, kinda sorta. You met my alter ego, who the world knows as Chai. She's out there so I can still enjoy my anonymity in my own skin."

"You can definitely do that," Shayna replied. "There's no way I'd know you two were the same person." And then, "I like your hair color."

"Thanks, girl."

"Hello, Shayna." Michael got up from his seat, walked over to where Shayna stood, and gave her a hug. "Wait until you see your new look. You're going to make a fashion statement on the track and start a trend in the streets."

"I don't know about all that," Shayna replied, not trying to hide her skepticism as she eyed the array of rhinestones and other flashy colors laid out in front of Choice. "I don't want to be out there looking like Cee-Lo Green at the Super Bowl!"

"Ha!" Choice stepped away from the bust and walked over to another table. She picked up two pieces of what looked to be a lightweight nylon fabric in understated gold, and motioned to Shayna. "Come try these on. You'll see that I incorporated your ideas about mixing fabrics. It works. The changing area is there in the corner."

Once inside the room, Shayna made fast work of shedding her drawstring pants and cotton tee. She liked the style of the outfit Choice had designed, the way the top cropped to just below the bust, and the boy shorts curved upward to expose more thigh. They looked comfortable and nonrestrictive, and the meshlike fabric gave the sexy illusion of showing more skin than was actually being exposed. The panels of Spandex added to the design's uniqueness. She put on the garments, turned to look in the mirror, and almost gasped. The material hugged her booty in a way that gave the effect of a neon sign. "Booty here, it's Shayna's boooooty here!" *Oh. My. Goodness.* The voice of Shayna's mother, Beverly, rose up in her mind. *That girl has a ghetto booty. Her ass is huge!* The neighborhood children had added to the teasing and by the time Jarrell tried to convince her that having a large gluteus maximus was a blessing, not a curse, it was too late. Beverly's damage had already been done.

After a few moments, Choice's voice interrupted Shayna's unplanned and unwelcomed walk down memory lane. "Shayna, is everything okay?"

"Yes, it's fine."

"Here, let me see." Shayna heard footsteps and soon Choice was pulling back the curtain. "Whoa, baby. You are rocking that outfit!" She entered and adjusted the bottoms. "Those shorts are on point! Come on out so Michael can have a look."

Shayna battled feelings of being modest, a new experience. Showing skin on the track field was something that the athletes rarely thought about. But now, with Michael in the other room, waiting to peruse her body up one side and down the other, she suddenly felt as though she should be wearing more clothes. These thoughts were processed in the time it took her to follow Choice out of the changing room and into the main area where Michael stood.

For a moment, Michael swore that the air left the room. Shayna walked toward him. He was positive that she had no idea the vision she presented: tight, chocolate body, toned abs, muscled legs. *Wow.* The decision he'd made to stay far and wide away from any type of romantic liaison with any of his clients battled the desire he had to sex Shayna and thus get her out of his system. He forced himself to remember his ex-client, the female basketball stalker, even bringing to mind the last time he saw the woman. All flailing arms and kicking legs—

subdued by Troy, his brother who owned a security business—she'd spewed words that burned his ears and launched threats that though she didn't follow through on, could have warranted her arrest. He swallowed hard, found his power, nodded his approval. "Looks good," he said, managing to adopt a properly casual tone of voice. That is, after he found it.

And then, at Choice's instruction, she turned around. *Damn.*

"Perfect," Choice gushed, walking around her muse and admiring her skills. "This outfit looks amazing . . . if I say so myself. What about the color?" she asked Shayna. "Do you like it?"

Shayna nodded. "There are some meets with more restrictive guidelines, however. So we'd have to have the more conservative navies and blacks as part of the line."

"No problem," Choice said, walking back over to the table where garments were strewn. She picked up two pieces of black mesh, like the material that Shayna wore. "Try on these."

She obliged, for not only the black two-piece but for a bright yellow iridescent, and even a pinstriped version of the same design, along with a daring one-piece for which Choice had borrowed from 1920s bathing suits for inspiration.

"Which style do you think would best suit the relay team?" Choice asked, as Shayna stood in the last look, a deep burgundy two-piece with bright pink satiny stripes up the side.

"Definitely the black or navy," Michael interrupted. "I want the bright flashy colors to be Shayna's signature, and that swimsuit-inspired design worn by her alone."

18

Michael pushed away the plate containing a half-eaten steak as he leaned back from the table. Along with his ability to get to sleep last night, had Shayna taken his appetite as well? He hadn't been able to get her out of his mind, that's for sure. Last night, he'd tossed and turned as visions of the one-woman fashion show danced in his head: her coy smile, graceful neck, perky boobs, taut abs, svelte hips . . . and that ass. *Lord have mercy, that ass!*

The waitress came over to refill his tea. "Mr. Morgan, would you like to see the dessert menu?"

"No, just the check, please." There was only one kind of dessert on Michael's mind and the restaurant couldn't deliver it. He reached for his wallet as the phone rang. "Yes?"

"Hey, boss. I've got Erin Bridges on the line. She wants to confirm your attendance at tonight's benefit, as well as the RSVP for two persons."

"Dang, I'd forgotten all about that." Since Shayna had become his client, Michael seemed to be forgetting about a lot of things. Not like him. Not good. Not to mention the women on his electronic address book that up until a month ago he'd sexed on the regular. But this event was important. Proceeds from it would benefit some of the inner city sports programs. And his date was the marketing director for XMVP, the newest player in athlete shoes and sportswear giving Nike, Jordan, and other classic companies a run for their money. He planned to use the evening to pitch Shayna as the next spokesperson for the company and model for their running shoes. "Yes, tell Erin I'll be there, along with a guest."

Later that evening, Michael arrived at the Ritz-Carlton Hotel, squiring an extremely attractive woman on his arm. Dina DeVore was a known force to be reckoned with in the world of retail, with clout that went far beyond Fifth Avenue and Fashion Week. Like Erin Bridges, Dina DeVore came from a wealthy, influential family. She was a strong, powerful woman who knew what—or in this case more specifically *who*—she wanted. They were less than an hour into the evening when Michael got the memo. Figuring he'd use this obvious interest to his advantage, he steered their conversation into the reason for their meeting.

"As you know," Michael said to Dina after they'd settled into dinner, "Shayna Washington made quite a name for herself at the London Olympics. I represent her now, and think she'd be a great addition for the XMVP brand."

"I don't know, Michael," Dina said, flirtatiously twirling a fiery red lock around her finger. "We're interested in showcasing new faces and the track world is definitely a place to look. But our research has shown a larger popularity among male athletes. Currently, we're considering Usain Bolt, of course, along with Tyson Gay, Richard Thompson, and others."

"Great choices," Michael quickly agreed. "But what if I told you that a couple Hollywood execs are eyeing her for a breakout role in an upcoming movie, and what if I said that in Tinseltown one of them is the number-two man? In less than two years, Shayna Washington will be a household name. And when she takes all the gold at the next Olympics, what if she's locked into a multiyear lucrative contract and your company appears genius?"

"I'd say that you're living up to your reputation." Dina placed a suggestive hand on Michael's thigh.

"Darling," he drawled, deftly moving her hand by lifting it to his lips for a kiss. "You have no idea." Then he tried to summon up the Morgan Mack, the kind he would use to seal the deal. Michael wasn't for sale, but in business deals he'd often given off the suggestion that he could be rented. That possibility alone often helped seal the deal, before the associate learned that he never mixed business with pleasure. But tonight, beyond the perfunctory kiss on the cheek upon greeting and this kiss on the hand before it moved to places off-limits, Michael couldn't seem to drum up a flirt for the life of him. With a sigh, he thought about long, toned legs, a tight, high booty, and a coy smile. Shayna. And he knew the reason.

Man, you're not going to be able to get that woman out of your system until you take her and do what comes naturally. And just like that, it was decided. He would make sure she understood the parameters, could handle a casual fling, and then he'd scratch the itch that had been bothering him worse than a poison ivy rash ever since she'd graced his home. Michael would break his own rule. He'd sleep with America's next sports sensation, Shayna Washington. That was the bottom line.

19

"I wouldn't sleep with him if we were the last two people on earth, it was subzero, and he was my only source of warmth." Shayna paced the room as she presented a convincing argument to her audience, the girls. The roommates who were acting crazy, and daring her to seduce her manager. Why? Because she'd finally let them in on her crazy attraction and increasingly frequent fantasies. She admitted to them that for the last week she simply hadn't been able to get him out of her mind. "He's too arrogant, too used to having everybody run when he snaps his fingers. I wouldn't give him the satisfaction."

"Forget about *him*," Talisha argued. "Sounds like you need to give *yourself* some."

"You've admitted that you like him," Brittney added, "and that you're feeling rhythm between the two of you. He's also single, gorgeous, and powerful. What more reason do you need?"

"I don't want to be like all the other women he's met. I'm sure most throw themselves at him."

"Then don't throw yourself," Talisha calmly replied. "Walk over to his ass all ladylike and request an appointment with his penis. I'd do him in a New York minute, faster than Trell Kimmons could run the one hundred."

"That would be some quick nooky," Shayna countered, "since brother man Trell is keeping it one hundred in less than ten ticks."

"I doubt anything about a romp with Michael Morgan would be quick. . . . " Brittney's dreamy expression made Shayna get up and deliver a playful punch to her friend's shoulder. "What?" Brittney continued in mock chagrin. "He looks like one of those long and strong kind of brothers. . . .I'm just saying."

Talisha leaned against the bar stool. "Shayna, you keep saying that you need to get over Jarrell, that you *are* over him, right?"

"I am over him!" Two pairs of eyes showing skepticism held her gaze. "I've forgiven him, but I haven't forgotten him," Shayna admitted. "I've known Jarrell over my whole life, dated him for almost ten years. We were best friends forever, and I'd be lying to say that words he's pounded into me over the years aren't still playing in my head—that no one would love me like him, treat me better than him. Just before we broke up, he reminded me of the promise I made him when we graduated high school."

"You were just a kid," Brittney insisted. "We all make promises when we're in puppy love. But as a woman, you should know that you have the prerogative to change your mind."

"I know, and I agree that I'm tripping, y'all. I'm messed up! Still trying to please a mother who isn't looking out for my best interests, still thinking about a man who scratched up my face. We've only been broken up since June. That's hardly time to get over what he and I had."

"Considering that his controlling, possessive, insecure ass cracked your ribs and bruised your face up, I'd say it was more than enough time."

"Not to mention that he seems to have moved on." Belatedly, Talisha realized that she may have just delivered a little TMI. "At least that's the word on the street. That he's dating some chick from his job."

"I don't care," Shayna said, in a voice that suggested she cared very much. "I know who she is and also know that he's been sleeping with her for months, from way before we broke up." Which pissed her off. That she knew, that he knew she knew, that he was trying to get back with her while still sleeping with one of the women who helped break them up! *How can I still have feelings for an abuser? And why can't I seem to get past this relationship and move on?* But Shayna knew the answer to that. Her mother, Beverly. As long as she was married to Larsen, Jarrell would be in Shayna's life, as a brother-in-law at least, even if one only recognized from a distance. The situation was jacked up, but it was what it was. "Maybe y'all are right," Shayna said with a sigh, walking over to the couch and crushing a throw pillow against her chest as she sat down. "Maybe I should have Michael Morgan sex me real good, pump Jarrell Powell, and this crazy hold he and Mom have on me, right out of a sistah's system."

Brittney jumped off the bar chair and slapped Shayna a high five. "Check out that Master P, girlfriend," she said with unabashed relish. "That's what I'm talking about!"

Shayna laughed at Brittney's use of their code word

for penis. "Okay," Talisha said, her natural planning skills bubbling to the surface. "Since we've decided that you're going to do the damn thing, let's make some plans. Where and how are you going to seduce him?"

"Geez, Tee, I don't know! It was only five seconds ago that I decided that I would."

"Well, a woman has to know these things."

"And like Brittney says, a woman has a right to change her mind. Which I think I'm doing right now."

"Why?" Talisha demanded.

"Because I don't want to be like every other woman he's met and been able to get in his bed. I think my not giving in to him is what will make me different."

Talisha gave Brittney a surreptitious wink. "Hmm, and you want to be different because . . . ?"

"Because I'm his client, and I don't want to cross that line. I told you guys that and now, instead of helping me be strong and stand my ground, you're trying to turn me into a . . . a . . . a floozy!"

"Ha! That's Big Mama talking right there," Brittney said, having spent enough time at Shayna's grandmother's house to know when the dear woman had gotten in her friend's head. "Big Mama wouldn't be mad at your trying to be happy," she continued in a softer tone. "That's all Tee and I want for you, Shay. We want to see the smile that these days is so rarely on your face. We want our girl back!"

"So if she was going to seduce him," Talisha continued as if Shayna hadn't changed her mind, "where would it be?"

"Why not his house, after a scrumptious meal created by the *chef*?" Brittney shrugged. "Sounds like the easiest, most logical choice."

"Not at all," Talisha argued. "You never want to meet

the man of your mission on his home turf. You want to choose someplace neutral and impersonal, where you can be in total control."

The room was silent as each woman pondered alternatives. Then Brittney spoke up. "Shay, didn't you say that Michael was going to the Cape Cod Classic?"

A squiggle went from Shayna's core to cootchie as she answered. "Yes, he's supposed to come and bring a potential sponsor, someone from XMVP Shoes and Sportswear."

"Hey," Talisha sang, dancing around the room. "Michael's going to the Cape Cod Classic and the brother's going to get some Cape Cod cootchie!"

Shayna deadpanned at Talisha. "Shut. Up."

"Cape Cod cootchie," Brittney sang, joining in with Talisha and dancing across the living room floor. "Some Morgan booty and some Cape Cod cootchie."

"Y'all have no sense," Shayna said with a frown. "I told you that I changed my mind. I'm not going to eff that man." But she could only hold it for so long. Soon, she was laughing along with her roommates and later, thought about "Morgan booty" and "Cape Cod cootchie" well into the night.

20

"Hey, Mom." Shayna raised her voice so that it could be heard through the speakerphone on the other side of the room. She'd been trying to pack for the past hour with what seemed like one interruption after another. This one, if the past was any indication of the future, was particularly one she could do without.

"Shayna, I left you a message two days ago. Why haven't I heard back from you?"

"I've been really busy, Mom, getting ready for the meet this week."

"Well, if you're too busy to call your mother back . . . you're too busy."

Shayna swallowed the sarcastic comment that threatened to spill out of her mouth. She knew where it had come from. On occasions too numerous to mention, Shayna recalled Big Mama saying that very thing to Beverly, when she'd gone too long without contacting mother or daughter. How many times had Shayna's mother been too busy for her daughter? How many times had Beverly Washington Powell put her own needs, desires, goals ahead of those of her child? Did

Beverly care that Shayna had found it embarrassing that her mother was dating her boyfriend's older brother? Being seven years older than Jarrell put Larsen just at a decade younger than her forty-three-year-old mother, but still! Had her mother once thought of how it felt for Shayna to find out from Jarrell and not Beverly that she and Larsen had married in Vegas? Did she ever think of the repercussions of a daughter feeling that her own mother was more of a competitor than a confidante? That the sexy good looks and vivacious personality of the mother had not only not been visited down on the daughter, but had made that daughter withdrawn and insecure, traits that she was still trying to shed in her midtwenties? No, Shayna didn't think her self-centered mother, Beverly, had ever considered such truths. Just like Jarrell had never placed her considerations before his own. Jarrell was quite a piece of work and as far as Shayna was concerned, her mother and Larsen were quite the pieces too.

"Shayna, what are you doing?"

"I told you, Mom. I'm packing for the meet in Massachusetts. Our flight leaves first thing in the morning."

"So when were you going to call me back about Thanksgiving?"

"Mom! We haven't even gotten to Halloween yet. What's the rush about the holidays?"

"I just want to make sure you're here, that's all."

"I hear that, but why?"

"Does a mother have to have a reason to want her daughter home for the holidays?"

When that mother's name is Beverly, then, yes, as a matter of fact. "As far as I know our schedule is clear that weekend, Mom, but it depends on Coach. He sometimes comes up with drills at the last minute and if that happens, then I'll need to be here."

"Hold on a minute, Shayna. Someone wants to talk to you."

"Mom, wait!"

But she'd already handed over the phone. "Hey, Shay."

Shayna didn't try to stifle her sigh. "Jarrell, what?"

"How's my baby girl?"

"I'm not your baby girl—"

"You've got a brother on lockdown or what? Can't get you to pick up the phone when I call directly."

"There's a reason for that, Jay. I don't want to talk to you. Damn! Sounding like a broken record is getting old!"

"I know you need time to cool off from what happened. I understand that. But we're going to get back on track, girl. By the time Thanksgiving rolls around, you'll be ready to take me back."

Whoa, back the bump up. Did this man just say "Thanksgiving?" Has Mom invited Jarrell to the same dinner she's inviting me to, knowing how I feel about him and how much I'm wanting, no, needing to move on from his grasp? Seriously? "Jarrell, tell Mom I'll call her next week, after the meet. I've got to go."

Shayna finished packing, then went into the kitchen.

Brittney was already there, making chicken salad. "Did I just hear the name Jarrell when I came out of my bedroom?"

"Unfortunately, yes." Shayna reached for a celery stick, leaned back on the counter, and munched it as she relayed the conversation with Beverly and Jarrell to Brittney. "I can't believe she's choosing Jay's side over mine, when I've told her that all I want to do is move on!"

Brittney stopped, looked her roommate straight in the eye. "Yes, Shayna, you can believe it. Your mother is a stone cold trip. I keep telling you that you don't have to stop loving her, but that you might need to do so from a distance."

"Yeah, I guess."

"I can understand it, though; you only have one mother and she's it."

"Lucky me."

"So are you going to do it? Are you going to spend Thanksgiving in Vegas, playing one big happy family with the Powells?"

"Right now, I just have one thing on my mind," Shayna responded. "And that's playing one big happy family with Michael Morgan in Cape Cod."

"So you're going to do it! Ha! Now you're talking, sistah," Brittney said, reaching into the cabinet for another plate. "You want some, right?" Shayna nodded. "Did you pack that dress that I gave you?" Shayna nodded again. "And the eff-me pumps?"

"Yes, ma'am," Shayna sarcastically replied. "Anything else, Mommy?"

"Just hoping that you got the bikini wax that I suggested. A brother doesn't need to take a dive at the Y and encounter grizzly fur!"

"Britt, you are a fool!"

Brittney winked, picking up her plate and bottle of water in the process. "I love you, too."

21

The Lighthouse Sports Center, a state-of-the-art indoor sports facility constructed on a picturesque piece of land in Falmouth, Massachusetts, bordering the Cape Cod Canal, was an athlete's dream. A multistory, multi-winged building of ten thousand square feet, the facility was now home to the state's preeminent sports teams, including several baseball franchises, the volley-ball league, flag football, and the hockey team, the Cape Cod Clubs. The California Angels track team, including Shayna, had taken full advantage of their top-of-the-line exercise facility, and after a full body massage, she was feeling a little less antsy about what would take place in about twenty-five hours.

But she wasn't thinking about the relay or her two sprints. She was thinking about the seduction of Michael Morgan.

After a fitful night's sleep, Shayna stepped onto the track ready and focused. As always, running was both her sanctity and salvation. She blocked out everything but her competition and her lane, forgetting about Michael, Choice, and a representative from XMVP in the stand, and even about the fact that she was debuting one of the more subtle outfits . . . a fashion line that would roll out under Shayna's own label—Triple S— which stood for Shayna's Sprint Sensations. (Thankfully, Choice had agreed with Shayna and nixed the *Sprintress* idea.) While some of her teammates preferred the standard issue track uniform, others applauded her daring fashion statement. Tomorrow, during the relay events, she would wear the navy shorts and tank top with the iridescent strip down the side, along with the others on the 4 x 100 relay team, Talisha, Brittney, and Kim. But today, she wore high-rise boy shorts in a barely discernible pinstriped design, with a matching tank top. She also wore on her feet a pair of Right Flights, a lightweight running shoe that Michael hoped Shayna would be able to endorse. She was ecstatic about her performance since wearing the shoes and, in a nod to Michael Johnson, was considering having her shoes made in an iridescent motif.

After a morning filled with throwing sports, jumps, and hurdles, it was time for the relays to begin: the 4 x 100, the 4 x 200, the 4 x 400, and the mother of all relays, the 4 x 1500. As always, Shayna was a bundle of nervous energy, vibes she'd channel into power once her fingers wrapped around the baton. She was the fourth runner of the relay team, the anchor. If her girls did their job, and they always did, then all she'd have to do is keep the lead and bring it home. As the officials directed them onto the track, Shayna did a variety of stretches and a couple half sprints before taking off the warm-up that Choice had designed. Once rid of the jacket and leggings, she tapped her thigh muscles, shook out her arms and legs, rolled her neck around, and pushed short bursts of air from her lungs. She elongated her body as much as possible, reaching to the heavens while standing on her tiptoes, before bending her midsection until her fingers made contact with the ground by her toes. She wasn't aware of the picture she painted, and how when she stretched her legs like this her boy shorts rode high, exposing quarter-moon mounds of chocolate goodness.

But somebody was.

Michael casually stretched out his long legs in front of him, or tried to. The indoor stadium's bleacher seats weren't the best place to try and hide a hard-on, especially one that seemed determined to ignore its master's command that it calm the bump down. He forced his eyes away from the vision in front of him and looked across the track at the other runners. He noted the eight lanes filled with toned bodies, a virtual smorgasbord to a bona fide player such as himself. *Maybe I won't go after Shayna,* he decided. The waters would be less murky if his conquest resided in another state.

"She looks good, doesn't she?" Choice asked, with a nod in Shayna's direction.

Well, so much for keeping my mind off the booty. "Yes, she does. Those uniforms look nice on all of the women."

"Comfortable, providing ease of movement . . ."

Michael nodded, as his phone vibrated against his hip. "Right." He looked down. *Felicia.* He never should have told that girl that he'd be on the East Coast. Good thing he'd left his exact location vague, otherwise she would have been on the first thing smoking to the Cape. He pressed the ignore button and had barely gotten the phone placed back in his pocket when it vibrated again. *Valerie.* He frowned. It had been a month since he'd been with any of his female crew and still they kept calling. Wanting to know what the deal was. Well, so did he.

"Complications?" Dina drawled out the word as if she already knew the answer.

"Business."

"Ha! If you say so." Dina leaned over so that only Michael could hear her. "I have some . . . business for us to handle later as well."

"I know. Shayna Washington. I've already arranged for our dinner tomorrow."

"You are a naughty boy, Michael Morgan. You very well know I'm not talking about your latest . . . acquisition, although you have convinced me that she might make an attractive and popular spokesperson." Her voice dropped even lower. "I'm talking about the matter that was so rudely interrupted at the benefit. As I remember, a phone call put an early end to our evening."

Michael remembered. He'd texted Troy for one of their emergency deliverances. More than once the brothers had come to each other's rescue when females became too aggressive. Dina was a hot, vibrant woman, to be sure, but Michael's focus was elsewhere right now. As if to underscore the point, the official motioned for the first runner of each team in the relay to get down into their starting blocks. *On your mark!* Michael's eyes drifted from that runner, Kim as he remembered, over to the others, Brittney and Talisha, before finally coming to rest on Shayna, the one closest to where he sat. He watched as she nervously shook her legs and twisted her neck one way and then the other. At this moment, he had an intense desire to help her work out those kinks, those in her neck and those decidedly lower as well. Mr. Big threatened to make his presence known again, so Michael shifted his focus from sexual to sprinting, before leaning forward to watch the race.

"Set." Michael noted that instead of watching the race's beginning, Shayna's eyes were temporarily glued to the track in front of her, as if she were mentally already running her leg in her mind. "Go!" The gun shot off and the race began. The crowd came alive, shouting, yelling, rooting their selective teams to victory. Michael was caught up in the excitement, his eyes glued to the speedy runners, watching lane three, which held the California Angels, quietly encouraging Kim. *Come on, Kim. Woman . . . run!* Kim's running was graceful, powerful, her five-foot-seven frame and long legs helping her eat up the distance between her and Brittney. As they rounded the curve, the women in lanes three, five, and six had established themselves as forces to be reckoned with. When Kim was about five feet from her, Brittney began moving forward, right arm back, palm up, waiting to feel the weight of the baton. As soon as she grabbed it she shot forward, trying to increase the lead between her and the other ladies. The runner in lane five wasn't having it. Obviously, the Angels weren't the only ones who wanted first place. The ponytailed blonde in lane one moved ahead of the sistah in lane six. Michael noted the determination on her face, her thin lips pressed into a straight line, her arms maintaining a one-two rhythm as she burned up the distance to the teammate handling the third leg of the race. Brittney reached Talisha, who began in second place. Now, he noted that Shayna was no longer staring ahead of her; she was nodding her head and waving Talisha toward her, calmly encouraging her friend to pick up the pace. Talisha read the telepathic text and by the time the baton was passed to Shayna, she and the woman in lane number five were separated by inches. Shayna put her head down, and later Michael would swear that a motor got turned on. Shayna hit the curve at around ninety, Michael reckoned, her movements smooth and purposeful, her body straight, her arms pumping, her feet barely touching the ground.

Michael was on his feet before he even realized it. "Go, Shayna!"

And she did. There was a good two feet between her and second place. After crossing the line, she did what would become her signature dance, a little hop, step, and body twirl as she pointed her fingers to the sky. Her teammates rushed over to join her at the finish line. The foursome celebrated coming very close to breaking an indoor record.

"Impressive," Dina said, once Michael had retaken his seat.

"Definitely," Michael replied. *And the race was pretty good, too.*

22

The following evening, Shayna waved good-bye to her teammates and nervously approached the waiting limousine. She felt strangely out of place, not joining her friends for celebratory pizza in Coach's suite. The day had been fantastic, with Shayna taking second in the 100-meter race, and third in the 200. Considering she'd not trained much for the past few weeks and had missed the platinum classics, she didn't feel too bad. Especially since she'd shown up and performed where it counted the most, the 4 x 100 relay with her girls.

She nodded a greeting as the driver opened her door, then she settled in for what she'd been told was a ten- to fifteen-minute ride. Retrieving the mirror from her purse, she eyed her reflection with a critical view. Turning this way and that, she finally agreed with Britt and Tee—the upswept do made her look more sophisticated and Talisha's makeup job was spot on. Rarely one to wear makeup, Shayna was pleasantly surprised how the smoky eye shadow made her large doe eyes stand out, and the mascara promising "lashes so long you will swear that they're fake" was pretty much living up to its name. She licked her lips, still getting used to the bronze-colored gloss that Brittney had sworn would be a perfect match for the dress she'd insisted Shayna borrow—a formfitting cream-colored jersey silk that highlighted her curves like a yellow marker and hit her legs a few inches above the knee. "This is too much, too sexy," she'd argued after first donning the garment. She'd turned in the mirror and almost gasped, feeling that her booty was way too prominent to be considered decent, and the neckline a little too plunging for her taste. Then both Brittney and Talisha had reminded her of the night's goal: seducing Michael Morgan. Back in Los Angeles, in the comfort of her condo, the idea had sounded genius. It had even still made sense this morning, when Michael had approached her at the track. But now, with her friends-barrier back at the hotel and the distance between her and Michael being rapidly eaten up by a limo driver on a mission, Shayna was now trying to find the mind that she'd lost.

"We're here, ma'am."

Shayna looked up to find what appeared to be a large, Victorian-style brick home with defined shingles, several gables, and a windowed turret. Her expression was dubious. "This is it?"

"Yes, ma'am. The Belfry Inne and Bistro is housed in what is called the Painted Lady, a reference used for Victorian homes back in the nineteenth century when this was built. I've brought my share of guests to this establishment, and haven't ever heard of one who left disappointed." He got out of the car to open the door for Shayna.

"Thank you," she said, and then realized that she hadn't even thought of the cost of the ride. "I'm sorry, how much do I owe you?"

"All taken care of, ma'am," the driver said, with a slight bow at the waist. "Go inside and enjoy."

As Shayna approached the building's front door, she took in the charm, elegance, and grace of the place. Now, she didn't feel her outfit at all out of place, and was thankful that Talisha had talked her into wearing the dress instead of the slacks or pantsuit that would have been Shayna's choice. She entered, and was immediately taken to a table where Michael and who Shayna assumed was the XMVP representative already sat. Michael stood as she approached, his eyes hooded and unreadable. She hoped hers were as well, since the scenario she was imagining was making her nipples tingle and nana ache. He looked positively decadent in a tailored black suit and gray shirt. The woman was attractive, Shayna noted, wearing something that Shayna imagined the price of which could feed a slew of Haitian children.

"Shayna, hello," Michael said, pulling her into a lightweight hug. "Let me introduce you to Dina DeVore, the VP of marketing for XMVP Shoes and Sportswear. Dina, this is Shayna, your next superstar spokesperson."

"A pleasure to meet you," Shayna said, reaching for the outstretched hand that resembled a limp noodle when grasped. Whatever their differences, there was one thing Shayna had in common with her mother. She could read a woman's face and body language like a Kindle Fire. Shayna knew envy when she saw it, and given this potential endorser's rather frosty greeting, wondered about the relationship between this woman and Michael. If something was happening between them, then three would most definitely be a crowd.

"You looked fantastic today," Michael said, once Shayna was seated. "Especially considering the fact that a month ago you were nursing cracked ribs. You should be proud of your showing."

"I did okay," Shayna said with a shrug. "This meet simply confirmed that I have a lot of work to do."

The three made small talk as the waiter came over to take their drink order. Both Michael and Dina opted for wine while Shayna stuck to sparkling water, her drink of choice. After ordering appetizers, Cape littleneck chowder for Shayna, mussels for Michael, and Dina settling for the sirloin carpaccio, Dina's mini-interrogation began.

"So tell me, Shayna. Did you grow up in Los Angeles?"

"Yes, in Inglewood."

"And did you always like to run?"

This question somewhat calmed Shayna's nerves. Talking about her passion, her first love, was easy. And it kept her from thinking about how that whisper of a mustache and goatee framed Michael's succulent lips. "I've been running for as long as I can remember," she said, with a smile. "First with the kids, and then later *from* them. A teacher encouraged me to join the track team and then later a friend of the family" —translated: one of Beverly's many lovers, but no need to digress —"noticed my potential and suggested I be entered into some citywide races. I was, and I won. My future was set and when USC came knocking, I never looked back."

"Where do you get your talent?"

Shayna took a spoonful of chowder as she pondered her answer. She noted the aroma of the soup, identified the celery root and chorizo, along with some spices that she couldn't name. Big Mama thought the gift of speed came from her father, a belief that her mother had routinely shot down. "He wasn't fast enough to run away from the hood, to run from the lure of the streets," Beverly had countered more than once. So many times, in fact, that Shayna believed her.

Any truthful answer she gave would be too complicated, so Shayna decided for a general approach. "I guess it's God-given," she finally offered. "I just always loved to run. It makes me feel strong, and free."

Michael ate his mussels and listened intently. In this moment, he realized that there was so much about Shayna that he didn't know. And he realized something else.

He wanted to know her—everything. Everywhere.

As their meal continued and the wine flowed, Shayna noticed that the cold around Ms. Ice Princess began to thaw. Having had the time to study her, Shayna's assumption that Dina was in her thirties had been replaced by her believing the executive was in her forties instead. According to Dina, she'd been in the retail business for twenty years, having graduated from the Fashion Institute of Technology and spending several years in Europe before settling on the East Coast. These days, Shayna learned, Dina split her time between coasts, having a home on Long Island and a condo in Beverly Hills. Michael eloquently stated the case for why Shayna would make such a great spokesperson and role model, and Shayna further won Dina over with understated charm.

As they finished their entrées of salmon, short ribs, and seafood risotto, Shayna pondered her next move. *How do I get Michael away from Ice Princess? Will saying I need to talk to him seem too obvious? Is trying to outlast Ice at the table not be noticeable enough?*

Just as she began to think there was no cool way to pull his coattail and therefore no chance of seducing Michael Morgan, Dina's phone rang.

Her expression changed as she looked at the face of

it. "Hello?" And then, "What is it, Jim?" She listened, appearing more worried as she held the phone to her ear. Finally she stood. "Michael, Shayna, excuse me. This will only take a minute."

Dina had barely rounded the corner before Shayna spoke up, quickly, almost urgently, before she lost her nerve and along with it the hundred-dollar bet—or "fun incentive," as Brittney had called it—lying on the LA condo table. "Michael," she said, lightly laying her hand on his muscled arm. "I need to speak with you privately. Is it possible for us to go back to your hotel room?"

23

For a moment, Michael didn't want to move. Because if he did, then he might wake up from what was surely a dream. Since seeing the vision enter the room wrapped in cream-colored loveliness, he'd basically had two things on his mind. Outwardly, to secure the deal with Dina DeVore and XMVP Sports. Inwardly, to get Shayna into his bed.

Had he just heard correctly? Had she just *asked* to go to his room? In his mind, her doing so was akin to the fly asking the spider for permission to visit his web. Thoughts bounced around in his mind like ping-pong balls. *What did she want to talk to him about? Had she hidden her interest and now wanted to get her groove on?* And then more sinister thoughts. *Is this a ploy to aid her professional success? Is there an ulterior motive to her wanting to get into my room? In the future, is there a way that she could use whatever happens between us against me? Or become a stalker, like what's her name?*

Shayna's next words brought him out of his paralysis. "I'm sorry, Michael. I shouldn't have asked."

"No, it's not that. It's just that I—"

"Probably have plans, or somebody waiting there for you already. I totally understand that. It was presumptuous of me to think any other—"

"Shayna!" Michael said, low yet forceful, reaching over to grab her gesturing hand. "There's no need to apologize. Your request took me by surprise, that's all. You're more than welcome to join me at the hotel. In fact, it will give us a chance to go over what was discussed tonight." Michael figured to go over something all right, and it wasn't a discussion. *I just need to think of a way to get out of Dina's crosshairs.* "Look, this is going to sound crazy, but I need for you to do something. Right now."

"What?"

"I need you to jump up from the table and run into the bathroom."

"What?"

"I'll explain later, but as soon as you see Dina returning, you need to do this."

Shayna's eyes narrowed. "Oh, so that's how it is."

"No!" Michael hissed through clenched teeth. "I'll explain about her later, Shayna. Just do it!"

"What, like a Nike commercial?" Shayna wiped her mouth with the pristinely white linen napkin before slowing rising from the table. "I don't know about this now, Michael. I don't want to interfere with whatever's—"

Hearing the click-clack of Dina's heels and seeing the flash of red out the corner of his eye, Michael gave Shayna a not-so-subtle push away from him. Her face registered mild shock as she almost instinctively turned and rushed from the room, partly because he'd asked her, but mostly because the forward-propelled motion of his push suggested she keep her feet moving or fall down on her face.

As it were, in the process of leaving, she almost knocked Dina down instead.

"What's going on?" Dina asked after righting herself and rushing to the table where Michael now stood.

"Not sure," Michael quickly replied, reaching for his wallet and pulling out a couple hundred-dollar bills. "She began to feel nauseous. It came out of nowhere."

Dina watched as Shayna fled the room with her arm raised, her hand over her mouth, Dina presumed. "Maybe she's pregnant," she drawled, partially believing what Michael told her, and partially not. The plan had been for her and Michael to spend the night together, but she'd seen the way he'd eyed her potential spokesperson all evening.

After tossing the money on the table, Michael placed a hand on Dina's shoulder. "Sorry, Dina, but I'm going to have to cancel our late-night meeting. I need to check on Shayna, make sure she gets back to her hotel okay."

"How convenient," was Dina's dryly delivered response, spoken to Michael's back as he rushed from the room.

He found Shayna near the foyer. With a firm hold on her arm, he ordered, "Let's go."

Within minutes, Shayna was ensconced in a limousine next to Michael, looking back at the Belfry Inne and Bistro. Whether from nerves, fear, embarrassment, or genuine humor, Shayna couldn't tell, but she burst out laughing.

"What?" Michael asked, a big old "cheese" spreading across his face.

The more Shayna tried to explain why she was laughing, the more hysterically she guffawed. Soon, Michael's deep chuckle joined hers and the back of the limousine was filled with laughter. After a few comical moments, Shayna regained control of herself and wiped tear-filled eyes. "This is crazy," she said at last. "I felt naughty back there, like I was lying to the coach to miss practice or skipping school or something."

Baby, I'm getting ready to show you how naughty really feels!

She sobered. "But now that I'm here, I don't know if asking to see you privately was the right thing to do."

"I'm glad you did," Michael quickly reassured her. "I wanted to see you, too, just . . . didn't know how to ask you. Didn't know how you'd feel about it and I didn't want to come off as being forward or presumptuous or . . . any of those things."

Shayna turned toward him, oblivious of the fact that when she did so, her dress rose up to midthigh and one juicy, cocoa orb peaked out from the dress's bodice. "So you first. What did you want to talk to me about?"

"Mine can wait," Michael replied, reaching for Shayna's hand and looking into her eyes as he continued. "What about you?"

"Mine can wait, too," Shayna replied, suddenly feeling shy and a bit lost under his intense perusal. She deftly slid her hand from his before turning to look out the window.

Sensing her nervousness, Michael placed them back on neutral footing. "This your first time to the Cape?"

Shayna nodded. Then realizing the gesture might not be seen on this dark night, replied, "Yes, you?"

"I'm not a stranger to the area; used to attend Sean's white parties on Martha's Vineyard, and have a friend who moors his boat near Chatham."

"What, a yacht or something?"

Michael shook his head. "Fishing boat. A little . . . never mind, it doesn't matter what type it is. One of my high school buddies fancies himself a fisherman and likes to go bass fishing in the summer."

"You like to fish?" Shayna asked, not hiding the difficulty she was having in drawing a picture of Mr. GQ holding a rod and reel, let alone bait.

"I can take it or leave it. But I do enjoy the camaraderie with my boys, hanging out on the lake. There's something peaceful about fishing, being out on the water. After dealing with business twenty-four/seven, and the pace of the city, it's a nice change that I try and enjoy at least once or twice a year."

Shayna eyed the passing scenery as she pondered Michael's comments. More than once, she'd thought she sensed a kinder, gentler soul beneath Michael's playboy personality and the fast-paced lifestyle. Before, she'd dismissed these as figments of her imagination, but now she wasn't so sure. As it were, there was no more time to ponder the issue. Surprising to Shayna, they'd reached their destination within minutes and with a quick thank-you to the driver, Shayna was being led up the stairs of a private home.

"Is this your place?" she asked.

"My friend's," Michael responded, placing the key in the lock and turning it. "After you, baby."

He'd probably used the term of endearment a zillion times, but that didn't stop a mini explosion from happening in her furnace of love. His hand at the small of her back as he entered behind her didn't help either. She hurried out of his grasp, trying to get in control of her emotions, trying to remember that she was the one who was supposed to be seducing him, and not the other way around.

Michael sensed Shayna's nervousness. Oddly, he too felt uneasy, something he hadn't experienced since giving Skittles to Robin before he was a teen. Michael pondered this thought as he observed Shayna. *Perhaps that's it,* he thought as he eyed the vulnerability seeping through the strong stare. The way her eyes flittered oh-so-briefly to the side before she determinedly locked vision again with him. Shayna was a most interesting mixture of opposites: athletically strong on the outside but emotionally vulnerable on the inside.

He tried to put her at ease. "Would you like something to drink?"

"Sure. What do you have?"

Michael walked to the bar. "I know you don't drink alcohol so—"

"I'll try something light."

Michael looked up at her. "Are you sure?"

"Yes, like maybe a . . . wine cooler?"

"Ha! I haven't heard that phrase since high school. Do they still make that alcoholic Kool-Aid?"

Shayna shrugged, feeling some of her nervousness leave on the wings of his laughter. "You know that I never was much of a drinker."

"No worries. I'll hook up something for you, something fruity with a little kick. How's that sound?"

"Okay."

While Michael made the drinks, Shayna took the time to look around her. The decor was simple and rather neutral; the place could have been owned by a man or a woman. There was an extra-long couch that sat beneath a bank of windows facing the street. On the right wall was a fireplace flanked by two wingback chairs. A small love seat and tree-stump end table sat between the living and dining spaces with the kitchen just beyond. The art reflected the area: seascapes and lighthouses, clam shells and fishing boats. The shades of blue and gray broken up with uncannily authentic-looking potted plants was soothing, and by the time Michael walked over with her drink, Shayna was fairly certain that her heart wouldn't jump out of her chest.

Then Michael handed her the drink, and their fingers touched. They both felt the spark.

Shayna took a sip of the drink that Michael had prepared for her. It was fruity, and carbonated, and tasted as if it contained no alcohol at all. "What's in here?" she asked.

"Perrier, fruit juice, and a splash of Grey Goose."

"That's vodka, right?"

"Right."

Shayna took another sip. "It's good." She noticed Michael had poured himself a glass of wine. "I see you like wine."

"Not so much. When I drink, which really isn't that often, I'm more of a beer guy. I just poured this because it's what I started with tonight."

"Oh." Shayna took another sip.

Michael lightly touched her arm. "Let's sit down."

They sat on the couch. Shayna took another sip of her drink and told herself to relax. Michael reared back against the sofa, sipping his wine, watching Shayna. "So," he began, his voice husky and silky smooth at the same time, "what did you want to talk to me about?"

Shayna took yet another sip of her drink, trying to buy time and remember all of the cute little lines her friends had supplied her with. In the light of reality, they all sounded . . . well . . . whack. She decided that the best approach was a straightforward one. So, taking another sip, followed by a deep breath, she turned to face him.

He was a good two feet away. Way too close.

"Nothing in particular. Just wanted to"—Shayna forced herself to look him in the eye—"get to know you better."

The message couldn't have been more clear had it been texted to his cell phone. Without breaking eye contact, Michael set down his glass on the coffee table. He lessened the distance between them, removed the drink from Shayna's hand. "There's something I'd like to know better, too," he murmured, running a finger along her cheek, across her jawline, and down her neck.

Shayna's swallow was almost audible. "What's that?" she whispered.

Michael ran his finger across her lips. "These."

His kiss was gentle, the merest of touching as he slowly moved his lips across hers. Shayna worked to control her breathing, content to let Michael take the lead in what she now knew was an inevitable dance. He pulled her to him, placing her neck in the crook of his arm while turning his body to better connect them. Still, the kiss was soft, a whisper really, even as he began to rub her arm, up and down, slowly, gently, massaging her shoulders, and back down again. He placed kisses on each side of her mouth, the tip of her nose and eyelids before raining them down her cheek until he finally nuzzled in the crevice of her neck. He lifted his head and looked at her. "You smell good."

As soon as she opened her mouth, he kissed her, his skillful tongue pushing back her answer. Shayna was surprised that such a forceful move could be delivered in such a sensitive way. His mouth was pressed firmly against hers, yet his tongue was tender, searching, initiating a playful dance with hers. He moved his head in the same circular motion as his tongue. Belatedly, she realized that his hand had moved from her arm to the front of her dress and his thumb was recreating the same lazy circle over the material of her nipple. It was just a kiss, but Shayna felt herself about to burst. Michael's approach was so different from Jarrell's, the only other man with whom she'd ever been intimate. Her ex-boyfriend's kisses were hard and unyielding, and while Shayna had thought she liked his rough-and-tumble caveman approach, she now realized that when it came to lovemaking, she had a lot to learn. As Michael's mouth left hers and once more began a journey down her neckline, she also realized that he was probably a very good teacher.

24

"Your skin is so soft," Michael murmured after placing kisses on her arm and hand. "I want to feel you all over."

"I want that, too," Shayna heard herself saying. *Oh, wait, did I say that out loud?* A drunken tongue speaking a sober mind, her Big Mama would say. Through the haze of her tipsiness she realized that somewhere the tides had turned and the seduction that she was supposed to be planning was being handled the other way around.

"Let's go upstairs."

They wordlessly mounted the stairway, hand in hand, both lost in thought. Michael was experiencing a rare moment where he was questioning his actions. He'd never thought twice before bedding a willing female, but with Shayna he was actually weighing the repercussions. *You said you'd never again do this, man. What if this causes insurmountable problems in your business relationship? What if she falls in love with you, man, and turns out to be like Ms. Lovin' Basketball . . . insane!* And then there was the thought that bothered him more than the others. *What if you hurt her?*

They reached the bedroom. Michael flipped on the light and then adjusted the dimmer switch to that of a romantic mood. Shayna sat down on the bed, then leaned back, resting on her elbows. "I'm kinda scared," she admitted.

"Me, too." Michael surprised himself with his own truth.

"We don't have to if you don't want to. . . . "

"Baby, I've never wanted to more in my life." He sat on the bed, gazing at this girl-child before him. She was twenty-five, but here, with her toned, compact body and vulnerable eyes, she seemed younger. He reached up and fingered her hair, feeling the tresses before pulling the pins away that held it aloft. He leaned down and kissed her, softly at first and then, as Shayna's hands began an exploration of his arms and back, with a little more urgency. She shifted her body until they were almost facing each other. Michael deepened the kiss as he began an exploration of his own, down her back, across her backside, thighs, and back again. Her skin felt softer than the jersey material covering it, Michael noticed, and realized that having any part of her body covered was a problem.

"Here, sit up. Let me undress you."

Shayna quietly obeyed, lifting her hips so that he could pull the material from around her thighs and then over her head in one fell swoop. Michael took in the perfectly formed breasts encased in a lacy black bra. Noticing the front clasp, he reached for it, undid it, closed his eyes against the beauty that greeted him in the form of large blackberry-colored nipples, already hard and waiting.

"You're beautiful." He leaned forward, kissing her gently as he lightly massaged one nipple and then the other. He ran his lips across her neck and shoulders before easing her body on the bed and immediately lowering his head to the nipples he'd just massaged. His long, stiff tongue circled one and then the other. Shayna hissed at the assault. Michael smiled and thought, *We're just getting started.* He stood and removed his shirt, slacks, shoes, and socks in short order. Shayna rose to remove her heels, but Michael stopped her. "Not yet." Still wearing a black silk undershirt and matching boxers, he rejoined Shayna on the bed. He moved her to the middle of the large, king-sized paradise and covered her body with his. Their tongues once again worked to get better acquainted as their hands traveled each other's bodies. Shayna became emboldened with desire, finding and squeezing Michael's round, taut buttocks, a move that caused Michael to grind his hardening desire into her stomach.

"Ummm." He lifted slightly from her and once again began a descent down her body. It seemed that he was determined to kiss each and every part of her, starting with her neck and shoulders before moving on to first one nipple and then the other, where he lingered for a while. He alternated between licks, nips, and a teasing rolling between forefinger and thumb, all while his other hand roamed across her stomach, hips, and the insides of her thighs. Shayna squirmed as Michael continued to come close to but not quite reach her heat. She gasped as his finger skimmed the top of her matching lace thong. Her body shivered as he slid a hand inside it, over her bare mound, down the inside of her leg, and back out. He moved his body lower still.

Licking, kissing, treating her body like the finest porcelain as his tongue touched her seemingly everywhere between her chest and hips. He reached her thighs and kissed the outside before spreading her legs apart and nuzzling the sensitive insides. His head rubbed her hot spot as he kissed her legs, on purpose, she thought. The friction of his head and the fabric of her thong was almost unbearable. Shayna had never been this turned on before, couldn't believe how hot she felt simply from Michael's kisses. But as he continued, she realized that there was nothing simple about them. She forced herself back into the moment, and focused on how he continued down her leg, massaging her stomach with his hands while he licked and then kissed her knees, ankles, and back up to the inside of her thighs. He pushed her legs farther apart and licked the triangle of her thong.

"Ahh!"

A deep, knowing chuckle escaped Michael's lips as he licked the fabric again, long and hard, and then a third time. Shayna's head went from one side to the other as she tried not to thrash around on the bed. Michael turned his head slightly until his tongue ran under the fabric, near her folds. And then more kisses, gentle, probing, until Shayna thought she'd burst. Finally, with one swift movement, he rid her of her thong. Within seconds, he'd tossed aside her heels as well. Then, with the precision of a seeker missile, he dove into her treasure, lapping, nipping, sucking its sweetness. He moved his head as he swirled his tongue, creating a sensation that sent Shayna shaking, blindly reaching for his head as her legs went into the air of their own volition. His tongue went deeper, making love to her body, each move seemingly orchestrated from one to the next. Suddenly, he was off her. Shayna's eyes flew open. Her body felt betrayed, bereft, like an addict needing a fix.

"What?" she asked breathlessly.

"This," Michael answered, holding up a square packet of golden foil.

"Oh," Shayna managed. She stared, transfixed, as she watched him shield his massive member. In that instant she wondered if she could handle the thickness and length of him, whether it was possible for all of that to get up inside her.

"Don't worry," he said, sensing her sudden unease. "We'll go slowly. I won't hurt you."

He lay back down and once again began his oral assault. Within minutes, Shayna had forgotten all about potential pain and was fully and completely focused on pleasure. Michael did a repeat performance, giving her a tongue bath that started at her upper lips and ended at her lower ones. His tongue was probing, unforgiving, relentless, until Shayna felt her body quaking from the inside, felt an intensity in her core unlike any she'd ever felt and before she knew it she was spiraling out of control, going over the edge of ecstasy. It felt like an out of body experience and while she was still up in that stratosphere, among the stars and the moons, Michael entered her.

Whoa.

His Master P was massive, weighty, stretching her with its girth. She tensed, instinctively, wrapping her arms around his shoulders and holding on for dear life.

"Shh, just relax, baby. We've got all night."

At this moment, Shayna felt it might take that long just to get past the head of this cobra!

They were still for a moment, with Michael's hips elevated and controlled, his legs baring the weight of him while Shayna's body adjusted. Then he began kissing her again, slowly, rhythmically, capturing her tongue and sucking it into his mouth. As she focused on this tongue-play Shayna began to relax and when she did so, Michael began easing his hips down ever so slowly, moving, grinding, around and around. He pushed in a little farther, and then pulled back out to the tip, all the while whispering endearments in her ear, and planting kisses everywhere his mouth could touch. With each push in and slow pulling out, Shayna relaxed more and more, and her body got wetter and wetter, until at last, with one long, determined thrust, Michael's hips touched hers.

And the dance began.

Michael's movements were slow and methodical. Shayna's were urgent, as if now that she'd expanded to accommodate him, she couldn't get enough. They fit together like hand in glove, their movements like a choreographed dance with him taking the lead, and then her, back and forth, seemingly forever. He placed her arms above her head and entwined his fingers in hers. Then he looked deeply into her eyes as he moved inside her, reaching places that were being touched for the first time, enjoying the eyes darkened with desire as they stared back at him before fluttering closed. He rolled over and Shayna sat up. She placed her hands on his chest, feeling powerful and womanly as she rode him, exulting in his hisses and exclamations. *Oh. Yeah. Damn!* The dance continued and neither was aware of the thin layer of perspiration that broke out on their skin. So caught up were they in mutual pleasure that they had no idea that one hour went by, and then another. They lost track of the orgasms. They lost track of everything but the fact that what was happening here was something new and different and special and . . .

more. After Shayna's final melodic scream and Michael's long moan, they settled their bodies in spoon fashion and within seconds were fast asleep. And though they weren't aware of it at the time, they'd both realized the exact same thing.

Tonight was a game changer. Big time.

25

Shayna was at once aware of the dichotomous atmosphere: soft bed, hard chest. The room so dark while her heart spilled sunshine. Had last night really happened? Had she really spent most of it making mad, passionate love? The soreness of her thighs and between her legs told her that indeed she had. But the immense pleasure had been more than worth the slight pangs of pain. Grabbing the pillow and cuddling it against her stomach, Shayna smiled as she remembered last night's events. How had she ever imagined that she'd be the one doing the seducing? The idea to come to his place might have been hers, but the lead on the loving? That all belonged to Michael. She'd known one man, but for all of what Jarrell had shown her about love, she might as well have been a virgin. That's how she felt in Michael's arms.

As though she'd never known love before.

She remembered how his eyes bore into hers as his powerful manhood pummeled her body. How they became almost black with desire, and how his mouth formed into a determined line. It was a face of passion she'd never forget. She turned to look at it, and was surprised to find two open eyes staring at her.

"Good morning."

Her smile was tremulous as she responded. "Morning."

Michael reached out and slid an errant strand of her hair behind her ear. "How are you, baby?"

Jarrell had called her "baby" all the time. So why did it sound so magical when Michael said the word? "A little sore, but . . . I'm good."

"I'm sorry I hurt you."

"No, you didn't. It's just that . . ."

"I know." A companionable silence, and then, "Did you text John?"

Shayna nodded. "I told him that I was staying to meet with a potential sponsor."

"Do you think that will be a problem?"

"We usually get the day off after a meet so, no, as long as I get back home tonight, I'm good."

Michael placed his arm underneath Shayna and pulled her close to him. "You mean I only get to have you all to myself for a few more hours?"

"I guess so." Michael began drawing lazy eights across Shayna's abdomen. The movement stirred something in Shayna beyond her ticklish inclinations. There was no doubt that she was in lust with him, but she felt if she gave in to him again, she might run the risk of falling in love as well. "Is there any food in this house? I'm starved."

So was Michael, but not for anything in the pantry. "I doubt it," he answered. "But we can go grab breakfast if you'd like." His fingers left her abdomen and grazed her navel before heading lower.

Shayna threw back the covers and moved away from him. "I'm going to take a shower."

Once inside the confines of the shower stall, with the hot water creating a curtain of steam around her, Shayna placed her head back against the cool marble and allowed the full range of her emotions to come to the surface. On one hand she was over the moon with happiness. Michael was one incredible lover. He made her feel like the sexiest, most desirable, most beautiful woman in the world. On the other hand, however, she was fearful. Now that she'd experienced this level of loving, could she go back to a detached, professional relationship with him? Could she keep herself from developing deeper emotions? And what about Michael? Shayna knew there were other women. But could there be anyone special considering what they'd just shared?

"Of course there's someone special," Shayna angrily hissed at herself as she reached for the soap and began vigorously scrubbing her body. *Do you think you're the first woman who's felt this way after a night with him? Do you think you're the only person he looks at with those bedroom eyes, the only one he caresses with those large, capable hands and whose body gets set on fire by his skillful tongue?*

And then as if conjured up they were now in the shower: those eyes, hands, and that skillful tongue. Her intake of breath was sharp as he came up behind her unnoticed in this large doorless enclosure. Yet she didn't mind the intrusion. She rested back against him, soaping his body with her own.

"Here, allow me," he murmured against her ear as he took the soap from her hand. With long sweeping strokes he lathered her body, all the while nibbling on her ear, nuzzling her neck, and kissing her cheek even as his free hand tweaked her nipples into hardened

pebbles. He soaped her thoroughly and then, after the
rinsing, took his tongue on the trail where the soap had
been: along her collarbone down to her shoulders, across
her breasts—licking, sucking, nipping his appreciation—
across the muscled outline of her abs, into her navel and
farther, until he swiped his tongue across her cootchie
curtain, parting the V like a Happy Meal to discover the
toy inside. He steadied Shayna's shaking legs by wrapping his arms around her thighs and at the same time
sucked her nub into a swollen bite of ambrosia until she
exploded.

"Let me do you," she managed to whisper, while
trying to remember how to breathe.

"Next time." He reached for the foil packet on the
shower floor, quickly sheathed himself, and then hoisted
Shayna up against the wall on the other side of the ten-
foot by ten-foot shower. Away from the water, the
marble was cool against her back, but no matter. Within
seconds Michael had pierced her insides with a log of
molten lava and continued to do so, over and again,
until his fire had lit her core and the familiar flames of
seventh-heaven style bliss began to ignite her body,
mind, and soul. Michael felt her muscles clench around
him. He reached around for the luscious cheeks that he
loved so much, captured one in each hand, and pulled
her even closer to him. His rhythm was ongoing and relentless. Shayna wrapped her arms around his neck and
held on for dear life. She heard music and at first
thought it was all in her mind. But no, music was all
around them. Had it been there since Michael entered
the shower? Shayna wasn't sure, but now the beat of
Trey Songz' "Sex Ain't Better Than Love" was unmistakable. Hmph. Right about now, she was willing to take

that lyric to a vote. Because she wouldn't fool herself
into believing that after twenty-four hours she was
in love with Michael. But she was sure as hell in sex
with him, and right now . . . as she screamed her
pleasure in sync with Michael's growling release . . .
she could think of nothing better.

26

An hour and a half later, Michael and Shayna sat at a casually chic restaurant, fresh off a quick shopping spree to buy Shayna some duds. She looked right at home in the autumn environment, her burnt orange sweater, multicolored striped turtleneck, black jeans, and low-slung boots presenting an acceptable nod to the East Coast chill. Michael wore a black turtleneck, jeans, and a satisfied smile. Since the shower, they'd engaged in small talk mostly. But now, as Michael watched Shayna's bright eyes take in the decor while sipping her orange juice, he realized that there was still a lot about this vixen that he didn't know. And he wanted to know everything.

"So, Shayna," he began, after a satisfying sip of java, "when we first met back in LA, our conversation centered mostly around your athletic achievements. Tell me a little bit about you, the person inside those fast running shoes."

"What would you like to know?"

"I don't know. Whatever else you'd like to tell me, I

guess. I remember your telling Dina that you grew up in Inglewood. Do you have siblings?"

"No, it's just me."

"You and your mother against the world, huh?"

"My grandmother is the woman who raised me. I lived mostly with her because Mom was always gone, either working or partying."

"It's an interesting relationship you have with your mom, if you don't mind me saying so. I'm trying to envision my mother being married to the sibling of someone I dated. That's a trip."

"If you ever get a chance to meet her, you'll understand. Mom is young at heart, still a party girl, where I've always been more of an old soul. Perhaps that comes from the time I spent with my grandmother, or it could just be my personality."

"Or you could get it from your father."

Shayna shrugged.

"My dad played such a pivotal role in my life," Michael admitted. "I can't imagine growing up without him. He died when I was twenty and that was still way too soon."

"I imagine growing up with him was special. But you can't miss what you've never had."

"Your mother never married? That is, before the man she's with now?"

"No. She always had boyfriends, though. Men were always coming and going."

"That had to be hard on you."

"It is what it is." There was a companionable silence as the two thought about fathers, and the lack thereof. "There were good times, though. I remember once, when I was about thirteen years old. We had an impromptu party in Big Mama's front yard, some of my mom's friends and some kids from the block. We were all dancing to Nelly's "Country Grammar" and Sisqó's "Thong Song." It was so much fun until . . ."

"Until what?"

Until my mother thought she saw her boyfriend looking at me and abruptly cut the music. And the fun time was over, just like that. "My mom was just never the overly maternal type. I think when they were passing out that gene, she must have left the room." They sipped their drinks in silence for a moment, Michael wondering what Shayna hadn't shared with him and Shayna wondering if she'd said too much. "What happened to your dad, if you don't mind me asking?"

Michael sat back in his chair, looked out the window, and fiddled with the coffee mug as he spoke. "On-the-job accident. My dad was a foreman down at the Long Beach shipyards. He worked there for thirty years without incident, never even took a sick day off. Then in a fluke accident, a large cable snapped, hit my dad in the head, in the only spot that could kill him instantly, the doctor would later tell us." After more than a decade, the memory still brought pain to Michael's face.

Shayna reached across the table. "I'm so sorry."

"I know, me, too. But like you said, it is what it is." He looked over at Shayna, realizing that she was the first woman since his last serious relationship more than three years ago where he'd opened up about his family. "Your mother told you that the streets claimed your father. What was it? Drugs? Gangs?"

"I don't know. Mom refuses to talk about it. But whenever I asked about him, that's what she always told me . . . streets got him."

And there it was again, Michael noticed, that flash of raw vulnerability in Shayna's eyes and with it, an overwhelming urge on his part to keep her safe, the way Sam Morgan had for his family. There was no doubt in Michael's mind that he was the man that he was because of his father; every valuable lesson he'd learned was at his knee. Part of the reason Michael hadn't yet married was because of his father's words: *Stay single until you're done playing the field. Because once you get married, you're playing for keeps.*

The waitress brought their hefty brunch order: eggs Benedict and hash browns for Shayna, a three-egg vegetable omelet, waffles, bacon, sausage, and hash browns for Michael. They agreed to split a fruit platter.

Ravenous when they'd ordered, the two now eyed the massive spread before them. "Are we really going to eat all this?" Shayna asked incredulously.

Reaching for his fork, Michael dug into his omelet. "We're going to try."

"Ha!"

For several moments, the click-clacking of silverware was the only thing heard at the table. After Michael had consumed a good portion of the omelet, a couple sausage patties and strips of bacon, and a third of his potatoes, he sat back, wiping his mouth in the process. "How's your eggs Benedict?"

Shayna nodded, chewing until she swallowed her bite. "Delicious. And if the way you're eating is any indication, yours is, too."

"I like my food, baby, no doubt. And for a little sistah, you're putting a good amount away yourself."

"Fast metabolism," she offered.

"For sure." Michael waited until the waitress had refreshed his coffee and then continued. "Do your mom and her husband live in Los Angeles?"

"No, Mom bought a home in Henderson, Nevada, two years ago, partly because of the attractive real estate prices and partly because that's where Larsen wanted to incorporate." It was also where Jarrell planned to begin his political career, gunning for the city council to start. But Shayna saw no need to share this tidbit. She wondered why it was that she even remembered.

"Sounds like the age difference isn't mattering much where their relationship is concerned."

"Not as much as their relationship matters to me."

"Jay's brother being your de facto stepfather a problem?"

Shayna saw the twinkle in his eye, knew he was trying to lighten the mood. "You think?" And then, "They are very close, Jarrell and Larsen. I believe in Mom's mind, Jay and I staying together helps secure her and Larsen's bond. Actually, some of the best times I've had with my mom were with the four of us, at least lately. Now that he and I have broken up, the mother-daughter dynamic is an understandably sticky situation."

"It's got to be hard for her trying to support you while not totally dissing her husband's brother."

"It would be if she were trying to support me. And maybe she is, in her own way. Maybe she truly believes what she says, that Jarrell and I should get back together. I didn't see it firsthand, but I know my mother endured her share of abusive relationships." She looked at Michael to know whether he understood what she meant. "Physical abuse," she added, just to be clear. "Big Mama made me promise to never allow a man to do that to me. I intend to keep that promise. Even with everything Jay did to me, my mother is still trying to help us get back together. When it comes to moving forward with my life, without him in it, I don't have her support."

Now, it was Michael's turn to reach across the table. "Don't worry about it, Shayna," he said sincerely. He paused before adding, "You have mine."

27

Shayna reached the door to her condo, bobbing her head to the sound flowing through her ear buds. "Family Affair" was one of Shayna's all time favorite songs by one of her all time favorite songstresses, Mary J. She hummed the funky hook as she unlocked the door, maneuvering her bulky canvas bag through the doorway with one arm while balancing the purse, take-out food, and drink with the other. It had been another long yet productive day and after spending an equally long and productive night with Michael last night, Shayna was more than ready to eat a delicious meal, take a hot bath, climb into a soft bed, and get a good night's sleep. Setting her food and drink on the counter, she tossed the canvas bag near the hallway that led to the bedrooms before ridding herself of jacket and shoes in quick order.

"'Don't need no hate. . .'" Shayna sang, as she removed the Chinese dishes she'd ordered from their container, placed a helping of each along with the egg rolls onto a plate and into the microwave, and danced down the hall to change out of her sweats. She put on the same extra-large Lakers T-shirt that Michael had given her to wear last night, shook her hair out of its ponytail, and returned to the kitchen. She'd just set her food on the living room coffee table and reached for the remote when her cell phone rang.

Upon seeing the number, she almost didn't answer it. Lately, whenever she and Beverly had talked, the conversation had not gone the direction she'd hoped.

"Hey, Mom."

"Hey, Shayna. Girl, what are you doing?"

"Just got home from practice, getting ready to eat. What's up?"

A sigh, and then, "It's Larsen. I think he's seeing somebody."

"Again?" Shayna stifled a sigh of her own. This wasn't the first time she and her mother had had this conversation. In fact, they'd often traded suspicions as Shayna knew for a fact that Jarrell had been unfaithful more than once. It was another reason why her breaking up with him had come a year or two later than it should have. Better late than never, she'd finally conceded. Both Brittney and Talisha had given Shayna the 411, along with the unsolicited advice to drop his ass like a hot potato while they were still in college. It hadn't happened until four years later. Like her mother, she knew, but didn't want to believe it. And like Shayna, her mother would have to get to that revelation on her own.

"What do you mean, 'again'? Has Jay told you something? Do you know something about what's going on that I don't?"

"I haven't talked to him since that time you put him on the phone. I've moved on from him, Mom, and his cheating ways is one of the reasons why." The obvious unspoken words hung in the air. Though her appetite had been impaired by the phone call, she picked up her chopsticks and dug into the kung pao. "I said 'again' because we had this conversation a few months ago, remember? Right before I broke up with Jarrell for the very same thing!"

"Y'all breaking up is the reason this is happening. Now that Jarrell is on the prowl, he's coming down here almost every weekend so him and Larsen can hit the clubs."

"He was going down there almost every weekend anyway. I'm surprised he hasn't moved there already."

"He would have if y'all hadn't broken up. Now he's delayed the move to try and get you back. He's probably doing it on purpose, Shayna, pulling Larsen away from me. Trying to hurt me just to get back at you."

"Seriously, Mom? Do you have any idea how crazy that sounded?"

"You know how close those brothers are. If you and Jarrell were still together, then he and my husband wouldn't be hanging out."

"This sounds like a conversation you need to have with Larsen. What Jarrell does or doesn't do is no longer my business."

"That's just it, Shayna. Everything isn't about you." Shayna looked at the phone with widened eyes and raised brows. *No. She. Didn't.* "This is about my future, too. Now I told you, girl, every relationship has its ups and downs. You and Jarrell were together for almost ten years. There shouldn't be anything too hard for y'all to work out."

"You also told me"—*and showed me*—"that men were like buses. That if one left, another one would be along in about fifteen minutes." The more Shayna listened, her mother sounded less ridiculous and more insecure. As often happened when her mother fretted over a man, the conversation with Big Mama came to mind. *Something happened that made her shut off her feelings. That's something she'll have to tell you.* Shayna wondered about the experience that had made her mother promiscuous in her youth and feel incomplete without a man. She believed it when Big Mama said Beverly loved her, but Shayna honestly didn't feel she was liked all the time. Even Beverly's going after Larsen had felt like a type of competition, like by dating Jarrell's brother Beverly proved that she could have anything that Shayna could. *What mother does that? What is that about?* And what was it about Shayna and her need for her mother's love that even now she was feeling herself weakening, planning to give in to her mother's wishes and spend Thanksgiving with the Powells. Beverly had demanded the very thing that Shayna had so often needed but didn't get: her support. Then someone else's voice rang inside her head. *You have mine.* The conversation that had continued once Michael and Shayna left the restaurant that late morning began to play in her ear. He'd been right when he said that her mother was an adult and as such, not her responsibility. Shayna's appetite increased. Her thoughts had blocked out what Beverly was saying, but when she tuned back in her mother prattled on. It had been this way since she could remember—Beverly sharing with Shayna about her man woes. She picked up and bit into her vegetable roll with newfound gusto.

". . . these young witches don't know a thing about boundaries. The fact that he's married? They couldn't care less. His phone rings all times of day and night and as much as his limo company is expanding, everybody isn't needing a ride at four a.m.!"

Shayna placed her sticks down on the plate. As much

as she wanted to shake some sense into her and call it a day, she could empathize with her mother's position. Six months ago, Shayna had been the one holding on to something that was way past its expiration date. Her mother had invested a lot in Larsen, had chased and chased him until he caught her. Like Jarrell, Larsen did have good qualities. He could be charming, attentive, and was the life of the party wherever he went. Women flocked to him, yes, but he was a magnet for almost any crowd. Add to that the fact that regular workouts kept his five-foot-ten-inch stocky frame in excellent shape, and regular trips to the barber kept his close-cropped hair gleaming and his goatee maintained, and one could see why Larsen presented a package that looked worth holding on to.

"Looks like you've got a situation, Mom," Shayna said at last. "What are you going to do about it?"

Beverly's demeanor changed as a chuckle replaced the frustration in her voice. "Girl, you don't even want to know."

"Oh, Lord. What are you thinking?"

"I was thinking about doing an Evelyn."

"A who?"

"Evelyn. That chick on *Basketball Wives* who married 'Spanish eighty-five.' Remember all the hoopla she caused when she talked about being open to his seeing other women as long as she knew about them?"

"No, Mom. You are *not* going there."

"When I think of the alternatives, I can understand her reasoning. It's better to know what's going on rather than have them sneak around. I met Larsen today for lunch down on the Strip. Saw this chick who looks younger than you are, giving him the flirty eye while looking at me like I was wearing shit for makeup. I asked Larsen about her and he swore she was just some chick he'd met at a club while picking up a client."

"Picking her up, more likely," Shayna muttered before she could stop herself.

"Exactly. Anyway, we finished our lunch and left the building. You know I lit into his ass as soon as we got into the car. I yelled and cried, he lied and denied, and now he's gone God knows where. That's what got me thinking. Who do I think I am to demand that he stay faithful when none of these other mother-brothers are keeping their shit on lock?"

"His wife, that's who."

"Living in la-la land is what got you single," Beverly retorted. "I'm not getting any younger, already competing with witches half my age, and am not even trying to be alone in this bitch, joining the Divorced Wives or Over Forty Club or hanging with a boyfriend called Slot Machine or Blackjack on a Saturday night! Every woman tries to front like her man is faithful, but bottom line is, if he's got one swinging, then he's probably flinging, whether they know it or not and whether they like it or not. Me? I'd rather know. Make ours an open marriage. Hell, I might even see me a cutie I want. This arrangement can end up working both ways!"

"Then why be married, Mom?" Shayna softly asked.

Instead of answering that question, Beverly asked one of her own. "You're still coming down for Thanksgiving, right? Because as pissed as I am, I've got a reason to want to keep Larsen around. But I want to share that in person."

Especially after this conversation, spending the holidays with her family was the last place Shayna wanted to be. But of all the holidays, Thanksgiving was one to be spent with family, such as it was. Maybe this year

would be different. Maybe Beverly and Jarrell would
see that she had moved on, that she was doing well and
that a woman could actually be single and happy. Or
working on it anyway. Maybe if Beverly saw what sup-
porting someone looked like, then she would support
Shayna the next time the need arose. "Yeah, Mom. I'll
be there."

"Alone, right? You know that Jarrell won't want to
see you with anybody."

"I can't make that promise, Mom. Like you, I don't
want to be alone, and end up with a man named Blackjack."

They laughed and thankfully the conversation turned
a bit lighter after that. Shayna shared highlights from
her latest meet and Beverly chatted about plans to head
to New York for a shopping spree. After the call ended,
Shayna reheated her food, finished it quickly, took a
hasty hot shower instead of the long bath she'd planned,
and crawled between the sheets. Sleep eluded her,
however, as she thought about the discussion she and
Beverly had had. *Every woman tries to front like their
man is faithful, but bottom line is, if he's got one swinging, then he's probably flinging. . . .* Shayna didn't believe this. She knew good men, men whom she believed
faithful: her coach, John, and Kim's husband, Patrick,
to name just two. But it made her wonder about another
man. She thought back to the day after the attack, before
she'd left the bedroom but heard various ring tones
going off, several times, when Michael's phone rang off
the hook. Was that all about business? Shayna seriously
doubted it. Brothah like him could have a bevy of chicks
and be rolling with a couple of prepaids and a Cricket
or two just to keep the roster straight. It had been almost
a week since Cape Cod and she and Michael had been

together almost every night. They hadn't put a label on what was happening between them, so the conversation of who he was or wasn't seeing had never come up.

But given the info her mom had put on Shayna's mind . . . it was about to.

28

Michael stood at the window of his seventieth-story offices in Los Angeles's tallest building, the U.S. Bank Tower, and gazed out on a stunning view that included the renovated area known as LA Live. This thriving community was built largely to complement its anchor, the Staples Center, home to the LA Lakers and other clients handled by MSM. He looked out the window, but he didn't see a thing. For the past ten minutes he'd ruminated on the horrible news delivered via his latest phone call: last night Cheryl had overdosed on sleeping pills. Ironically, she was rushed to UCLA Medical and while Gregory hadn't been on duty then, he'd found out about it this morning, and had immediately called to tell (or warn, advise, relay—pick your poison) his brother of her still critical status. Not so much physically—the on-call emergency physician had pumped her stomach and stabilized her vitals—but mentally. She'd been heard murmuring about not wanting to live and, as a precaution, had been put on suicide watch. Michael had been shocked, then devastated. True, he'd never lied to Cheryl, had always told her that what they had, though steadier and lengthier than most of his affairs, was neither exclusive nor lasting. More than once he'd assured her that he had no plans to turn in his bachelor card, and when she called wanting to see him, he often admitted that he was on his way to a date. He felt being upfront and keeping it real was the best way to deal with his multiple-partner lifestyle, and had never considered himself a cheater because he had always told the truth.

Yeah. Right. But look what's happened. Of course, Gregory tried to tell him that it wasn't his fault. And of course Michael felt totally responsible.

"Excuse me, Michael?"

At the sound of his second assistant's voice, Michael turned around. "Yes, Nadia?"

"Your eleven o'clock appointment, Ms. Chase, is here. Should I show her in or do you need more time?"

After talking with Gregory, Michael had advised Nadia to hold his calls. He'd totally forgotten about Samantha Chase, the soccer standout whom he'd met in London, the same time as Shayna and others. She'd sought him out, and he'd been impressed with her knowledge of him, the business side of sports, and her desire to develop a solid postcareer trajectory. Before, he wouldn't have given the meeting and possible work arrangement a second thought, but news of Cheryl's overdose had him rethinking all things female. Did this woman really want to work on her career path? Or had she sought him out in London to work on *him*?

"Uh, why don't you set us up in the small conference room? Give her a client packet and make sure she's as comfortable as possible. Tell her I'm dealing with an emergency, but I'll be in there as soon as I can."

Once Nadia had left the room, Michael returned to his desk. He pulled out his electronic address book and went to a folder simply titled "The List." He opened it and began to scroll. *Bree. Jessica. Felicia. Mandy. Tamera. Susanna. Ashley. Paige. Peyton. Kayla. Natalie. Chloe. Kamela. Victoria. Sandra. Faith.* . . . It continued, the list of women Michael had known in the past seven, eight years. By today's standards, it wasn't an overly egregious amount of women. Some he'd only been with once or twice. Others he'd dated and afterward they had become friends. Still others had been business associates with whom he was still friendly, even having met some of their husbands and children once these partners had moved on. Healthy sexual appetite aside, Michael considered himself an honorable man, a good guy. He never lied to these women. Always stated the rules before engagement. Never led them on. Always treated them with dignity and respect. Never went without protection. And when he had to let them go, he always tried to let them down easy. All these years, these points had sounded okay to his conscience. But with Cheryl lying in a hospital, these facts sounded like the pitiful excuses of a spoiled boy, and a selfish man. Like someone who took what he wanted, whenever he wanted and from whomever he wanted, consequences be damned. True, all the women were grown and no, no one had put a gun to their heads and forced them into whatever bedroom. Now, in the light of a brand-new overdose, this detail seemed minor at best.

Cheryl had come by his house last night. Even with his declarations that it was over, and with his admission that he was seeing someone else, she'd begged to enter. Just to talk, she'd said. He'd looked at his camera, had seen her there in the short minidress and the high spike heels and, if she were true to habit, nothing on underneath. But Michael had been with Shayna the night before, and the night before that, and before Cape Cod, Shayna had been the only woman he'd wanted. Even with come-and-get-it-you-can-have-it-all-you-can-eat-pussy just outside his door. It was late, he was tired, and he didn't let her in.

As he gathered himself and headed out of his office, he allowed one more thought before he slipped on his business mask. *I wish I had.*

29

Had it only been twenty-four hours since she'd seen Michael? Not according to the body part that fairly pulsated with excitement as Shayna turned into her new lover's drive. Even though he'd seemed preoccupied when they spoke earlier, something he said he'd tell her about later, Shayna still intended to do what she'd planned, what had been on her mind ever since getting off the phone with Beverly last night. For the past seven days, she and Michael had mostly been screwing. Tonight, it was time to talk.

"Hey, baby," Michael greeted her as soon as he opened the door. She stepped inside and into his waiting arms. He hugged her fiercely, breathing deeply while running his hand up and down her back. "I'm glad to see you."

His voice was low, husky, and filled with . . . *what?* . . . Shayna wondered. *Worry? Sadness? Grief? Pain?* Pulling away from him, she looked into his drooping eyes. "What happened?"

He reached for her hand. "Come here." They walked into the living room and sat on the couch. He turned to face her. "There are some things I need to tell you," he began after taking a deep breath. "About my lifestyle, and some of the people who've been a part of it."

His lifestyle? Surely this man isn't getting ready to tell me he's gay! "Okay," she replied, drawing out the word.

"I've always considered myself the consummate bachelor—no commitments, no ties, no promises, no problems."

"Whoa." Shayna released Michael's hand at about the same time her mother's voice piped up in her ear. *These young witches don't know a thing about boundaries.* But Shayna did. And hers began and ended with the fact that she was not going to date a nonexclusive man with a lifetime player membership.

"Wait, Shayna, please." Michael reached for her hand and once again placed it between his two. "I know this is going to sound crazy, but hear me out first. I'm not asking you to agree with it, or even understand it necessarily. All I'm asking right now is that you listen, with an open heart. I need to share this. Can you do it?"

Taking a deep breath, she answered, "I'll try."

"Over the years, there have been a lot of women in my life. Some have come and gone, others pop in and out for days, weeks, or for a month or two at a time. There are others whom I've known for years and we were friends before we, uh, took things to another level, and some who remained friends after we decided to put that aspect of the relationship on ice. I lay out where I'm coming from up front, so that there are no misunderstandings down the road. That usually involves understanding three things. One"—Michael held up his pinky finger—"I'm not exclusive. Two, I've never been married and am not looking to get married. And three, protection is always used, not only as precaution against HIV and other sexual diseases but to make sure I don't catch the biggest virus of them all—fatherhood." He'd hoped the smile that accompanied this line would lighten the mood.

It didn't. He went on.

"I always ask the women I'm dealing with if they understand, and if the answer is yes, then do they want to stay. A couple have left after learning there'd be no destination wedding at the end of the rainbow, but most of them stayed. And the ones who did, I thought were cool with everything."

"But somebody wasn't?" *Somebody with some damn sense, I presume.*

"Over the years there have been one or two women who tried to hang on long after the fire died, who didn't want to hear that the relationship was over. But eventually, they got the message and left me alone, moved on with their lives. One of my talent scouts, a former tennis player, is just such a woman; we hung out for one, two months. She wanted more. I didn't. She moved on— marriage, kids, the whole nine. I've met her family, we've even shared a box at the U.S. Open. What I'm saying is that I'm cool with most of my liaisons both past and present."

Shayna wasn't sure how she felt about that, but okay.

Michael released her hand and stood. Walking toward the patio doors that opened onto his oasis, and looking out at the placid waters and spouting fountain in search of peace, he continued. "There is a woman who fits into the former category, the one where understanding that we were done was not an option and there was no part of the word *no* that she understood. Her name is Cheryl. We go back several years. I met her when I regularly worked the city's club and party circuit. She's a product of Hollywood; mother is an actress, father a producer. She grew up in the lap of luxury and is used to getting everything she wants. When she finally encountered something that she couldn't have, namely me, she took pretty drastic action to show her displeasure." He paused, watched a couple sparrows thrash in the yard's birdbath.

"What did she do?" Shayna quietly asked, standing and walking toward the stiff back before her.

Michael turned as she neared. "Last night, she tried to kill herself."

Shayna stopped short. "Oh, no." She'd expected to hear something common like she slashed his tires, broke a window, or showed up where he was and made a scene. But to be so desperate for someone's affections? And she'd thought Beverly cuckoo for entertaining the idea of an open marriage. No, this, what Michael had just shared, was truly crazy. Now Shayna understood the look in Michael's eyes and what was emanating from his hug when she'd walked in the door. It had been all of what she'd imagined—worry, sadness, grief, pain—and more. "Michael, I'm so sorry." She wrapped her arms around his waist, and lay her head on his chest. His heart beat rapidly, his breathing was shallow. "How'd you find out?"

"Gregory called me earlier today." He relayed their conversation, shared more of the history between him and Cheryl, ending with the fact that he refused her entry when she came by last night.

"I told her that I was taking a break from all that, all the women, the juggling, and the constant back to back dating, told her that it wasn't personal, that I was reevaluating my life. That has never been truer than it is in this moment. You should know something, Shayna. Even before we made love last week, all the way back to last month and the first time you came here, I haven't wanted to be with any of my old hookups. It had been a month since I'd had sex, which probably hasn't happened since I was fifteen, sixteen years old. I guess what I'm trying to say is that there's something about you that is different from how it was with the other women. You do it for me, everything, and I don't want to be with the other women, don't even want to think about other women. If you're willing, baby, I want to do two things: something I said I'd never do again and something that I've never done in my life. Even though you're my client, I want to date you. And I want us to be exclusive, for it to be just me and you." He paused, gazing at Shayna for a reaction. When she remained silent, he asked, "What do you think about that?"

She nodded. "I'd like that."

His breath of relief was audible. "Come here." The kiss was tentative at first, and then deep and scorching. He ran his hand down her back until it reached his favorite part of her, the luscious booty of which he'd now made extensive acquaintance. They made their way back to the couch and continued the kiss. Her acceptance of him after baring his soul and sharing his story was like being blessed by a priest, or in this case, a priestess. He covered her face and her neck with kisses, wanting to be on top of her, inside her. But then he remembered her earlier phone call and knew that there was something she wanted to discuss with him.

"You know I want to get in that hot spot, right? But first, what is it that you wanted to ask me?"

Shayna cupped his strong jaw while looking into his vulnerable eyes. She gave him a peck on the lips and smiled. "You've already answered my questions. Every single one."

30

"Hey, Shayna! How's the packing coming?" Talisha obviously figured there was no need to walk across the hall when a loudly asked—translated: screamed—question worked just as good. All three ladies were preparing for their flight to Spain, and the Barcelona Indoor Classic.

"Girl, I've repacked three times. Coach has to be crazy telling us we can only take one bag."

"It's budget cuts, ladies," Brittney chimed in from her room. "And extra baggage charges. Y'all are just going to have to leave your ratchet clothes at home. Ha!"

"Oh, no, you didn't go there," Talisha huffed, walking out into the hallway in a red-hot stretchy spandex number with about as much material as a handkerchief. "I'll have you know that I'm very much a lady."

Shayna and Brittney came out of their respective rooms, took a look at Talisha, each other, and said in unison, "Ratchet dress!" They high-fived while laughing, dodging Talisha's playful swings before darting back into their rooms.

"Forget y'all heifahs," she replied, laughing herself before returning to her room. "Hey, Shay. Is Michael bringing his fine ass to Barcelona?"

"I don't think so."

"Damn. I still can't believe y'all are dating! Let alone the fact that your face is getting ready to grace a cereal box. You need to step up your game, sistah, get the relay team signed so we can all make more paper."

It was true. While he and XMVP Shoes and Sportswear were still in negotiations, and he was talking to a flavored-water company about her participation in a TV commercial, they'd just received word that Organic Health, a new line of cereals appearing in high-end stores such as Whole Foods and Sprouts, were ready with an offer to have her on their bran flakes box. Partnered in business for only two months and Michael had already delivered. Just like he said he would. "I already told him that y'all were interested in being represented. Don't think I'm going to bug him every day."

"I don't see why not," Brittney snipped playfully. "You're banging him every day!"

Laughter abounded.

"I know you're not in there laughing, Tee," Shayna said. "Not with those creaking springs I heard last night."

"That's why I bought you that fan. So my man and I can have some privacy."

"Privacy is called your own address, Tee," Brittney offered. "I heard y'all, too. Why does Cameron always have to be all Badu up in here?"

"How's that?" Talisha tried to make hers the voice of innocence.

"Going 'on and on and on and on,'" Brittney sang.

"Whew!" Shayna said, with a laugh. "Good one, Brittney!"

"Forget y'all! Brittney, you're just mad because you're not getting any."

"Uh, that would be a negative. I'm focusing on the run, believe that."

"Please." Shayna removed a couple sweaters from the suitcase and replaced them with two less bulkier ones. "You're focusing on DeVaughn. I saw you hanging back after practice today, watching the boys put through their paces."

"Not true. We both run the four hundred. That's what we have in common."

"If things go your way, you and I are getting ready to have something in common."

"What's that, Tee?"

"Some creaking springs!"

Shayna's phone rang. She looked at the caller ID and smiled. Time to head over to Michael's and make a little "spring" music herself.

A little over a half hour later, Shayna sat in Michael's master suite, chilling out while Michael showered after a very long day. She loved everything about his Holly-wood Hills abode, but aside from the backyard that had been landscaped to within an inch of its life, this room was her favorite. The designer had paired warm, burnt orange with shades of brown, two colors that Shayna would not have put together and had she not seen it first-hand, would have thought odd choices for a man's abode. But here, it worked: the low-slung platform bed in urban maple, with dark chocolate coverings and a burnt orange, tan, and dark brown pinstriped duvet. The light brown silk-covered walls were offset by a stark white ceiling. Bronze-colored lamps sat on Moroccan-inspired nightstands and a Bokhara-styled Persian rug separated the sitting area from the rest of the space. There, the color scheme continued with two coffee-colored leather accent chairs, a love seat, geometric tables, and a custom-made mini-fridge with a chestnut finish.

Bringing everything together was the artwork, especially a stellar uniquely drawn piece that hung behind the love seat. It drew her to it, the oversized images in earth-tone colors, drawn it seemed with thousands and thousands of penlike strokes. *Where have I seen this type of work before?* She leaned forward, reading the name scrolled on the painting's left-hand side. *Oh, right. Charles Bibbs.* Now she remembered where she'd seen this artist's work, at the Leimert Park Village Book Fair the previous summer. After traveling with Talisha to where her cousins lived in this area of Los Angeles, which was bordered by the Crenshaw District, View Park, Jefferson Park, and Vermont Square, they'd driven down Degnan Boulevard and then followed the crowd to a large tent filled with authors and their books. There had also been food vendors, a children's stage, and another stage where panel discussions were held and celebrities were interviewed. NeNe Leakes was on the stage when they arrived and as she exited, Shayna recalled Talisha's comment, "Lord, that sistah is six feet tall!" And she was, Shayna remembered. And they'd figured that was without the five-inch heels she wore.

A ringtone caused Shayna to jump out of her skin. She'd been eyeing the artwork intently, and hadn't even noticed the two cell phones sitting on one of the end tables flanking the love seat. One phone had barely finished sounding off before the other started. Shayna ignored them and turned to walk back toward the bed. And then both phones began ringing again. No longer able to hold back her curiosity, Shayna walked over and picked up the slender black iPhone. She tried to remain detached as she eyed the name. Shrugging, she put down that phone when the other one vibrated. *Wow, somebody really wants to talk to you, Mikey boy.* She looked at the screen on the BlackBerry. When the call stopped, the screen jumped to Missed Calls. Almost of its own volition, her thumb began to scroll the list. As it did so, Shayna's heart began to beat faster as her frown deepened. She hadn't meant to invade Michael's privacy by looking at his phone. But she had. And, yes, he'd told her about all of his past liaisons. He'd also said he was not seeing any of them. So why were they still calling?

A few minutes later, a decadent-looking Michael wrapped only in a stark white towel strolled out of the shower. Shayna sat on the bed, trying to appear casual despite her rigid back and crossed arms.

"What is it, baby?" Michael asked, dropping the towel in unabashed fashion and joining her on the bed. His brows raised when he reached for her, as she pulled back. A first.

"I have a question," Shayna said, her voice low and calm.

"Ask me anything, baby."

"If you're no longer with them, then why are Ashley, Paige, Chloe, Victoria, and all these other women blowing up your phone?"

It was Michael's turn to act indignant. "You checked my phone?"

"Didn't intend to, but when they kept ringing and buzzing back to back to back curiosity got the best of me. And before you try and turn the tables, I apologize. Now, will you explain why all of these women are still calling the man who told me he wanted to be exclusive?"

31

The following day, Shayna called a powwow with her girls. They'd congregated in Talisha's room, the largest, a master suite with en suite bath that she'd gotten by default because at the time she was the only one who'd had a man and nobody wanted to take the chance of seeing Cameron's goods at two or three o'clock in the morning. They'd split the rent accordingly, and the arrangement had worked out for everyone involved.

"Okay, so what is going on?" Talisha asked, after setting a bowl of popcorn in the middle of the bed. "This must be about Jarrell, because just last week you floated in here talking about you and Michael being exclusive. So I know that's not the problem."

Shayna reached for the popcorn, even though she wasn't hungry. "Looks like I may have spoken too soon." She told the girls about finding all of the names on Michael's phone.

Talisha reacted first. "My Aunt Claudette says if you go looking for shit, you'll find shit."

"Doesn't excuse him if he's playing her," Brittney said, hurrying to Shayna's defense.

"I didn't go looking, not exactly. We were in his bedroom and his phones started ringing—"

"Hold up," Talisha said, one hand in the air and another on her hip. "'Phones,' as in plural?"

"Well, you know, for business . . ." Shayna offered, but considering where she was going with the conversation, her defense sounded out of place at best. "I knew he had more than one. That wasn't what got my attention. What happened is they started ringing at once, or almost at once anyway. Hell, it sounded like a datgum ring tone concert. After the fourth or fifth one, I don't remember, curiosity got the better of me and I picked one up. When I touched the screen it went to Missed Calls. That's when I saw the names."

"How many?" Brittney asked, not even trying to hide her nosiness.

"Too many," Talisha interjected. "Unless they were all clients—which, since Shayna is here with us instead of where she's been spending nearly every night, I'd say isn't the case." She popped a handful of popcorn into her mouth. "What did he say when you asked him about it?"

"He assured me that he hadn't been with any of them since we got together, and that it would take time to . . . handle that whole situation. Some of them he's slept with, but had business with as well—"

"Been a busy little bee, sounds like," Brittney offered, rolling over for her water bottle on the nightstand. Shayna cut her a look. "What? Just saying . . ."

"I think you're overreacting," Talisha said.

"Me? Wasn't your hand on your hip just a moment ago?"

"You know how fast I jump to conclusions. But think about it. You just met the man, what, a month ago? Y'all just decided to become an exclusive item or whatever a week ago. The man wasn't a monk when you met him, Shayna. I don't think it's too much to ask for you to give him some time to get his past squared away. He knows you still have interactions with Jarrell and he isn't tripping about that."

"That's different!"

"How?"

"Please, Tee," Brittney interrupted. "You know how. Shay's ex is also her brother-in-law."

"Technically, uncle-in-law," Shayna corrected.

Talisha grunted. "That's some messed up reality TV stuff if I ever saw it."

"Tell me about it," Shayna admitted. "But—"

All three women finished the sentence together: "It is what it is."

"What did you tell him?" Talisha asked.

"I may have overreacted. I told him that I wanted us to cool things off until he handled his business."

"Um, risky move there," Brittney said. "Man like that don't seem like the cooling off type, if you know what I mean."

"Britt has a point, Shay. I'm not saying that you don't have a right to want what you want and to put down your rules, but are you really ready to turn back the clock and go back to a manager/client relationship only? How will y'all work together if that happens? Won't that be kind of . . . you know . . . awkward?"

"If it weren't for ya'll, I wouldn't be in this mess in the first place."

"What do you mean?" Britt asked.

"It was your suggestion to seduce him!"

"Yes," Britt answered, "but it was your decision to go back for seconds and thirds. . . ."

"And fourths and fifths," Talisha chimed in.

"And now I'm all wide open and everything, with a man who's more desirable than a winning lotto ticket." Shayna grabbed a pillow and hugged it to her chest as she fell back against the bed. "Geez, here I was trying to straighten my life out and now it's more complicated than ever."

"Don't worry about it," Talisha said, her voice as calm as a mother soothing a child. "Things like this have a way of working out. Just go with the flow."

32

Barcelona, Catalonia, lazily rests against the Mediterranean Sea and is the second largest city in Spain. Founded as a Roman city (by either the mythical Hercules or Hannibal's daddy, depending on who's asked), it is a rich cultural mecca known for its unique architecture—most notably the works of native artist Antoni Gaudí and his signature creation, the Sagrada Familia, the Church of the Holy Family, which even now, after more than one hundred-sixty years, is still considered unfinished. Popular tourist attractions include the Columbus monument and La Rambla. This tree-lined boulevard boasting eateries, shops, souvenir-selling kiosks, and dozens of street performers, was a haven for tourists and locals both day and night, often played out to a soundtrack of a street-performing band. As beautiful and notable as the city was, however, for those attending the indoor track meet, their only scenery was the Estadi Olímpic Lluís Companys, formerly known as the Barcelona Olympic Stadium, and their only attraction was whatever event they'd come to conquer. For Shayna, Brittney, Talisha, and Kim, that event was the 4 x 100 relay, the next item up on the day's agenda and one of the highlights of the meet. The track world's eyes were not only on the U.S. team, but also on Jamaica's ultratalented, record-busting relay squad, along with countries Trinidad and Tobago, France, and the Ukraine. The stadium held a capacity crowd of more than 55,000. But there was one particular man watching one particular woman's every move.

Michael wasn't aware of his serious expression as he watched Shayna go through her paces. His world had felt slightly off its axis for about a week now, ever since her last visit to his home when she heard an unplanned phone symphony that needed an explanation rather than an encore. He was still trying to figure out just how many gods he'd pissed off for events that night to go down the way they had. In all his years of bed hopping, he'd never encountered a cellular traffic jam of this magnitude. But it had happened, with Shayna as witness. To that he'd had only one thought.

There was a first time for everything.

Later he'd learned that Jessica, the flight attendant, had called just after touching down in Los Angeles. She was only going to be there twenty-four hours, which might have accounted for the reason that she called him three times in five minutes. Ashley had broken up with her latest sponsor and even though he'd told her there was no interest in rekindling the relationship, she'd obviously not believed him. Paige and Victoria, well, they'd always been every-now-and-then diversions. While it was true that Chloe was an ex-lover, her call was the legitimate one in the group. She was now dating a football player and was checking to see if there was room for another client on Michael's roster. Michael had explained this to Shayna, had told her that it would take

time to totally break all of his past ties. When her reaction
to this statement was skeptical at best, he asked how he
was supposed to make people quit calling him. Changing his phone number would only result in their calling
the office.

"Just give it time, babe," he'd gently requested.

"How much?"

"I don't know, Shayna. You'll have to trust me."

"Unfortunately, Michael, from watching my mother's
life and through my own experience, I'm not sure that is
something that I can do."

If there was one thing Shayna was an expert at doing,
it was finding her focus before a race. No matter what
had gone on in the week, day, or moment leading up to
when she stepped on the track, she could bring all of her
energy into the singular importance of the moment and
force out all distraction until there was nothing but her,
the track, and the wind.

Today, this was not happening.

Shayna squinted her eyes as she shook out the muscles of one leg and then the other. She raised her hands
high above her head, standing on tiptoe, and then bent
at the waist until her palms were firmly planted on the
polyurethane track. She let her head hang loosely, turning it this way and that. She forced her breathing to be
slow, steady, forced her thoughts to become singular. Or
tried to. The truth of the matter was nothing had been
quite the same since the phone call last night, the one
where she learned that Michael was here. When she'd
boarded the plane two days ago, it was with the knowledge that she'd have several days to not think about "the
conversation," that she could put any decisions that

needed to be made on the back burner until after the meet. After learning about all of the women still blowing up Michael's phone, Shayna had not spent the night at Michael's house, a rare occasion in itself since they'd become a couple. But this revelation had come too close on the heels of the conversation with her mother, had drawn the unavoidable comparison to a lifestyle that she'd grown up witnessing and didn't want to lead. They'd talked a couple more times since, and then she'd told him that she needed to focus on the upcoming meet and that they'd talk when she got back.

But Michael was here. In Barcelona. And Shayna didn't quite know how she felt about that.

"Come on, Kim," Shayna commanded, glad that the race had begun and her focus had shifted. "Keep your head up, girl, let's do this!" She watched as her teammate gracefully rounded the first curve of the track, fists pumping, legs churning in a fluid motion, her braids flying horizontally in the breeze. Kim reached Brittney and the handoff was flawless, practiced hundreds of times. "Go, Britt!" Shayna forcefully encouraged, her voice low, energy contained, when she really wanted to shout and jump up and down as her girl flew ahead of Jamaica, their primary competition, giving the United States a slight lead as she handed off to Talisha. Talisha took the baton, shifted it to her other hand, and was off like a canon shot. She ran straight up and down, similar to Usain Bolt, her tall frame and lanky legs providing the much needed assist to create more distance between her and the shorter Jamaican running the third leg. The group of eight runners rounded the curve at different intervals and hit the straightaway. The Jamaican runner's arms swung back and forth in an interesting, staccato motion, her face a mask of concentration. But Shayna didn't see that. All she saw was Talisha coming at her. She turned and threw back her arm, palm up, feet moving as she waited for the smooth feel of hard plastic to slap against her flesh.

"Go, Shay," Talisha commanded as she handed off the baton. Her roommate and bestie hadn't said nothing but a word. Out of the corner of her eye, Shayna saw a flash of green, gold, and black. *Jamaica.* She shifted her focus, eyes becoming fixed on nothing but the track and the tape. The sound of the crowd receded.

Up in the stands, Michael's eyes were trained on Shayna. She ran like a machine, all arms and legs and fluid motion, her face holding the same type of intensity he sometimes saw when they made love. By the time she busted the tape at the finish line, he knew what he had to do. And he wanted to do it before the meet ended tomorrow and he took Shayna to the next level of her career.

Back at his suite at the W Hotel, Michael sat gazing at the nighttime view of Barcelona, the lights twinkling from the buildings beyond his hotel, the vast darkness of the sea just beyond them. He'd been walking back and forth from the sitting area to the bedroom area, on the phone for the better part of an hour, trying to do what he'd promised Shayna he would and end the liaisons with all of his other women. It sounded easy enough in theory, but the reality of it was proving harder than he thought. First there was the matter of reaching them and if not, leaving a message for them to call him as soon as possible. Unlike some of the guys he'd heard about, he wasn't going to send a text message or break up by voice mail. No, a son of Sam and Jackie Morgan would never go out like that.

Michael looked down at his blinking phone. For the umpteenth time he wished that the ringers on his cells had been silenced when Shayna had come over that night. But Michael had never played those kinds of games, never thought to silence his phones unless he was in a meeting. Had surely never thought to silence his phones so that one female wouldn't know that another was calling. *It was probably best that it happened,* he thought, seeing that it was Paia who'd returned his call. *This had to happen sooner or later, so it might as well be happening now.* He touched the screen. "Hello, Paia." No "baby," "honey," or "darling" on these calls. It was time to address each and every one of these women by their first names.

A brief pause, and then she said, "You sound . . . serious."

Michael attempted a chuckle, but it sounded more like a cough. As confident as he was, and as up to any task that came in his direction, these waters had never been charted and he didn't mind admitting that it was taking him a while to get used to rowing upstream. He decided to ease into it. "Where are you?"

"Paris. Where are you? Wait, don't tell me you're in Barcelona! Was that this week you were going to Spain? How long will you be there? The last show ends here tomorrow night. I could hop on a plane or if it's too late, take a charter."

"That's okay." Immediately he knew that he'd answered too quickly.

"What kind of call is this?" she asked bluntly.

"Not the type of call I'm used to," he honestly replied.

"What kind of call is that?"

"One where I'm ending a liaison to . . . focus on someone special." Silence. Several seconds passed. "Paia, you still there?"

"Yes, and I'm trying to figure out who this imposter is who stole Michael Morgan's phone. Because this doesn't sound like the guy I know at all."

"Yeah, well, the guy you heard about is turning over a new leaf."

"Wow. She must be pretty special."

"She is."

"What—a famous actor or pop star? Or wait—do I know her? Is it another model and you're trying to keep things from getting messy?"

"No, none of that. You don't know this girl." She would eventually, but Michael knew this fact needn't be a part of the conversation.

"I'm happy for you, Michael," Paia said at last. "I mean that. No matter how we play in the fast lane, I think all of us would like to find that one true love, and experience happiness. If I'd known that's where you were in life, I would have tried harder to be the one you found that with."

"You're good people, Paia. I wish you the best." Three quick beeps sounded in succession. "Listen, that's my other phone. Take care of yourself, okay?"

"You, too, lover. You, too."

Michael ended that call and quickly reached for his other phone. "Valerie, thanks for calling me back. There's something I need to discuss with you."

Before the night was over, Michael was well on his way to making good on his promise to Shayna. He'd talked to Cheryl for over an hour, including about the suicide attempt, and was thrilled to learn that not only had she joined a professional dating service, but also that a world-renowned therapist was helping her sort out her life. And as he finished taking his shower to spend an unlikely night in his bed alone, he was hit with the most unexpected thought. Jackie Morgan just might get what she wanted. She might get to witness one of her sons stop sowing his oats.

33

"You were amazing out there." Michael had borrowed the patience of Job and waited more than three hours after the last race for the chance to speak with Shayna. Alone.

"Coach said that you were here. Why'd you come here, Michael?" Usually one to shy away from the presses, Shayna had talked to every reporter, stood for photo ops, and gave an impromptu speech to a group of children, all in hopes that Michael would take the hint and leave. But he hadn't. And the situation she thought could be dealt with later had to be handled now. She wasn't ready. Hadn't had time to think about what she should do, what she could do, considering the truth she'd finally dared admit to herself.

Oh, so we're going to play it like that? Taking in her cool facade, and the back that now faced him as she gathered her things, Michael's voice became detached as well. "What, are you no longer my client? Because as of this very moment, I don't remember receiving a call from your lawyer or yourself that the status has changed. If it has, let me know." A slight clenching and unclenching of his jaw was the only outward sign of his anger. She turned and glared at him. His eyes held her gaze.

Shayna blinked first. "Yes, I'm still your client."

"All right, then. As my client, you need to realize it's important that I witness these major events firsthand, that I have the right PR people in place in order to raise your profile. The magazines, TV stations, and Internet bloggers clamoring for your attention weren't just doing so because of your three first-place finishes today, as impressive as they were. There are people working behind the scenes for you, Shayna. I'm one of those people."

Okay, there was no way she could be rude and not acknowledge that more press seemed to talk to her than some of her other teammates, even though there were others with multiple first-place finishes, namely Alonzo Snead, who'd dominated the long jump, triple jump, and the hurdles. "Thank you."

"I heard of a restaurant that serves a stellar seafood paella. Would you join me?"

"I really should get back to the hotel. We—"

"I spoke with John."

This got Shayna's attention. "You what?"

"You heard me." He took a deep breath and tried to calm down. Stalking-basketball-player-slash-ex-lover aside, this was the very reason why he didn't date the people he represented. Women tended to not be able to keep business and pleasure in their respective corners. True, he'd phoned a friend and "created" the business opportunity with Shayna as a way to get her to talk to him. But this type of beneficial mixing for what he wanted was beside the point. Michael clarified his position. "I tried phoning you, Shayna. When you didn't return my calls, I contacted John so that he could tell you about the photo shoot happening tomorrow. He didn't tell you?"

What her coach had said was to call Michael. She hadn't.

"We're slated to take a flight tomorrow morning for Rome. Italian *Vogue* will be doing a shoot with several female athletes on the Spanish Steps near Trevi Fountain. You'll be modeling Chai's Fashions, both formal wear and athlete designs. It's going to be an all-day shoot, then we'll fly from there back home tomorrow night."

A thrill of excitement ran down Shayna's spine. At least that's what she called it. Since childhood she'd held a secret ambition to be a model, something that because of her height she thought would never happen. She wouldn't dare attribute the feeling to the way Michael was looking at her, the way his jeans carelessly hugged his lean hips and long legs, the way he absentmindedly nibbled on those thick, capable lips, or the way the dimmed lighting made his eyes glow. Knowing she had to do something to cool this growing ardor, Shayna raised herself to her full five foot four, crossed her arms, and acted way angrier than she felt. "Don't you think you should run things by me before you commit to my participation? What if I'd had something else planned, or needed to be back in the States right away?"

"John said that—"

"John is my coach, not my spokesperson or my father! You shouldn't have booked this shoot without my okay."

"Is that so?"

The calmness of his tone sent another shiver down Shayna's spine. "Yes, that's so."

"Well, I did. And since I know you're the consummate professional and all, able to control any feelings you have for me, I know that you'll be there. Isn't that so as well?"

Shayna couldn't disagree with a thing Michael had said. Which is why later she'd question why in the heck she kept arguing with him. Insecurity? The lack of feeling in control? Mistaking his confidence *in* her as condescendence *to* her? All or none of the above could apply. No matter, at the moment she felt that she'd gone too far to turn back now.

"I'll be at the shoot, Michael, but you need to remember that I'm your client, not your employee. You work for me, not the other way around. You sought me out to represent; I didn't come looking for you. Now, I realize that we've crossed some boundaries, but since *you're* the consummate professional and all, able to control any feelings you have for *me,* I know you'll keep what I've said in mind for the future, and not make any more decisions about my life and career without my input. Is *that* so?"

"Did anyone ever tell you how fine you are when you're angry?" Shayna's eyes narrowed to slits. "Yes, Ms. Washington. Your observations as to the workings of this business relationship are duly noted. Now, can we have dinner?"

Shayna had a feeling that dinner might be in a restaurant, but dessert would take place in Michael's bed. It had taken all of her energy to stand up to him—something that happened only because her feigned anger had turned to real chagrin—and if he hit the panties, she wasn't sure she'd have the energy to do it again. So, she gave him the only answer that made any sense. Short. Simple. Unmistakable. "No."

34

Almost twenty-four hours had passed since their heated exchange, but the two had had little to say to each other and even now barely spoke two words during the short walk from the Spanish Steps to the five-star Hotel Rafael. Reaching the door, Michael opened it to let Shayna pass. As she did so, she could have sworn she felt the heat emanating from his body. She'd certainly felt the heat of his stares during the shoot—desire palpable and untamed as she stood in her mini and five-inch heels. She could understand the desire—she was feeling the same. Which is why she couldn't fathom the range of her emotions, and why she was acting immature and irrational. Michael had done a wonderful thing in arranging this shoot and additionally had secured an interview with the Italian press. He'd done nothing but act professional, just as she'd asked, nothing but focus on business, the way she'd said she wanted. Except right now, with them enclosed in the small space of the elevator and her body on fire, she knew that there was something else she wanted—something primal and untamed, something beyond the calm restraint Michael had shown her since they landed in the Eternal City. And as much as she knew what she wanted, she knew that he wasn't going to offer it to her. He'd tried once, this morning when they'd checked into the hotel, and her rebuff had been instant and absolute. *Yeah, how's that working for you right about now, Miss Shayna?* That's just it; it wasn't working for her. Not at all . . .

As soon as they entered the suite, Michael turned toward his room. "Good night, babe."

Just like that? Seriously? She watched his proud, straight, receding back. *What did you expect him to do after turning him down this morning—beg for it? You wanted professional, and that's what he's giving you.* "Good night."

She walked into her room, began to undress, and moments later heard water running from down the hall. A mischievous smile formed on her face as she tossed aside the nightie in her hand and walked bold and buck naked toward the shower.

Michael snatched the hand towel off the rack and angrily soaped his body. Here he'd worked his behind off setting up an amazing shoot and interview for Shayna and what had she done? Basically ignored him all day. Here he was in one of the most romantic cities in the world, where no less than half a dozen women had come on to him (and he had a couple hotel room numbers to prove it) and here he was with a woman tripping because of a few phone calls. Hadn't he told her that he wasn't seeing anyone, that it would take him a minute to untangle from years of living like a consummate bachelor? And even after he'd handled the women he'd seen in the past, there would be others. In the world of high-caliber celebrity sports management, it came with the territory. *I need someone who is confident enough to not trip out every time there's a female nearby.* He'd thought that woman was Shayna. Now he wondered if he'd thought wrong.

The soft click of the shower door was his only warning, and until he felt her lips against his back, he'd even thought that it was his imagination. Now it was his turn to cop an attitude. He turned around. "Yes, may I help you?"

She reached for his limp member and squeezed. "I sure hope so," she said silkily, squeezing the sleeping monster and encouraging it to awaken.

"Oh, so when I wanted it this morning, you didn't feel like it, but now that you want it I'm supposed to handle my business. Is that it?"

Shayna reached for the soap and began lathering Michael's body. "I'm sorry, baby. Seeing all of those numbers come in, all those names one after another just made me crazy. You were up front and told me about them, and we're both grown so we both have a past. I don't know why I let it get to me as much as it did."

"And my coming to Barcelona—why were you tripping about that?" Michael's voice was stern, but his hips had begun to betray him by guiding his stiffening dick in Shayna's hand.

"Because I didn't think I was ready to see you, thought I needed more time to decide how I felt about . . . everything."

"Uh-huh." He reached up and tweaked a nipple, brought lazy, lust-filled eyes up to meet Shayna's half-lid stare. "And how do you feel?"

Shayna began a slow kneel to the tub floor. "I think we'll both feel better in a minute." And with that, she filled her mouth with the width of him, and as much of his length as she could stand. A growl escaped Michael's mouth, and he steadied himself with one hand on the cool marble of the wall and the other on the glass side. The warmth of the water cascaded down his back and the heat of Shayna's mouth almost caused him to explode at once. Shayna put as much focus on the task at hand as she would the 100-meter dash or the 4 x 100 relay. She eased him in and out, rolled her tongue around his massive tip, kissed his weighty balls, and balanced herself on the balls of her feet while clinging to his thigh. She was totally oblivious of the water that was taking her hair from its bone-straight press to a curlicue do. All she wanted in this moment was to satisfy her man. She reached around and caressed his buttocks, adding pressure to the way she was sucking him in. He placed his hand on the back of her head, encouraging her on. And as much as he loved the way she was loving him, he felt it was way past time for her to be satisfied. He guided her up and amidst long, wet kisses they soaped each other's bodies and then made quick work of rinsing off the suds. Opening the glass shower door, he lifted a wet and dripping Shayna into his arms and quickly closed the distance to the bed. As he lay her down, his focus was as singular as hers had been just moments before. He spread her wide and buried his head between her legs, using his tongue with an archer's precision, branding her heat with his skillful determination. She cried out in pleasure, thrashing against the high-count sheets. Michael gave no quarter; instead he upped the ante by parting her folds and licking long and hard, while simultaneously teasing her with his long middle finger. Shayna cried out in ecstasy.

But Michael wasn't finished. He was just getting started.

"Come here," he growled, guiding her to her knees and

positioning himself behind her. He brought them together with one strong push, and immediately set up a fast-paced rhythm. "I missed this," he whispered, cupping her cheeks while driving home the point. "I missed you."

"Me, too," Shayna huffed.

"Who does this belong to?" Michael asked, branding her insides to prove the point.

"Ah . . ."

Michael pulled out to the tip. "Whose is this?" He tickled her opening with his tip.

"Yours." She wiggled her butt to reclaim her prize.

He sank back in, fully, completely. "Are you ever going to deny me again?"

Shayna's head swung back and forth. "No!"

"Good. Now arch that back, let me give you a couple more inches."

She did, and he did. And they did. It would be morning before Shayna would learn about the names that had been deleted from Michael's phone.

35

"Are you sure you can't do Thanksgiving with us?" Michael asked Shayna, while watching her get dressed.

It had been three weeks since their explosive makeup sex in Barcelona. During this time, Michael had had "the conversation" with all of his exes. Like Shayna's ex, Jarrell, some of his former lovers also had a problem taking no for an answer. Some of the calls continued, and he'd reluctantly changed his phone number. It caused a pain for his assistants to have to inform all of his legitimate contacts, but at the end of the day, it made Shayna happy and that, in turn, pleased Michael immensely. Not only that but the Triple S line had been featured in *Women's Running* magazine and was slated to run in an upcoming issue of *O*. Add to that the fact that Michael had signed Rashad Walls the star running back for the Los Angeles Sea Lions and the current boyfriend of one of his exes, Chloe Sinclair, and that another client had just picked up sponsorship from JP Morgan, and one could say his life was pretty much perfect.

"If I don't tell Mama I'm bringing a date, she's likely to try and set me up."

"Seriously?" Shayna said, with a laugh. "Your mom is playing matchmaker?"

"She's trying to own the game! And not just with me but with Gregory and Troy, too. She's a trip. But you'll like her, and I know she'll love you."

"You think so?" Shayna thought about this as she walked over to the closet that was slowly becoming filled with her clothes and took out a pair of shoes. Since Barcelona, she'd practically lived at Michael's, so much so that her roommates were threatening to make double money by renting out her room if she didn't check in soon. Since Big Mama died, she'd not really felt that warm-fuzzy feeling that came with family. Larsen liked to party so the get-togethers with him and her mom were usually loud, rambunctious, and filled with too much T & A. She fondly remembered that last Thanksgiving in Inglewood, just Big Mama, Beverly, and Shayna. The turkey was fall-off-the-bone tender, the dressing was sinfully good, and Shayna still longed for those sweet potato pies. It was a melancholy heart that thought about what dinner would be like in Vegas, especially since her mother had asked her not to bring Michael. Part of the holiday, she knew, would be convincing Jarrell yet again that there was no chance of reconciliation. She was losing her appetite just thinking about it.

"Why don't you spend half your day there, then catch an afternoon flight and come to my mom's?"

"That's a great idea, Michael, but I haven't seen Mom in a while and she has something she wants to talk with me about. I'd better keep the whole day open so I can play it by ear." She walked over to where he sat, leaned down, and kissed him. "But I'll miss you."

"I'll miss you, too."

The next day, Shayna touched down at McCarran International Airport in Las Vegas and, as she'd figured, Jarrell was there to pick her up. His gentlemanlike, hands-off demeanor should have made her grateful, but instead, she was immediately suspicious. *What type of game is dude trying to play?* One thing was for sure: Shayna would keep her guard up.

"So how have you been, Shay?" Jarrell asked, once they'd settled into his sports coupe. "I checked out your line at the local XMVP. I gotta admit your stuff is bangin'. You're doing the damn thing, girl, for real!"

"Thanks, Jay." Shayna rubbed the soft tan leather of Jarrell's brand new ride. "Looks like you're doing pretty good for yourself as well."

"Yeah, I'm trying to do a little sumpin', sumpin'. Larsen's business is booming and I've developed a celebrity arm where we're the exclusive service to most of the celebrities coming from Cali and New York. We've already purchased two additional town cars and I think we might need four more in about six months." He glanced at Shayna. "I always told you I was going to be a success one day, that it was just a matter of time. This gig is just the beginning. After I help Larsen get his business solid, I'm going to start a franchise of luxury car services in the South and Southeast. It's going to be called Nothing But Bentleys, and it's going to be off the chain!"

"What about politics? I thought you were moving down here to run for city council?"

"I'll do that eventually, but first I have to build up a name for myself, and owning the company that squires around the muckety-mucks is one way to get to know all of the players. I figure a couple years, three at the most, and one of those seats is as good as mine."

"I'm happy for you." And she meant it. Shayna had decided before getting on the plane that she was going to do her best to enjoy this trip, and make it a nice holiday for everyone.

"I always saw you with me when I made that climb."

"Jay . . ."

"I'm just saying, Shayna. I know that you don't want to hear it. I heard about you starting to see Michael—" Shayna showed her surprise. "What—you don't think that wouldn't get back to me? Some people couldn't wait to let me know what was going down."

"Who, the woman you're seeing?"

"I don't want to argue with you, Shay. I know I did you wrong and I'm really sorry. We were both young—"

"I wasn't cheating."

"I know. I got scared, Shayna, once other people started pulling on you and you became so involved in track. It was the first time since we were teenagers that you didn't need me. Taking care of you had always been my job and all of a sudden I was unemployed. I started talking to other women just to prove that I still had it, you know, that I could still pull." He glanced away from the road to look at her. "It was the worst mistake of my life."

Shayna was silent as she absorbed this truth, the first time since his infidelities began that he'd come out and owned them, and apologized. Jarrell had been so nasty in those last few months, for the last year of their being together actually, that she'd never thought to look at what was happening from his point of view. It didn't make it right, that he was propping his manhood up against her achievements . . . but she understood it. "What's done is done," she said at last. "And, Jarrell, I have moved on."

"Uh-oh. You're just like my mom. Whenever she calls me 'Jarrell' and not 'Jay,' I know she's serious."

"Yes, I am. But that doesn't mean that we can't treat each other in a civil manner, keep things peaceful for the sake of the family."

"So you're saying that we can be friends."

"Anything's possible."

"I'll always be your first love, Shayna. Your big-shot boyfriend can't take that from me. But I'll take friendship, if that's what I can get."

The small talk continued as they drove to Henderson, a tony suburb about twenty minutes from the Strip. They turned into a cul-de-sac and parked in the driveway of the largest house of the group. Shayna was a bit surprised to see only two other cars in the driveway. She expected there to be at least a dozen people over for dinner. But it was still early, she figured, looking at her watch. Just a little past noon. Dinner wasn't until three.

"Hey, Shay!" Beverly looked up from where she lounged in the living room. She was looking radiant in a brightly colored, thigh-length caftan. Her hair was fixed in a bone-straight style and hung down her back. Sometimes Shayna had to remind herself that Beverly was her mother, and not a chick round the way.

"Hey, Mom." She walked over and gave her mother a hug. Soon Larsen came around the corner and also greeted her. "Hey, sis."

"Hey, Larsen."

Jarrell walked in with a bottle of expensive bubbly in one hand and a bottle of orange juice in the other. He set them down on the bar that separated the living and dining areas. "Well, now that you're here, let's get the party started! Who all wants a mimosa?"

"You know I'm down with the Cristal," Larsen said.

"I know you, Shayna. A drop of champagne and a lot of juice."

"Yes. Like a fourth of the bubbly and the rest orange juice."

"Just juice for me," Beverly said. When three pairs of eyes turned to her, she smiled shyly and added, "I'm on the wagon."

"Well, there's a first time for everything," Larsen replied, giving Beverly a skeptical look. "You sure you're not sick or something?"

"I'm fine, lover," Beverly said, rising smoothly from the couch and walking over to plant a kiss on Larsen's cheek. "Come here, Shay. I want to show you these new outfits I bought."

As soon as they got to the huge master suite, Shay closed the door. "All right, Mom. Out with it."

"What?" Beverly's voice was innocent, but her eyes twinkled.

"With whatever has you not drinking. You're usually the first one to have your glass out for some fine champagne. If you keep that up all day, we'll start to think you're pregnant."

Beverly smiled, and lifted a brow.

"No." Shayna just knew her mother wasn't saying what she appeared to be saying. "Oh my goodness, Mom. Please tell me that you're not pregnant."

"I can tell you that, but I'd be lying." Beverly giggled like a schoolgirl, twirled around, and sat on the bed. "You're getting ready to have a baby sis or brother in about six months."

Shayna stared at her mother. Now the oversized caftan, something her mother never wore, made sense. And as she looked closer, Shayna noticed Beverly's face was more full and she definitely had a glow about her.

"I take it Larsen doesn't know yet."

"No. That's why I wanted you here. I'm going to announce it at dinner."

"How do you think he'll feel about it?"

The smile faded as Beverly stood and began to pace the room. "Honestly, Shay, I don't know. A part of me thinks he'll be happy; he hardly ever sees his daughter since they moved to DC. Plus, she's ten years old and he hasn't ever been that involved in her life. I'm hoping it's a boy. Men always like having a namesake, and a little Larsen would be just the ticket I need to make sure the daddy always finds his way back home."

"Really, Mom? You honestly believe a baby will keep your marriage together? How many women have made that mistake? I only hope that it brings you closer instead of pushing you farther apart."

"I know it's a lot to adjust to, for everybody. Try and be happy for me, okay? Try to be excited, and say what a wonderful thing it is for me to be having his child."

"But how can I say that when I'm getting ready to have a sibling that's twenty-five years younger than me? You're forty-three years old, Mom. When the child's sixteen, you'll be . . . oh my God . . . almost sixty years old!"

"Yeah, and by that time sixty will be the new forty. Look, I think that everything will be all right. Let's just try and have a good time today, just the four of us."

"What? There's only going to be us for dinner?"

"Yes. It's going to be just like old times."

"No, not quite. Not without Big Mama."

A shadow passed across Beverly's face.

"What is it, Mom?" Beverly shook her head. "What is it about Big Mama that you're not telling me? Does it have to do with why there always seemed to be a rift between you?"

"It's in the past," Beverly said, pasting on a smile again. "Let me show you my latest purchases, then we'll go find our men and have some fun."

Shay followed her mother into the dressing room where she'd stashed some designer maternity clothes she'd already bought, and even a few items for the baby. Shayna tried to share in her mother's joy, and she wanted to make the best of the day. But things surely wouldn't be the way they used to. Big Mama was gone. Her man wasn't there. And in this moment she missed him more than ever.

"Mom, I need to share some news myself."

"Oh?"

"Yes. I'm now dating my manager. And I'm in love."

"Son! It's so good to see you!" Jackie walked toward Michael with arms outstretched. Michael hugged her, looking over her shoulder at Troy, who was gesturing toward the living room.

"You just saw me last week," Michael replied, somewhat dryly. "What's got you so excited to see me today?"

"You know how much I love the holidays; for me Thanksgiving is the official start of the season. Now get on in here. Someone is waiting to see you."

Michael stifled a groan and flipped the bird to Troy, who was laughing and gesturing out of his mother's sight. While walking to his mother's front door, he'd seen that he'd missed a call from Troy. But because he knew he'd be seeing him shortly, he didn't bother to return the call. Now he wished he had, so that he could have heeded what he now knew was a warning. His mother was at it again!

He walked over and greeted his father's image, lingered awhile and asked for his help with his mother's latest shenanigans. By the time he turned the corner, Michael had fixed his face into a polite expression. It quickly turned to surprise. "Alison?" As they hugged, he remembered the conversation from a couple months ago, when Jackie had mentioned Alison's divorce and return to California. "How have you been?"

"Getting better every day since I left some no good baggage at the curb for the trash man to pick up." They laughed. "It's good to see you, Michael. You look better than I remember."

"You look good, too, Alison," he said, stepping away and for the first time noticing another woman in the room.

Jackie continued the introductions. "This is Alison's friend Diane." Michael nodded, and shook the other woman's hand. His eyes quickly swept over the women, who were attractive, but seemed a bit nervous. Alison had always been a pretty girl: curly brown hair, slim physique, and dimples. Diane, whom he assumed his mother had snagged for Troy, was tall and wore glasses. She too was attractive, and he immediately felt sorry for her. Because knowing his brother, she'd get tapped real good tonight and then more than likely turned out tomorrow.

"You know Mary's in Africa," Jackie said, seeming quite satisfied with herself as she looked from her sons to the guests.

"No, Mom," Michael said, sitting down and resigning himself to the fact that he'd be entertaining his ex-girlfriend for the afternoon. But maybe that wasn't all bad. It could be fun to catch up with a woman he'd grown up with but hadn't seen in years.

Shortly after Michael and Alison began catching up, Gregory showed up. Unbeknownst to the other two brothers, he'd told his mother he was bringing a date and had thereby been relieved of the blind hookup. Lakshmi Privrata was an OB-GYN doctor at UCLA Med whose husband and son had traveled to India two days ago. Due to a conflict with the schedule, it was going to be next week before she would be able to join them. Thus the impromptu holiday invite from Gregory, an appropriate one since they were both on call and even more appropriate for Gregory, who was tired of his mother trying to provide him with a wife.

The Morgans enjoyed a traditional Thanksgiving meal with all the trimmings and Jackie was especially excited to not be the only woman in the room. Michael had been correct about Troy, who offered to take Diane and Alison out for a night on the town. Alison boldly stated that she'd rather spend her time with Michael, maybe take in a movie or head to the beach like they did in the old days. But Michael declined, citing work responsibilities. It was only a partial lie. The old days were gone. And his mind *was* on a client. He only hoped that surrounded by memories of her "old days," Shayna's mind was also on him.

36

It wasn't, not at this particular moment anyway. At this moment, Shayna's mind was on trying to figure out what cards her partner had in his hand and of which suit she should lead. It had been a while since she'd played spades, though she remembered it being one of Big Mama's favorites.

"Just show me some love, baby," Jarrell said casually. "Show me some love."

"Stop talking across the table," Beverly said with a girlish laugh. She'd been in a good mood ever since announcing her pregnancy and having Larsen's reaction be one of true joy.

"Who's talking?" Jarrell asked, trying to remember what innocence sounded like so that he could put some in his voice. "I'm just looking for some love."

"Shayna, if you put down a heart, we'll know y'all are cheating."

"It doesn't matter, love," Larsen said, eyeing his hand. "Because I can dig us out of wherever we end up."

"He's holding spades," Jarrell said with a shake of his head. "And probably the jokers."

"Yeah, whatever, man. Come on, Shayna. Hurry up and play!"

And for the next hour they laughed and joked and sold "wolf tickets," as Big Mama would say. In the end, Jarrell had been right. His brother had been holding enough spades to dig up an acre of land. He and Beverly had won easily, but what was really a miracle was that they'd gotten through dinner, a pregnancy announcement, and an evening of cards without anyone getting cursed out, beaten up, or dying. As they got up from the table Shayna thought, *So far, so good.*

"All right," Larsen said, walking over to Beverly. "Me and Jay are going to the club to have a quick drink."

"Why do you have to go out drinking when we've got a full bar right here?"

"Come on, now, you know we boys have to go do our thing. Besides, you know you don't like me smoking, and after that delicious meal, I need my cigar fix." Beverly pouted but did not argue. Larsen kissed her on the cheek and then the mouth, first a peck and then a little longer smooch. He wrapped his arms around her and whispered in her ear. Whatever he said must have placated her because Beverly laughed as they broke the embrace. "Don't keep my husband out too late," she said to Jarrell.

"I won't," Jarrell answered, walking over to Shayna with arms outstretched. She hesitated for only a moment before giving him a hug. "We almost got them, partner," he said, referring to the card game. "Next time, okay?"

"Y'all be careful," Shayna replied. Next time, in reference to family gatherings, she hoped that Michael would be there.

After the men left, Shayna and Beverly got something to drink and then settled in the living room. It was

the first time mother and daughter had been truly alone
since Shayna had arrived in Nevada and the first time
they'd enjoyed time in each other's presence all year.

"That went well," Shayna offered, sipping the cran-
berry juice she'd poured. "Larsen seems happy."

"For now," Beverly said, a slight scowl on her face.
"Wait until I start growing and can't give it to him like
he wants it." Shayna wasn't going to touch that statement
with a ten-foot pole vault. Before conceiving, her mother
had been beautiful and toned and, if Beverly's suspicions
were correct, that hadn't stopped brothah man from slipping anyway. Shayna only hoped that this baby on the
way would bring her mother the happiness she wanted.
"Jay was happy," Beverly continued. "He was almost
beside himself just having you here. I know," she hurried
on when Shayna would have stopped her. "You're in love
with your manager. Jay had already told me that, by the
way. Told me all about how he was rolling in the big
leagues. Girl, if you think I've got problems with Larsen,
I can only imagine the witches who are after your man.
Fine and rich and with a high profile? Shit." Beverly
drew out the word until it was almost three syllables.
"You might want to take a page out of your mother's
book and get you an eighteen-year insurance marker."

"It's true that Michael was a player," Shayna offered.
"But he's stopped all that. We've decided to see only
each other."

"Ha! Is that what he told you? Girl, you'd better get
your head out of the clouds."

Her first thought was to get defensive, but she went
with her second thought instead. "Mom, what happened
with you and Big Mama? I know you don't want to talk
about it, but maybe if I understand that I'll understand
why our relationship is . . ."

"Is what?"

Shayna shrugged. "I don't know. Not like other mother/daughter relationships."

"Ours might be better than most—you don't know. Besides, you didn't need me. You always had Big Mama."

Again, the attack, and again, Shayna almost took the bait. But she was using the same skills here in her mother's living room that she did on the track. Focus. She remained silent, kept looking at her mother and waiting for an answer.

"Oh, girl, I don't know why you want to bring up the past anyway. I chose Daddy," she finally said.

Shayna's brow furrowed. *Huh?*

"Right before I got pregnant with you, Mama and Daddy got divorced. He married the woman he'd been cheating on Mama with and I asked Daddy if I could stay with them. I chose him over staying with Mama. I don't think she ever forgave me for that."

"I always got the feeling that Big Mama and her husband divorced a long time ago, like when you were a child."

Beverly shook her head. "No, they divorced when I was sixteen. Me and Mama pretty much didn't speak until a year or so later, when I got pregnant with you. By that time Orsella—that was Daddy's wife's name—had talked Daddy into moving back to St. Louis, where she was from. He got killed in a car accident a few years later."

Shayna absorbed this news, more confused than ever. Why had her mother been so hesitant about sharing this, and why had Big Mama skirted around it as well? Something wasn't right, something wasn't adding up. "I don't get it, Mom. I can understand your feeling guilty about abandoning Big Mama, but why was that such a secret? I thought it was something horrible like incest or something."

"It was close."

Her mother had spoken so softly that Shayna almost didn't hear. "What?"

"Daddy's brother. My uncle. He sexually assaulted me when I was ten years old." Shayna stared at her mother, not wanting to believe the words coming from her mouth. "When Mama found out she wanted him arrested, but Daddy, your grandfather, didn't believe it was true. Even after my uncle admitted what he did, Daddy continued to interact with him and this infuriated Mama. Orsella was the woman who Daddy went with, but his and Mama's marriage was over long before she came along. Anyway, the fact that Daddy didn't defend me after his brother's assault made my going to live with him all the more traitorous in Mama's eyes. But I always was a daddy's girl. Me and Mama never had that closeness." Beverly looked at Shayna. "Maybe that's why I don't have it with you."

Shayna and Beverly talked for two hours, until Larsen and Jarrell returned from having drinks at the club. Larsen and Beverly went to bed shortly after and then, perhaps because the day had gone so well and perhaps at one time it had been the most normal thing to do, Shayna and Jarrell sat up talking, laughing, and reminiscing the way they used to do. For Shayna, it was a sign that the family could and would survive her and Jarrell's breakup. But later she'd learn that, from that night on, Jarrell believed that getting back together was just a matter of time.

37

The beautiful people were out and the party benefiting the Pediatric Society of Greater Los Angeles was in full swing. Shayna sat in the back of the limousine, satiated and satisfied after her and Michael's marathon sex session. Michael had been right, Shayna's mind had stayed on him during her visit to Vegas, and the night's endless loving had proved just how much they'd missed each other. She'd always viewed her mother as a sex kitten, having been embarrassed by the sounds coming from her room on more than one occasion. But who knew that Shayna possessed an inner freak, one that Michael brought out full-force? She laughed at the thought.

"What's funny?" Michael reached for her hand as he fiddled with his bow tie.

"Nothing. Just happy is all."

"That's my job, babe. Making sure you stay that way."

"Oh, really? I thought your job was to make me rich and famous."

"Ha! That, too."

They arrived at the Beverly Hilton and joined a long line of town cars and limos carrying a veritable who's who of not only LA's medical field but also the movie and music industries. This was a popular fund-raiser, one that was known for having stellar music, a decadent buffet, and gift bags valued in the thousands of dollars. Since becoming Michael's client, she'd attended many high-end functions, but this was the first one where she was doing so strictly as his guest. She was nervous, not so much because she didn't feel in her element—though that was part of it as well—but mainly because Michael had warned her that she was more than likely going to come face to face with one or more of his exes. Shayna ran a hand down the front of her silky Chai original, set her red-bottomed shoes on the pavement, and pulled up her big girl panties. It was showtime.

Ironically, it wasn't one of Michael's exes they ran into first. It was hers.

"Jay?" They'd not taken two steps from the town car when Shayna saw her tuxedo-clad ex-lover coming toward her.

He stopped just two feet away. "Hey, Shayna," he said, though his eyes were on Michael.

Okay, Shayna thought as she felt Michael stiffen beside her. *This is the epitome of an awkward moment.* But then again, maybe not. She and Jay had not only been civil in Las Vegas, the word *cordial* could have even been used to describe their interactions. He'd behaved, for the most part, and seemed ready to acknowledge that the ex-lovers were now just in-laws and casual friends. Jarrell rose up to his full five-feet-nine and squared his shoulders, reminding Shayna that it was the first time these men had been face to face. *Uh-oh.* Though no introductions were needed, she still spilt them into the awkward, tension-filled silence. "Michael, this is Jay, Jarrell Powell. Jay, Michael."

"I'd say it was a pleasure, but I'd be lying," Michael said, his low calm voice a stark contrast to the instant anger Shayna felt emanating from his six-foot frame.

"I don't give a damn what you say to or about me," Jarrell countered before finally turning his eyes back to Shayna. "You're looking beautiful, Shayna. It's good to see you again."

Michael took a step toward Jarrell, and Shayna quickly placed herself between the pissing contest that was well underway. "Michael, I see your brother. Let's go inside."

"You should call your mother," Jarrell said as Shayna passed him. "She hasn't been feeling too well."

Shayna kept a firm hand on Michael's arm as they entered the ballroom. "Was that necessary?" she hissed as soon as they rounded the corner.

"Look, you may have a history with him and a cause to be friendly, but I don't. I don't like him, and I don't care if he knows it."

"Let it go," she whispered, noting the coiled muscle beneath his jacket arm. "I told you that during my visit to Vegas we'd agreed to bury the hatchet, let the past be the past. And then here you go being an asshole."

"Oh, you're defending him now?"

They reached Gregory, who was standing with a stunning brunette. *Just in time.* "Hi, Gregory!"

"Hello, Shayna," he said, bending over to give her a hug. He introduced his date and then turned to his brother. "What's up, big man?"

Michael gritted his teeth and remained silent, though he had given a curt nod and handshake to Gregory's companion.

"Uh, excuse us for a minute," Gregory said, and then began walking away from the women without waiting for a reply. "What's going on, man?" he asked Michael, as soon as they were away from the hubbub.

"We just ran into the punk who beat up Shayna," Michael spat, hands flexing into fists as he searched for Jarrell's whereabouts.

"Here?" Gregory asked, obviously surprised.

"Yeah."

"Why?"

"I don't know," Michael said, spotting the back of a familiar-looking tux beneath a head covered with close-cropped swirls. "But I'm getting ready to find out."

"Michael!" Gregory turned to catch up with his brother, who was making fast tracks out of the ballroom and across the lobby. "Damn," he hissed under his breath. He'd just purchased his tuxedo and would hate to get it ruined in a fisticuff.

Michael reached the lobby doors and exited. He looked around just in time to see Jarrell getting into a limousine. He was driving it.

"Ah," Gregory said as both of the men watched the limo leave the circular driveway. "So he's a limo driver."

"He's a brother who's going to get his ass kicked if he bothers my girl again."

Gregory cast a concerned eye in his brother's direction. Troy was the hothead of the family; Michael, though not one to back down from much of anything, was normally the objective one in the bunch. Gregory was cool, calm, and collected. Which was a good thing because that's exactly what Michael needed right now. "Come on, brother. He's gone. Don't let that chance meeting ruin our evening. Let's get back in before they begin the silent auction. I've got my eye on a painting I want you to buy me."

"Oh, is that right?" Michael asked, visibly relaxing after taking one more glance toward the front of the hotel. He smiled. "Your birthday isn't for another month, man."

"It's for a good cause, Michael. Let's spend some of that money you and Shayna have made."

38

"Hey, Jarrell, you want some of this?" Beverly scooped out a small helping of the lasagna that had been delivered by her favorite Italian eatery. She'd had a horrible bout of morning sickness and was just now regaining a bit of an appetite.

"Naw, I'm good." Jarrell sat brooding in the living room, flicking through the television stations and not seeing a thing.

"What's gotten you in this foul mood?" Beverly walked into the living room and plopped down on the opposite end of the couch where Jarrell sat. "You've barely had two words to say since returning from LA."

"You know why."

"You're still mad about running into Shayna and her manager?"

"Manager," Jarrell all but spat out. "The dude is managing something all right, and it's more than her career."

"He's hitting it—so what? You remember how she was with you during Thanksgiving. She still loves you, Jay. If you play your cards like I told you, she'll be back.

Just wait until Mr. Big Shot gets restless, and goes for some new meat. A man like him can't be faithful, and you know a woman like Shayna can't stand sharing her man. The minute he hurts her, and he will, she'll come running right back into your arms. "

"You're right about that," Jarrell agreed, calming down a bit.

"And didn't you say that Shayna sent a text apologizing about what happened?"

Yes, there was that, Jarrell admitted. She had sent a text. But aside from when she landed and called to let him know that she'd gotten home safe, as he'd asked her, she still wasn't taking his phone calls. Jarrell had never been much of a patient man. "They don't care about nobody but themselves," he offered Beverly. "You know that nobody is ever going to care about your daughter the way I do."

"And in the meantime you're taking care of business yourself." Beverly sighed, taking a bite from a slice of garlic bread. "Larsen told me about the girl at the office and I already knew about the limo driver. So it's not like you're twiddling your thumbs until Shayna comes back. Her manager is just a diversion. You need to chill."

"Oh, yeah? Is that what you were saying a month ago when Larsen was stepping out with the exotic dancer? Before he found out you were pregnant and you were begging me to get him to put on the brakes? Or what about just last week, when you wanted me to drive by the office and see if old girl was still working there, the one he was screwing for six months."

"That's cold, Jarrell."

"It's the truth."

"Me and Larsen are different."

"How so?"

"We're married."

"Me and Shayna are supposed to be married. Isn't that what you told me, Beverly, all those years ago when I set you up with my brother? That we were all going to be one big happy family and have each other's back? Do you remember saying that?"

Beverly nodded. "And I meant it, too, at the time. But things changed, Jarrell. I told you to stop being so possessive with Shayna, to stop trying to control her. I was working on getting her off the pill so that you could get her pregnant. And then you had to go and put your hands on her."

"I told you how that went down. I didn't hit her! I just wanted to talk to her, but she fought and jerked away from me and that's how she got hurt!"

"Whatever happened, it made Shayna not want to have anything to do with you."

"She doesn't really feel that way, Beverly, and you know it. That girl will always love me." His eyes narrowed as he looked at Beverly. "And you told me that you'd help me get her back."

"I told you that I was on your side and that I would do what I could. And I will. Like I said, I think that when this big-time agent is through with her, he'll dump her on the side and be on to the next flavor. Until then, just keep being the charming man that you can be and stop acting all needy and possessive and crazy in the way that got you kicked to the curb in the first place."

39

"Hey, Mom. Just calling to check on you." It had been a week since Shayna had run into Jarrell, and his parting words had haunted her. She'd called her mother almost every day since then, and was cautiously optimistic at the camaraderie existing between them these days. "How's the little one?"

"The way it's tossing and turning, kicking my insides, I'd say extremely pissed off!"

"Ha! He'd better enjoy himself in there. These are some of the best days of his life." Shayna tensed at the sharp intake of breath from the other end of the phone. "Mom, you all right?"

"I'm rather miserable, to tell you the truth. Having a baby at eighteen and having one in your forties are two totally different things. With you, I worked and partied right up until the due date, was in labor two hours, dropped you, and was back on my grind in less than two weeks. This one has me feeling all kinds of aches and pains. The doctor is threatening to put me on bed rest."

"For real?"

"I wish you were here, Shayna. But I know you've got your life and all," Beverly hurried on. "I'll be all right."

"You sure?"

"It's only a couple weeks till Christmas. I'll be okay till then."

"Mom, we've already had this conversation. I spent Thanksgiving in Vegas. I'm spending Christmas with Michael and his family. I've never met his mother. She's expecting me."

"Oh, right." There was about as much enthusiasm in her voice as that of a graveyard corpse.

"You know what? I don't get this attitude where Michael is concerned. You've never seemed to like him. You don't ask about him. But he's a good man. He's doing great things for my career. I'm happy. Why can't you be happy for me?"

"I'm sure he's cool and all, Shay. But you know I love Jarrell like a son, have known him since he was a child. Y'all grew up together."

"What we had is over, Mom. I thought this was all settled with my trip in November."

"He still misses you."

"Mom . . ."

"But he's trying to move on, Shay. He's dating a girl from the office. She's the receptionist at Larsen's company."

Shayna's sigh of relief was audible. "That's nice. I'm happy for him."

"You should be. You both deserve to be happy. She's a pretty girl. And nice, too. She knows about you and is cool with the fact that the boss's wife is Jarrell's ex-girl's mother."

Shayna wanted to say whup-the-frickin'-do, but decided against it. This had been a fairly civil conversation after all. Hearing the call indicator beep, Shayna looked at her phone. "This is Michael, Mom. I've got to go. He's heading out of town tonight, so I'll call you back tomorrow."

She accepted the incoming call. "Hey, baby."

"Hey, you. That was crazy—your phone didn't ring."

"I was talking to my mom."

"How is she?"

Shayna relayed the gist of their conversation. "I know she wants me to come down there. Maybe after Christmas with your family we can go down there for a couple of days. I want you to meet her."

"Sounds like a plan, babe."

Shayna heard water running in the background. "What are you doing?"

"Washing my hands. I'm going to eat and then take a shower."

"Ooh, sounds like the perfect time for me to head over."

"I wish, but I've got some business to handle before I head to the airport."

Shayna heard another sound. "What was *that*?"

"Troy came over with a couple of his friends."

The tinkling sound of women's laughter continued along with what Shayna imagined was either the stereo or TV. "Oh, is this the business you need to take care of?" She didn't even try and hide the pout in her voice.

"Don't even start. He's dating one of them and her friend wanted to meet me because she has an advertising company and wants to network."

"Yeah, I've got her network, all right."

Michael laughed, his voice low and sexy. "I like that you're jealous, baby. It means I've been hitting it right."

"Whatever, nucka," Shayna said, smiling. "Just make

sure she understands who that weapon you're firing belongs to."

"Michael, the steaks are done!"

"Oh, so y'all grilling and the whole nine? What, are they chillin' by the pool in bikinis? Or are they wearing thongs?"

"Baby, I'll call you when I'm on my way to the airport."

"Michael, don't—" But it was too late; he'd already hung up. "Stop trippin', Shay," she said aloud, walking to the kitchen and grabbing a cold water out of the fridge. *You just told your mother that you've got a good man.*

She had told Beverly this, and she was right. But across town, someone else had a different idea. Somebody else was trying to talk Michael into being a very bad boy.

40

"Oops, I'm sorry. I was looking for the bathroom."

Michael stood by a dresser in his bedroom, about to put on his signature simple jewelry: a two-carat stud earring, his Rolex, and a thin platinum cross. That would have been three additions to his present attire; the only thing keeping the stranger before him from seeing the family jewels was a stark white towel wrapped securely around his waist.

"But then again," Ms. Advertiser cooed while brazenly walking into the bedroom dressed in a barely there bikini top and a thong bottom, "I'd much rather use the one here, in the master suite."

"The guest bathroom," Michael began with a scowl, "is back down the hallway, on your left. Which you probably know since you had to pass it to get here."

"I like your place." Ms. Advertiser turned and sauntered toward the painting on the wall. The fact that she wanted Michael to check out her tush was about as subtle as a neon sign in front of a strip bar. Unfortunately for her, Shayna was working with a badonkadonk where girlfriend here only had a donk. "I'm thinking about having my home redone. Who's your designer?"

"Someone who would take the hint and leave where she's not wanted. I suggest you rejoin my brother. I'll be out shortly."

"Sorry," Ms. Advertiser said in a way that suggested she was anything but. She gave his physique the once-over before heading for the door. "But if you need someone to help you dry off, just let me know."

Minutes later, a jeans-clad Michael stood in the patio doorway. "Troy, come let me holler at you for a minute." He stood, hands on hips, taking in the scene at the pool: both women topless, with surgically enhanced breasts that if needed could easily be used as flotation devices. Shayna's voice came floating into his mind. *Is this the business you need to take care of?* If Shayna saw this, she'd be furious. "And tell your friends to get dressed."

Troy, who'd been taking the medium-well steaks off the grill, turned to the women. "Cover up, ladies. These ears of corn are almost ready to turn over; I'll grab the salad and be back out in a minute." He followed Michael inside. "What's up, man? Since when did you not enjoy a titty show?"

"Since I went exclusive with Shayna. How many times do I have to tell you that I've chilled on that mess?"

"Damn, man. I guess I can't believe you actually turned in your player card."

"Well, believe it. In fact, it feels pretty good. You might want to try it."

Troy raised his hands in mock surrender. "I've still got a few wild seeds to sow. I'm not sure just one woman could satisfy me."

"When you find the right one, she can." Michael looked at his watch and started for the bedroom. It was early yet, but he'd rather hang in the lounge at the airport than stay here and deal with drama. "You've got your keys, right?" Troy nodded. "Okay, be sure and lock up."

"How long are you gone for this time?"

"A couple days."

"New York?"

"Chicago."

"Oh, yeah. The dude who just got signed with the Bulls."

"Exactly."

The brothers shared a fist pound and a shoulder bump. "Okay, be safe, man."

Michael arched his brow and cocked his head in the direction of the pool. "*You* be safe, my brothah."

Troy's laughter followed him down the hall.

Had Michael not taken the shortcut through the side street that placed him closer to the 101 Freeway, he would have seen Shayna's shiny red Hyundai as it wound around the snarly curves and pulled into his driveway. But by the time she knocked on his door, he was on the 101, headed to the 110 and the Los Angeles International Airport.

Shayna bopped up to the door with a smile on her face. She still felt quite good about her ingenious idea to give Michael a ride to the airport. She knew that for these short trips he preferred driving himself to using one of the company cars. She also knew that he was one of those last-minute passengers who'd valet their car, breeze through the first-class security line, haul all kinds of you-know-what to the gate, and then flash that piano he called a smile at the would-be-angry flight attendant before taking his preferred seat: 2B. Today would be different. She knew from the female who'd announced dinner that he'd eaten. She'd left the house as soon as she'd hung up the phone so he should be showered, dressed, and just about ready to go.

"Oh, hey. You must be Troy," she said when he answered the door. When he stepped toward her, she gave him a quizzical look before brushing past him and going inside. Sensing that he'd remained by the door, Shayna turned. "I'm just here to pick up Michael. I assume he's—"

"I knew you wouldn't be able to stay away from the festivities!" a playful voice rang out from just beyond the hallway. "I know you said to get dressed, Mike, but . . ." As topless Ms. Advertising turned the corner, the would-be come hither faded from her lips, ending with a breathy "Oh." Hardly an introvert, she lifted her hands to twist the wet hair splayed around her shoulders into a brunette bun atop her head. "Sorry, I thought Mikey had come back for more fun."

Mikey? That's the first clue that you don't know him, witch, because anyone who did would never ever call him Mikey. Without responding to the distraction, Shayna turned back to Troy. "I take it he's not here."

A slow, lazy smile spread across Troy's face. "And you must be Shayna. Michael's on his way to the airport. He left awhile ago."

Shayna's head nod to Ms. Advertising behind her was barely discernible. "I figured as much."

Troy caught the gesture and laughed out loud. Ms. Advertising turned around and flounced back toward the pool. "I've heard a lot about you. It's nice to meet the woman who's elicited traits from my brother that I never thought I'd see."

"Such as . . ."

"Stability. Commitment."

"Thank you," Shayna replied, walking to the door.

Troy followed Shayna out of the house, walking her to her car. "Michael would think I'm a fine one for giving advice on relationships, but can I tell you something?" Shayna nodded. "For all of the women who throw themselves at us and all of the partying and all the fun we like to have, our mother didn't raise no fools. When we find that special someone, we know how to treat her. My brother is seriously digging you. So you don't have anything to worry about. You feel me?"

Shayna nodded. "I feel you, Troy. It was nice to meet you. Thanks again."

41

The drizzle began just before Shayna reached her destination. She turned on the wipers, absentmindedly reflecting that the rain pouring down the windshield mirrored the tears falling on her face. Time had passed, but the leaving still felt as fresh as it did on that unseasonably warm day in December three years ago when Shayna, her mother, Jarrell, Larsen, some cousins, and a few dozen members from the Good Hope South Central AME Church had stood by a flower-strewn grave and bid Willie Jean "Big Mama" Washington a fond farewell. That entire week had gone by in a haze, starting at the moment she'd gotten the call that her grandmother had suffered a heart attack and then getting to the hospital forty-five minutes later only to find out that she was already gone. That night, Big Mama had appeared to Shayna in a dream. In it she hadn't spoken, but had simply patted Shayna's hand, given her a big hug and smile, and then turned and walked across a foggy meadow. Shayna waved and waved, until she could no longer see Big Mama. Upon awakening, there was a hole in her heart. But for the one Willie Jean Washington

had called her favorite grandchild even though she was
the only one, that last meeting was like manna from
heaven, its memory just about the only thing that could
bring her solace during that bleak time.

Shayna reached the slab of black granite engraved
with roses, a cross, the name and date: WILLIE JEAN
WASHINGTON, DECEMBER 20, 1947–DECEMBER 28, 2009,
and lastly the inscription: FOREVER ALIVE IN OUR HEARTS.
"Hey, Big Mama," she whispered, kneeling down and
placing the dozen pink heart roses against the stone.
"Happy birthday. I can't believe it's been three years
already. Seems like just yesterday we were over at your
friend's house, Miss Josie, remember? Eating your favorite German chocolate and listening to your favorite
Billie Holiday. I haven't played her much lately," Shayna
continued, pulling the weeds from around the stone as
tears continued to fall. "I guess I don't want to wish a
heartache good morning." Finding a comfortable spot
near the smooth, cool slab, Shayna placed a plastic bag
she'd found in her back seat on the ground and sat on top
of it. The winter rain had stopped as quickly as it had
begun, and streaks of sun were trying to pierce the gray-
ish sky. She looked around at this "community" of souls,
different markers signaling a life come and gone, the dash
in between the dates, Big Mama once told her. Before her
death, Shayna had considered graveyards morbid, and
wasn't one to watch murder mysteries or horror films.
But on the times she'd visited, three in all, she'd felt an
overwhelming peace, like now, like her grandmother was
right here with her brimming with love.

"I met someone, Big Mama. You remember I broke
up with Jarrell, right? Well, my new guy, his name is
Michael and he's also my manager. He's gotten me in
magazines and on TV, and I even have my own clothing

and shoe line. I so wish you were here to meet him, Big Mama," Shayna said, a tremor to her voice as she tried to replace her tears with happy memories. "But then again, if you were here you'd be dealing with the fact that your daughter is getting ready to have a baby. Yes, Big Mama. Mom is pregnant—can you believe it? I'm trying to be happy for her, but her being with Larsen indirectly keeps me connected to Jay and it's just one big mess. I know you liked Jay, Big Mama, but he changed after you died, became more possessive, controlling, especially after I turned pro. But I remember how well he treated you, how he tried to look after you. You always told me that everybody had some good in them. I guess that's one good thing about Jarrell that I can remember. That he loved you."

The rain started up again and after a few more moments, Shayna returned to her car. As she opened the door, the phone was ringing. She wasn't totally surprised to see who was on the caller ID.

"Hey, Jay."

"Hey, Shayna. You know I had to call you today."

"Yeah, I know."

"Gotta say happy birthday to Miss Willie Jean." Shayna smiled. "Have you gone to vist the grave yet?"

"I'm here now."

"Ah, baby. I wish I would have been able to go there with you. You know I loved Big Mama like she was my own, knew her my whole life."

It was true. Big Mama used to parent all of the children in the neighborhood, and she'd send Jarrell to the store for her unlikely favorite, Jolly Ranchers. Jarrell's mother often worked overtime, so Jarrell was a regular for Big Mama's spaghetti, meatloaf, or fried chicken dinners and would always make her smile by asking for seconds, sometimes thirds. After that, they'd entertain her with talent shows in the living room: Shayna singing—translated: butchering—"Butterfly" by Mariah Carey, Jarrell rapping Biggie's "Hypnotize," and their teaming up for Puff Daddy and Faith Evans's "I'll Be Missing You."

"Hey, remember that time I stole those cookies that Big Mama made and sold them to the neighborhood kids?"

"Ha! How could I forget that one?"

"Big Mama was ready to whup me until she saw my profit. That wrongdoing ended up being the basis for my first business. She's probably the reason I sold sweets instead of drugs."

The two continued to chat about old times. Shayna had forgotten just how funny Jarrell could be, not to mention how much at one time their lives had been intertwined. Before she knew it, an hour had gone by. She started her car and hurried out of the cemetery.

"I need to run, Jay. I was supposed to be at Michael's office by now."

"All right, Shay. When are you coming down here?"

"I don't know. But tell Mom I'll call her later."

They ended the call. Shayna headed downtown, thinking of Jarrell. Before being lovers, they'd been the best of friends. A part of her would always love him. "I hope you're happy," Shayna said aloud, thinking that maybe it was time she visited her mother in Vegas. And for the first time in a long time, she even looked forward to seeing Jarrell again.

42

A jazzy rendition of "White Christmas" could be heard playing just beyond the door as Michael and Shayna reached his mother's house. They'd awakened to a bright and shiny Christmas morning and while they'd agreed to exchange gifts at his mother's house, they'd given each other an extended morning present of the physical kind. It had both of their moods chipper, had made Shayna's cheeks glow, and put a little extra pep in Michael's steps.

"So nice to finally meet you," Jackie said, once her son and friend had stepped inside and she'd given him a hug. She embraced Shayna as well before stepping back to look at her. "You're shorter than I imagined. Who would have thought it'd be a short cup of chocolate to tame my son?"

Michael groaned. "Ah, here we go."

"It's nice to meet you, too, Mrs. Morgan."

"Please. Call me Jackie."

"Come over here and meet my father," Michael said, taking Shayna's hand.

Shayna walked with Michael over to the fireplace. She

looked at the painting, an older, darker version of Michael
and Troy, and was immediately struck with the intense,
kind eyes of Michael's father even as she realized that
Gregory got his good looks from his mother's side.

"This is Samuel Morgan," Michael said, reaching up
to stroke the frame that contained the exquisitely
painted image. "My father and one of the finest men I
ever knew."

"You look like him." Michael nodded. Shayna stepped
closer to him and said, "I bet you still miss him."

"Every single day."

He and Shayna eyed the painting for another silent
moment. Finally, Shayna whispered, "It's a pleasure
meeting you, Mr. Morgan."

Michael smiled, kissed her temple, and led her to the
kitchen, where his mother and one of her friends were
cooking up dinner. On the way, they noticed that Gregory
was out on the patio with his date. After a quick hello,
they joined Jackie and her two women friends, one widowed, the other divorced with a child overseas, from the
old neighborhood. Thankfully, Jackie had agreed to
Michael's request not to invite her best friend, Mary. He
knew that Mary coming meant Alison's presence as well
and with the way she kept bugging his mother for his cell
number, seeing her again this lifetime might be too soon.
He and Shayna had just joined the other guests, who
were chatting while munching on vegetable sticks, when
in walked a surprise: Troy. Alone.

Jackie made a big show of looking behind him.
"Where's she at?"

"Who?" Troy walked over to the stove and lifted up
the lid on a pot of chicken and dumplings before opening the oven to find a roasting duck, winter vegetables,
and a chocolate cake.

"Your latest arm candy," Jackie replied, walking over and swatting Troy away from the oven before closing the door. "Where is she?"

"I'll be his arm candy," Jackie's widowed neighbor said. "What do they call 'em these days? Tigers?"

"Cougars," offered the Navy officer's mom. Her only child was the same age as Michael, and the mother's friendship had ridden the coattails of the sons.

"Yeah, honey. Get me some of those five-inch pumps."

"Please," Jackie dryly replied. "I don't need a visual."

Troy walked over and playfully hugged the woman who'd been his neighbor and sometimes babysitter from the time he was born until he was twelve years old. "You can be my date anytime, Miss Linda. But Mom is the jealous type. We might have to keep it on the low."

Shayna came around the corner. "Do you need any help, Mrs. Morgan? I mean, Jackie."

"Sure do. I was just getting ready to make the salad."

A short time later, Jackie's dining room was filled with the sound of clinking silver hitting china and laughter all around.

"Remember that time when Michael and Otis thought they were going to run away? They got as far as the freeway before the cops brought them home."

"You were arrested?" Shayna asked in surprise. Somehow she couldn't imagine her man behind bars.

"He should have been," Jackie replied. "But no. Linda's cousin is a policeman. We sent him to instill the fear of God in them, which he did."

Linda shook her head at the memory. "For about five minutes. After that, they wanted to ride around and show off in the squad car."

"Which they did, even managing to handcuff one of their friends to the fence and then lose the key."

"Perry, Linda's cousin, just locked Michael up beside him. They didn't get loosed until Sam got home."

"Trust me, after that I'd rather have been in handcuffs," Michael said.

The afternoon passed quickly. Shayna loved watching the easy camaraderie between Jackie and her sons, and the brothers with each other. Aside from the time at her grandmother's, she'd never witnessed such familial love and was appreciative of how much Jackie made sure she felt a part of the Morgan clan. When the time for gift-giving arrived, Shayna was surprised to see that all of the brothers had purchased her a gift.

"Michael didn't tell me that we were all exchanging," she chided, offering Michael a stern look.

"Don't worry about it," Jackie admonished. "It's a family tradition."

A collective breath was held when Michael handed Shayna a small, wrapped box. She tore open the paper and instantly recognized the blue box. With slightly shaky hands, she opened it to reveal a pair of perfectly cut yellow diamonds. "They're beautiful," Shayna exclaimed with tears in her eyes. She showed around the box to the women before reaching up to replace the earrings she wore with this holiday gift.

"The diamonds are lovely, son," Jackie said, already loving the spunky young woman who seemed to fit her son to a tee. "But I can think of another setting with a more . . . forever kind of message. If you know what I mean."

43

Michael knew exactly what his mother was talking about and if he hadn't, he surely did now, after just getting off the phone with her. Shayna had gone over to Brittney's cousin's house to exchange gifts with Talisha and Brittney. Michael and Shayna were meeting back up tonight and heading to Vegas the following morning to meet Shayna's mom. It was hard to believe that this time last year he was juggling a dozen women and now he was getting ready to meet a potential mother-in-law. That is, if his mother had her way. He mixed himself a cocktail and thought about what his mother had said, starting right into her case as soon as he answered the phone.

"Can you talk?" Michael said yes. "I like her, Michael. She kinda reminds me of me at her age."

"How's that?"

"She has a sparkly personality, but I detect a shyness, and a bit of a sadness about her. Am I right?"

"You always could read people, Mom." Michael relayed to Jackie about how Shayna's father's absence and her mother's competitive indifference had affected Shayna's personality and outlook on life. "Most of the children on her block were being raised by single moms. But for whatever reason, Shayna has really missed not knowing her dad, or having him around."

"I always wondered how those mothers did it. You boys were basically grown when Sam passed and it was still a struggle. Had it not been for his strong hand before he left, who knows how y'all would have turned out."

"Probably like a lot of our friends." While the Morgan brothers and a few others had gotten out of their middle-class surrounded by lower-class neighborhood, the widowed neighbor's children had had their share of problems. Even now, her daughter was on probation for passing bad checks.

"I wish Dad were here to meet Shayna."

"Me, too, son. I miss him every day."

"Do you think you'll ever marry again, Mama?"

"You do, then I will . . . okay?"

"Ha! Okay, Mama."

The two chatted for a while longer and when Michael ended the call, he thought about everything his mother had shared, especially her last comment: "Baby, if you love her you'd better do like that girl Beyoncé said and put a ring on it."

Michael laughed out loud as he dialed his brother Troy. Time to find out what had his playboy youngest riding solo. "Hey, man," he said once his brother had answered. "How is it that you ended up the lone ranger today?"

"No big deal," Troy replied. "I'd asked this one sistah if she wanted to join me and she said that she would. Then about fifteen minutes before I was supposed to pick her up, she called and canceled."

"What? Someone had the nerve to cancel on you?"

"I know—can you believe it?"

"What's the world coming to?"

"It's getting hard out here for a pimp."

"Ha!"

"On another note, I like your girl, Shayna. She seems real cool."

"Yes, she made it through an afternoon with Jackie Morgan, got her approval. That's not always easy."

"You know I still have her ex's info on file. Let me know if you ever want me to do something with it."

"Wasn't much there, just the personal stuff about jobs, his family. I could have Googled and found that out."

"Oh, so now we've got jokes, huh? Bottom line is that the dude was pretty clean. So was his brother, Larsen."

"I didn't know you checked him, too."

"Then you need to Google the fact on how thorough the people who work for me are. Even if it's family, I put my stamp on anything connected to Morgan Security. And it's got to be top notch, believe that."

"I appreciate it, man." Michael smiled, grateful to have the type of relationship he did with his brothers. "Hey, what's Gregory doing tonight?"

"I don't know, but he left the house rather quietly. Might be making a house call if you know what I mean."

"Or somebody might be at his house."

"You want to pay him a surprise visit?"

"Yeah. Why don't you come over and we'll ride together. If he's not home, we'll go out and see what kind of trouble you can get into."

"Me? What about you?"

"Naw, man. When it comes to trouble . . . I'm good."

"Oh, Shayna's got it like that, huh?"

"Yes, Troy. It's like that."

* * *

"Ooh, girl, I'm so jealous," Brittney said. She, Shayna, and Talisha were hanging out on her cousin's screened-in patio.

"Cameron got me"—Talisha used air quotes—"a trip to Hawaii. Y'all know his ass has been wanting to visit there for years!"

"I think it's a very romantic present," Shayna countered. "Who knows? While there he may even propose."

"She's right," Brittney added. "Cameron has shown a romantic streak over the years."

"I know. . . . I'm sounding ungrateful, huh?"

Shayna laughed. "You think?" She looked at Brittney, proudly sporting the leather jacket that Shayna had bought her. "What about you, Britt? Don't you think it's time to finally get back into the dating game, and let DeVaughn hit it?"

The last serious relationship for Brittney had ended when the "legally separated" attorney went back to his wife. "I'm focused on my career right now," she answered truthfully. "There will be plenty of time later for kicking it with my boo."

"Speaking of," Shayna said, looking at her watch and rising. "I'd better go. Michael and I leave first thing tomorrow for Vegas."

Brittney gave Shayna a look. "That should be interesting."

"Very," Shayna admitted. "But he's not meeting Mom right away. He has friends there, and after a couple days on our own, we're going to spend the next two hanging out with them. As far as Mom knows, we're not getting there until the twenty-ninth."

"Do you think it's going to be okay for Michael and

Jarrell to be in the same room? Remember they almost
went to blows the first time, at the Beverly Hilton."

"Michael has promised to be on his best behavior,
and according to Mom, Jarrell has moved on, too. So I
hope so."

"Girl, I still can't believe your mom is having a baby.
So how will that go? When you have a child, his or her
uncle will probably not be more than five years old! Ha!"

"It will be some kind of madness, but you're getting
ahead of yourself. There's the small matter of something
called a wedding before I entertain a baby. Let's do first
things first."

"So you'd say yes if Michael asked you?" Talisha
asked. "Considering all of the women he's had and all
of the splits still sniffing around him, you'd have no
reservations?"

"No reservations," Shayna said. "After seeing the way
he treated his mother, I'd say yes in a heartbeat, with no
doubt at all."

44

Upon meeting Michael, Beverly Powell was her typically flirty self. That she was almost five months pregnant didn't matter at all. "Wow," she said after the introductions. "You're even better looking in person than you are on TV!"

"It's a pleasure to meet you, Mrs. Powell," Michael answered.

"Oh my God, you make me sound so old. Mrs. Powell is Colin's wife. Call me Bev, or Beverly."

It was the evening of the 29th, and Michael and Shayna had enjoyed a wonderful time in Vegas. After holing up like two lovebirds at the Aria Resort, they'd joined one of Michael's college buddies who now owned a profitable technology firm and flown to Reno, Nevada, and yet another friend's palatial estate. It was Shayna's first time riding in a private jet and as they leveled off at thirty-thousand feet she'd one thought: *I could get used to this.*

They arrived back in Vegas, rented a car, and headed straight for Henderson. Shayna had been pleasantly surprised to see that for now it was just the four of them:

her, Michael, Larsen, and Beverly. Beverly and Shayna had rarely shared casual chitchat so she was almost thankful when the men took over the conversation with the topic of business.

"We should work together," Larsen said after fixing drinks. The doctor had told Beverly she could have one small glass of red wine a day. She took ladylike sips, relishing its sweetness. Shayna nursed a sparkling water and listened as the men went on. "Athletes love Vegas. I could draw up a contract for First Class Limo to be the exclusive ride for all your clients. We could also include a concierge service of sorts, say for anything that your clients needed that couldn't be found at the hotel. And I do mean anything."

"Whoa, you're rolling like that? You've got some girls on your payroll or what?"

"Yes," Beverly drawled, "or what?"

"Come on, now, baby, don't even be like that." Larsen looked at Michael. "A buddy of mine owns an exotic dance club. We're all trying to pool our resources— know what I'm saying?—and boost everyone's revenue potential. I'm talking a similar deal with some of my connections at the hotels. My business has grown steadily over the past five years and I think the next five will be off the charts!" He threw back his drink. "So what do you say? We're almost like family. Think we can do a little business together?" Just then, the doorbell rang. Michael looked in the direction of the foyer before answering, "We'll see."

A few seconds later and Jarrell walked in, accompanied by a very attractive woman sporting high heels, a long weave, and a smile as fake as snow in Southern California. After introductions had been made, Jarrell walked over to where Shayna and Michael sat on a love seat. "Hey, Michael, can I talk to you for a minute?"

"Jarrell, please," Shayna began.

"No, it's all right," Michael said, rising as he spoke. "I need to speak with Jarrell as well."

The two men went out to the backyard, into a cold, starry night. "Look, man," Jarrell said, pulling his jacket together against the chill, "I know there's no love lost between us, but it looks like you might be around for a while. And since my brother is married to Shayna's mother, that means I'm going to be here as well. I just want you to know there's no hard feelings where that whole situation is concerned. What I want more than anything is for Shayna to be happy."

"I see." Michael looked into Jarrell's eyes, searching for sincerity. Couldn't say that he found it, but he was a bigger giver of the benefit of the doubt. "No worries then, man. As long as you stay cool with Shayna, you'll be cool with me."

"Oh, me and Shayna are going to be cool. We've known each other all our lives, so nothing is going to change that."

A little bit of that benefit slipped as Michael responded, "Yeah, well, Shayna and I are very happy together. And nothing is going to change that either."

Jarrell nodded. He held up a fist. "So I say we call a truce then. Do a Rodney King and all try and get along."

Michael hesitated briefly before raising his fist to give Jarrell a pound. "Okay, then. Truce."

"Baby." Long Weave sauntered out into the frigid night, her long legs fully exposed beneath the mini that she wore. "It's cold out here. I'm afraid you'll get sick. Let's go inside."

"Nothing like a woman to take care of you," Jarrell

said. He kissed his new thing on the lips before going inside. Michael followed them in.

"Is everything okay?" a worried Shayna asked as soon as Michael returned.

"Everything's fine. We called a truce."

"Oh, good." Shayna was visibly relieved, so much so that when Jarrell offered glasses of champagne all around, she participated in the rare indulgence. That her childhood friend and the love of her life were going to try and live in harmony was a cause for celebration. As the days passed and they welcomed in the New Year, Shayna only hoped that the peacefulness would last.

45

The atmosphere in Madison Square Garden was electric. It was the U.S. Open Track and Field event, the first meet of the new year. A sold-out crowd packed the stands, and the grounds were filled with athletes decked out in their team colors, ready to set the bar for what was to come, and move themselves one step closer to being a participant in the 2016 Olympics, happening in Brazil. Still a long time away, those who hoped to make their name there had been preparing for their event since the day after the 2012 Olympics were over. Members of the California Angels were no exception. Shayna, Brittney, and Talisha were hyped about the coming year and had eagerly embraced their new fourth 4 x 100 running mate, Chantelle, for what they felt would be a record-breaking season. A former standout at the University of Texas, Chantelle had replaced Kim, who was now expecting her first child.

"Come on, Shayna!" Talisha yelled, as Shayna made her way to the starting blocks for the 200-meter race.

"Let's do this!" Brittney added, clapping her hands and nodding her agreement that Shayna could win.

Michael stood near Coach John, an unflappable demeanor belying the nerves that churned inside. For all of his finesse as a businessman, he knew that the success of these partnerships depended largely on the success of the athlete. As long as your star was shining brightly and the accolades continued, folks in the office were happy and the money flowed. But most who enjoyed success in sports were only a scandal or injury away from downfall. It was a fine balancing act, one that Michael had honed to perfection. Not only Shayna's, but also his name was on the line. The Triple S sports line was doing well, but its continued success depended on Shayna having a winning season. *Nothing to it but to do it,* he thought as the women knelt into their starting blocks. Let the games begin.

Once again, Shayna was finding it hard to pull her focus into the singular act of making it around the track in record time. This time it wasn't Michael; it was the message Jarrell had left on her phone shortly before she'd left the hotel. Her mother had cramped throughout the night and was going to the hospital. For all of the talk Shayna had done about having a brother younger by two decades plus, she wanted her mother to have a healthy baby and she wanted Beverly to be healthy as well. Having never known her father and already lost her grandmother, if Shayna lost her last connection with true family, she didn't know what she'd do.

Less than a minute later, Shayna still didn't know the state of her mother's health, but she knew that she'd won her heat and was headed for the final race two days later. Earlier, she'd qualified in the 100 meter. Now it was just up to her and her girls to secure their spot in the 4 x 100, and she was also pulling for Chantelle in the hurdle event. The Angels were on a roll, and if this week's times were any indication, it was getting ready to be a stellar year.

Shayna ended the day having dinner with her team and after returning to her hotel room to change, joined Michael on Broadway for a hot new play about the mother of a superstar R & B artist who determines to go after the dream she'd put aside when her only child gets killed. Everyone had been talking about how Patti LaBelle performed with standing O precision. Talks of Tony Awards had led to sold-out shows, but as always, Michael had a connection. They enjoyed the show from front-row seats and afterward, Michael took Shayna's hand and they walked a short distance to a hotel bar overlooking the bundled and bustling Times Square crowd. Shayna sipped hot chocolate while Michael enjoyed the subtleties and nuances of a hundred-year-old Scotch. About halfway through their casual chatter, when after a flirty remark Shayna gave Michael a coy look and shy smile as she had dozens of times, the atmosphere changed. Michael's eyes darkened with desire. He finished his drink and placed it on the table. "Come on, there's one more place I want to take you." He tossed money on the table and took her hand.

"Wait, Michael . . . where are we going?"

"You'll see." They stepped out into the crowd, reached another signature hotel, and entered its upscale lobby. They approached a lounge area spotted with comfortable chairs.

"Wait here," Michael said. Shayna watched as he walked over to the concierge. Minutes later, a nattily dressed gentleman joined them at the counter. He shook Michael's hand and listened as Michael explained something of which Shayna could not imagine. She yawned, suddenly realizing how long the day had been and that she'd run three top-caliber races. The team was flying out first thing in the morning and Shayna would be on that plane. Michael was due to stay in the city on business a couple extra days. The well-dressed man, obviously a hotel exec, walked over behind the lobby counter where people were checking in, went into an office, and came out with what looked like a room key that he handed Michael.

Shayna's look was sarcastic as he walked back toward her. "I told you that I'm not sleeping with you," she admonished just before he kissed her on the mouth. "Our flight leaves at seven a.m. and I've got to work. So just slow your roll, randy man."

Without a word, Michael reached for her hand and started for the elevator. Shayna didn't want to make a scene so she had no choice but to follow along. "What, did you get a room for a couple hours? Why didn't we just go back to your hotel?"

The elevator door closed and Michael backed her up against the mahogany wood. "You'll see," he whispered before crushing his lips against hers. He swallowed her gasp of surprise and thrust his tongue inside her mouth. The kiss was hot, urgent. He lifted her up and pinned her against the wall, searching for and finding the rapidly moistening folds just inside her thong panties. He'd just begun an exploration with his middle finger when the elevator stopped.

"Michael!"

He eased her back and managed a couple of inches of space between them when the doors opened. "Good evening," he said to the well-dressed couple who got on.

"Good evening," they replied in unison.

The couple got out four floors from the top. When

they did, Michael slid the card into a slot and pushed a button. Shayna watched in silence, wondering what he was up to. She didn't have long to wait.

"Let's go," Michael said when the doors opened.

"Where are we?" Shayna asked once they'd stepped outside the elevator. It looked like a large storage space, with what appeared to be electrical boxes, wiring, and other machinations lining the wall. "What are we doing here?" she hissed.

"I came here once as a teenager," Michael explained as they neared a door with the word EMERGENCY EXIT emboldened in red. "Heard about stories of what sometimes took place up here. Always wanted to see if what I'd heard could happen."

He opened the door and a blast of cold air wrapped around Shayna's face and slipped inside her coat. "Whoa! It's freezing up here!"

"I know, baby, but come on. It's one hell of a view, probably the best you can get outside of a helicopter or the Empire State Building. But this one is magic because it's right in the middle of all that is happening."

"I don't know, Michael . . ." Shayna wasn't particularly fond of heights, especially on a cold dark night on the roof of a building and especially when said roof was more than forty stories high. Another blast of wind hit her. "It's so cold!"

Michael led them over to a corner where the city of Manhattan lay out before them, a dazzling array of blinking lights and blaring horns. He placed Shayna against the brick and, opening his coat, he covered her with his body before snuggling them inside the leathery warmth. "Isn't this beautiful, babe?" He nuzzled her neck, pressed himself up against her. "They say that this used to be a place where dares were made. Brothahs had to bring their dates up here and sex them, and then come down with their panties as proof."

Shayna turned, making sure to keep herself within the warm confines of his knee-length leather coat. "No way."

"Yes." There were those eyes again, smoldering, twinkling like gems of pristine black onyx.

"You don't want to . . ."

He pressed himself against her, the thought of her naked butt in the cold air above the most dazzling city in the world already turning him on. "Yes, I do." He unzipped his pants and unleashed the hardened beast, proving his point.

"Babe!"

"Warm it up, baby." He pressed himself against her thigh. "It's cold." He pulled them back against a chain-link enclosure around a large, metal boxlike device. Shayna instantly felt a blast of hot air around her feet, to go with the hot piece of fleshy steel against her thigh. Michael seared her with another hot, wet kiss, grinding himself against her, reaching around her to cup her cheeks and press them even closer together.

"This is crazy," she murmured against his lips.

"Crazy is good," he replied, and then, "Take off your panties."

"No!"

"You're going to leave me hard like this? It might freeze and break off, baby."

Shayna laughed in spite of herself. *This is what he had in mind,* Shayna thought as she lifted up the ankle-length dress made of soft beige mohair. Michael had given it to her earlier, said he'd seen it in a shop with her name written on it. It had been a perfect fit, looked great with the suede chocolate boots she'd brought on the trip.

Shayna lifted her dress. Goose bumps popped out on

her naked skin, quickly replaced by the feel of Michael's hot hands massaging her butt. He slid a hand around and down and soon a determined middle finger was massaging her jewel, creating a delicious friction between the cold on her legs and the heat in between them. He kissed her, hard, long, his tongue swirling in the same way his fingers were. His hardened flesh slapped determinedly against her bare stomach even as a gust of heat from the generator wrapped itself around them. Michael allowed his pants to drop to his feet as he lifted Shayna off the ground, balanced her butt in his hands and placed her against the chain-linked enclosure. Then, with one swift thrust, he was inside her.

The contrasts were delicious: the cold air, his hot shaft, the feel of the hard chain-link against her coat, Michael's hands kneading her booty while he sucked her tongue into his mouth. He stroked her slowly, circling his hips in a lazy fashion, running a finger along the crease of her thick rear and then slipping it inside. Shayna reached back, wound her fingers around the cold metal of the fence. She felt deliciously impaled and explicitly trapped, and felt that Michael was reaching for her very core with his love, felt him growing even longer as her inner walls clenched him tighter, pulling him deeper still. Through the haze of love Shayna realized that this was the first time she'd felt him this way, skin to skin, the first time there had been no barrier between them. It felt right and good and as it should be. His log exploded into her heat, causing the furnace of their love to block out the chill of the night, and send up a fire that rivaled the skyline of the New York lights.

"Damn, that was good!" Michael breathed, as he pulled up his pants and Shayna pulled down her dress.

"That was crazy," Shayna corrected.

"But you liked it."

"Yes." Shayna laughed, her eyes twinkling with devilment as she looked into Michael's eyes. "I liked it a lot."

She picked up her purse from where it had fallen and she and Michael joined in the laughter as they headed back down to earth via the elevator with the special card that yet another of Michael's contacts had provided. *The girls won't believe this!* Shayna thought, her legs still wobbly from the impact of a Big Apple orgasm. They reached the elevator, began the descent. Shayna felt her phone vibrate. She'd totally forgotten to reset the volume and hadn't given a second thought to the fact that the phone hadn't rung all day. She pulled out the phone and was surprised to see that she had more than a dozen missed calls. She touched the screen and saw that most of the calls were from Jarrell. "Uh-oh."

"What is it, baby?"

"Jay. He's called several times." *I thought we were over this. I thought he said he'd moved on. Now here he is blowing up my phone again.* Then she noticed that one of the missed calls was Larsen's number, another was her mother's, and a third was a Las Vegas number that she didn't recognize. It couldn't be her mother because when she'd called after the meet, Larsen had answered Beverly's cell phone, told Shayna that she was asleep and that everything was fine. Shayna tapped Jarrell's number and while the call connected, forced herself to remain calm.

"We've been calling you for hours, Shayna," was Jarrell's hello.

"It's Mom." A statement, not a question. She'd heard the stress in his voice. "What's happened? Is she okay?"

"No," was Jarrell's clipped reply. "You need to get here, Shay."

Shayna felt her legs about to give way. She sank against Michael. "What happened, Jay? When I talked with Larsen earlier, she was fine."

"She woke up bleeding. He took her to emergency. They might have to do an emergency C-section. You need to get here."

"Tell Mom to hang in there. I'm on my way."

As Shayna hung up, there was no way for her to know the depth of Jarrell's anguish. It was irrational, but he felt responsible for Beverly's illness. He had once suggested that she feign sickness to get Shayna down there, alone, away from Michael. He'd thought that if he could be with her for an extended period of time, under the same roof, he could get her back. They'd somewhat put the plan in motion, dropped hints here and there, leading up to the phone call that was going to come next month, when Beverly would tell Shayna she'd been put on bed rest and needed her help. It wasn't supposed to be true. But it was. Beverly Powell, Shayna's only living relative, was in the University Medical Center in Las Vegas, the same hospital where rapper Tupac Shakur had taken his last breath. Unbeknownst to each other, both Shayna and Jarrell were praying that it wasn't the place where Beverly breathed hers.

46

"They said it's placenta previa." Shayna was on the phone with Michael, having gone to the hospital as soon as she landed in Vegas. She was still wearing the mohair dress and chocolate boots, the panties she'd shed during the tryst while overlooking all of New York still in her coat pocket. Once he'd learned what had happened, Michael had chartered a jet so that Shayna could get to the hospital as quickly as possible. She'd arrived in Vegas at two in the morning. Jarrell had picked her up at the airport and whisked her to the hospital. "She's still in danger of severe hemorrhaging; they're considering a cesarean section, even though the baby is less than twenty-four weeks. But that will likely cause major complications for the baby, so they're only going to use that as a last possible option."

"Baby, I know I told you that I had to stay here, but if you really need me—"

"No, Michael, it's okay. Larsen hasn't left the hospital and Jarrell has been in and out with his girlfriend. I called Coach, told him what was going on and that I'd be back at practice next week. I just want to stay here until everything with Mom and the baby stabilizes."

"How long will that be?"

"We don't know." Shayna looked up and saw Jarrell coming toward her. "Look, I have to go. I'll call you later." Her questioning eyes made words unnecessary. "She's okay," Jarrell said, enveloping Shayna in a tender hug. He'd done that quite often since this arrival: at the airport, when Shayna teared up after seeing her mother in the hospital (a first for this only child), after he'd accompanied Shayna to a private visit with the doctor, and now. It was an act that Shayna barely noticed; her entire focus was on her mom. But every nerve ending in Jarrell's body was on full alert, aware of everything—the feel of her hair, the way she smelled, the softness of the body-hugging dress that he wanted to remove, and the way her curves fit his frame perfectly. Every time he held her he remembered how it had been for them to make love. Every time they parted he vowed that it wouldn't be long before they made love again.

"Shayna, have you eaten?"

"I'm not really hungry."

"Yes, but you need to eat something, babe, to keep up your strength. Let's go grab a little bite, okay?"

"Okay."

A short time later Jarrell and Shayna sat in the booth of a popular diner. When they'd ordered, breakfast sounded good. But now Shayna pushed around the French toast on her plate while Jarrell made quick work of his steak and eggs. She watched him, and thought of Michael, thought back to their first breakfast in Cape Cod. And missed him.

"Don't be sad, babe," Jarrell said, mistaking the

lonely look in her eye. "Your mother is going to get better. But I want to ask you something, Shayna."

"What?"

"Would you ever give consideration to moving down here, to help your mom with this new baby?"

"Why, did Mom say something about that?"

"Not exactly, but she talked about how different it would be raising a baby now than when she was eighteen. And that was before she got hit with this complication. I mean I know you have your life in LA and all, and Beverly said that it wouldn't be right to ask you to move, that even if she did, you probably wouldn't say yes."

"So you guys have talked about it."

"The subject came up. I'm just telling you what she said."

Shayna took a bite of French toast and pondered what Jarrell had told her. Did her mother really need for her to be around like that, and could Shayna answer the call if it came to that? For sure there were a couple months that she could do it, a couple meets that weren't qualifiers. If she didn't compete in every event, it wouldn't affect her bank account, or her career. The more she thought about it, the more Shayna felt that spending time with her mother and the little sister or brother that she was carrying might be a good thing, might help them to form the type of family bond that Shayna had always wanted, the type of relationship she felt the Morgans shared. It was the first time in her life that Shayna could remember her mother possibly needing her. For some inexplicable reason, the thought felt good. "If it came to it, I probably could get some time off," she eventually said to Jarrell.

"You'd do that? You'd leave LA and move here?"

"Not move," Shayna clarified. "But I could probably

arrange to spend a good amount of time down here, get to know my sibling and reestablish a connection with my mom. The way we used to be when you and I were growing up."

"She'd like that," Jarrell said.

"You think so?"

"I know so," he assured her as he pulled out his wallet to pay the check. *And so would I.*

47

Three days passed before Shayna caught a flight back to Los Angeles. Ironically, Michael was arriving home the same day, at about the same time. They'd ridden together in his town car, to her house, where she was staying just long enough to get her schedule situated with Coach, pay some bills, check in with her roommates, and throw a few clothes together into a suitcase. Then she was heading back to the airport and back to Vegas. And even though Michael had asked her the question what seemed like a million times, the answer was the same as the first time: "I don't know how long I'm going to be there, Michael. I guess as long as she needs me."

Michael tried to remain calm. He'd told himself that he was tripping, that he was being inconsiderate given that Shayna's only living relative was critically ill. But his drawers had been in a bunch ever since he'd called Shayna's phone and Jarrell had answered. *Why had she let that asshole answer her phone?* She'd told him, but before he could stop the words, they came out of his mouth. "Tell me why Jarrell had your phone again?"

Shayna pulled—translated: yanked—a sweater off a hanger. "Why? Have you forgotten the answer I gave you an hour ago?"

"Come on, Shayna, I—"

"I told you, Michael. I had gone into the room to see Mom. My phone was in my coat, which was next to where Jarrell was sitting. I didn't ask him to answer it. I told you that I don't know why he did. Maybe he thought it was one of my roommates, who knows? Maybe he thought it was you and wanted to piss you off." She huffed out of the walk-in closet and tossed the clothes in the suitcase lying on the bed. "Looks like he succeeded."

"Baby, I'm sorry about your mom and I know he's her husband's brother, but I just don't trust that dude. He's the type who will try and take advantage of the situation."

"How's he going to do that?" Shayna walked into the bathroom, tossed the necessary toiletries into a bag, walked out, and placed them in her carry-on. She said this, but once she'd gotten on the plane her mind had gone back to the times that Jarrell had hugged her— especially the last time when she felt him kiss her cheek. She'd asked him about it.

"Girl, you're trippin'," had been his answer.

"I'm still with Michael—happily so."

"No doubt. And I'm with baby girl."

"Where is she?"

"She had to work and then she's going out of town. Don't worry about her though; we're good."

That's what Jarrell had said and Shayna wanted to believe him. And even though she felt now was not the time to tell Michael, she too had reservations about Jarrell's helpful ways. What she didn't doubt was that he loved her mother. And right now, that's who Shayna had to focus on. Bottom line.

"Remember when we first got together and I found out about *all* of your women?"

"Shayna, this isn't about me—"

"No. It's about trust. And just like you asked me to trust you when it came to all of the lovers that came before me, I'm now asking you to trust me with the one"—strong forefinger in the air for emphasis—"other man that I've had."

Her argument was sound, but this didn't make Michael feel any better. If possible, he'd put all of his meetings and appointments on hold and head straight to Henderson. But he couldn't. The event of the football season was happening in two weeks. Skipping the Super Bowl was not an option. Aside from the two clients who'd be playing in the big event, the days leading up to the Sunday prime-time game were awash with networking, partying, and lining up deals. Michael had planned to take Shayna, who along with him had been invited to sit in the XMVP-hosted suite. When the women found out he was rolling solo, especially any exes who might be in attendance, things were going to get crazy. He already knew.

He walked over to where Shayna stood zipping up her luggage and put his arms around her. "I'm trying not to sound unreasonable, baby. I know your mother is the priority. I just lo—"

He stopped.

She stopped.

Did the earth stop spinning? If Michael were getting ready to say the *L* word, then the axis on old terra firma might need to get checked!

Shayna recovered first. "You just what?" There was a hint of a smile and a sparkle in her eye as she asked this. No pressure much.

"I just lo . . . okay at the situation and—"

"That's not what you were getting ready to say!" she exclaimed, delivering this keen observation with a slap on Michael's arm.

The tension was broken. He laughed and pulled her into his arms. "Okay, I'll admit it. I love you, Shayna Washington. There, I've said it. Now, will you somehow find a way to stay away from Jarrell while you're handling your mom?"

Shayna sighed. "Hmm, now you're getting a little taste of how it feels to have somebody clamoring all over your significant other."

Good mood shifted, smile replaced. "Oh, so he *has* been trying to talk to you."

"No, Michael! I'm just saying that how you're feeling now is how I felt when we first started dating—what wiggled in just a little bit when Ms. Boobs came around the corner from your living room."

"I wasn't there, Shay." *And when I was there, I made sure the women put their tops back on.*

"I know." She raised up on tiptoes and gave Michael a kiss.

"Uh, don't you have something that you want to say to me?"

"Yes," she said. Michael smiled. "I wonder where the girls are? I need to talk with them before my flight leaves."

"Somebody considers themselves a comedian."

"Ha! I'm just messing with you, Michael." The sound of keys jingling in the door signaled her roommate's arrival. "Do you have to leave or can you hang out for a while with me and my friends?" she asked.

"I'll make time." Shayna turned to leave, but Michael reached for her arm. "I'm going to miss you, Shayna. Don't stay too long, okay?"

"Okay."

48

Beverly sat in her pink satiny tower, otherwise known as her king-sized bed. She'd just gotten released from the hospital and had been given instructions for strict bed rest. Getting up to use the bathroom was pretty much it. Otherwise, for the next eight to ten weeks, her bed was her new throne. She looked around the room and wondered how she'd gotten here. Getting pregnant to keep her husband had sounded like a good idea at the time. But things had changed in the twenty-five years since her last pregnancy. Namely, her body. She hadn't planned on being sidelined, with even less of an opportunity to keep tabs on her husband than she'd previously had. Larsen had been attentive, for the most part, but the way he'd been talking and texting on his cell phone, she wondered who else was on his mind. Shayna's visit was probably the best thing that had come out of her sickness. It hadn't been her idea, but having her daughter here had turned out to be a good thing. And maybe it was the way her hormones were fluctuating, but last night they'd connected on an even deeper level than her previous visit. Beverly had to admit that her daughter had grown up to be an amazing woman, and didn't miss the irony that she was just now actually realizing this fact.

Reaching for one of the dozen or so magazines on the bed, Beverly picked one up and began flicking through it. But she wasn't really seeing the pictures on the pages. Her mind's eye was going through the photos of her own life, memories that had been dredged up by Shayna's questions, both from her last visit and this one, memories that she'd buried a long time ago. Not so much the things that she'd shared with Shayna, which were bad enough, but that which had remained unsaid. She'd told Shayna the truth about the uncle who'd assaulted her. She left out the part about how her mother tried to help her and Beverly refused, why the reason she went to stay with her father had less to do with her being a daddy's girl, which she was, and more to do with her being wild. Wanting sex, liking it, and not wanting to be under her mother's strict hand. Beverly's father had taken her in and then pretty much left her alone. He was too busy setting up his own house to notice what was going on in Beverly's world. Shayna had not been her first pregnancy. She didn't feel her daughter needed to know that either. It was a secret that not even Big Mama knew about. Beverly knew that she hadn't been the best mom, and wasn't the best daughter, but she also knew that at all times of her life, at any given moment in her past or her present, she was doing like everybody else was doing . . . the best that she could.

And it wasn't all bad. Lying back, she thought of what had turned out to be a great time. Shayna's recent visit.

"How are you feeling, Mom?"

It was after midnight, but because sleeping was just

about all she'd been doing, Beverly was wide awake. "I'm okay. Where's my husband?"

"He said he had to make a run. One of the drivers called in sick."

"Where's Jarrell? Why didn't he go?"

"We sent him to get the food, remember?"

Beverly nodded, then winced a little as she shuffled the pillows.

Shayna was immediately by her side. "Hold on, Mom. Let me help you."

"I would rather Jarrell had done the run. I want Larsen here. Where I can keep an eye on him."

Given her mother's condition, Larsen's faithfulness or lack thereof was the last thing that Shayna wanted to discuss. But clearly her mother had other ideas. "Why do you think he's cheating? Maybe he's working, just like he said."

Beverly snorted. "I see there's still some things about men you need to learn."

"Not all men are bad, Mom." She talked about Michael, and shared some of what she'd learned about his father, Sam Morgan. "You've never wanted to talk about my father, Mom. Why not?"

"Oh, Shayna . . ."

"I'm not asking for a year-by-year account of his life. Or even about your relationship with him. But no matter what you felt about him, he was my father, Mom. You're getting ready to have Larsen's child. Would you not want the baby to know its father? Unless there's something dark, or evil . . . like he was a rapist or murderer or something. And even then—"

"No, Shayna. He was none of those things." Beverly let her head fall back. She looked at the ceiling so long that Shayna thought she wasn't going to answer. "I loved your father," she said at last. One tear rolled down her face, and then another. And then her mother was sobbing, with her head in her hands.

"Mommy, I'm sorry. I didn't mean to upset you." She climbed onto the bed and over to her mother. She hugged her before repositioning the pillows and running her hand over her mother's shoulder and back. "Shh. We don't have to talk about it."

Beverly gazed at Shayna through her tears. "Yes, Shay. We do need to talk about it."

"But it's making you so upset. Why would you want to continue?"

"Because there is something I need to tell you. Something you need to know."

"What's that?"

Beverly looked away from Shayna as fresh tears followed. "I don't know any other way to say it except straight out." Shayna's heartbeat raced as she thought of the possibilities. Had her mother been raped, and that's how she was conceived? Was her father also a relative, and was she the product of a sexual assault? In the span of a few seconds she thought of one outcome after another, each one worse than the next. But nothing prepared her for the truth when her mother spoke it.

"Shayna, your father is alive."

49

Your father is alive. The words were an ongoing mantra in Shayna's ears, continuing well after the conversation with her mother had ended, a long time past when she'd left the room so that her mother could sleep. Four simple words, yet their combination so impacted her world that there was barely room left to breathe, none left to think. Shayna knew this because from then until now she'd tried to process the words her mother had told her, had tried to go from realization to rationalization, tried to figure which emotion she should hang on to the longest: anger, sadness, confusion, all of the above?

Your father is alive.

She had not even cried yet, and she felt she should. All these years that she'd longed for him, had ached for knowledge of the other half of Shayna, dreamed of what it would have been like to talk to him, hear his voice, know his full name. *Not what it would have been like, what it will be like.* Maybe it was the impending birth of a life from a man whom Beverly loved and wanted to be around the child, maybe it was her love for Larsen and desire—no, desperate need to keep him—that had finally loosed this particular part of her mother's tongue from the place of secrets it had occupied for twenty-five years. Whatever the matter, Shayna now knew more than she ever had about the man who helped make her: Antonio Bell, whom most of the world called Slick.

"I met him at a club," Beverly had told her. "I was barely out of high school and he was twenty-five." Shayna hadn't missed the irony that she was learning this truth at the age her father had been when he and her mother had met. "I was crazy about him right away and even though my friends warned me not to do it, I got with him that very night. We were hot and heavy, and then I was pregnant. Everything happened so fast, which is why I had no time to learn that he was married, with a baby already on the way.

"I was so in love with him, Shayna. Your father was my life, my very breath. I told him I was pregnant, and that he would have to make a choice—her or me. He chose her, and it devastated me, took me to a place I never thought I could be. I hated him, for years, and wanted to hurt him the way he'd hurt me, which I'm sorry to say that I used you to do. I saw him one day, shortly after you were born. When he asked about you, I lied and said I'd miscarried. He didn't learn about you until almost a dozen years later. By then he was locked up, so it was easy for me to ignore the messages he sent through his cousin, my only remaining contact to that life. Several years after that, he stopped trying to contact me. And I tried to forget the awful thing I'd done."

"But all those years I asked about him, how could you tell me he was dead?"

"I never said that word."

"You implied it! 'The streets took him.' That's what you said. When you said there was no way I could ever see him, that he was gone forever, what did you think that would mean to someone who was eight, ten, fourteen years old!"

A premature contraction had happened then, doubling over Beverly and ending the conversation. Well, almost. Shayna did have one more question before she left the room. "How do I find my father?" to which Beverly had replied, "I'll help you." And Shayna gained a parent . . . just like that.

"Why are you sitting in the dark?" Shayna hadn't heard the front door open, hadn't been aware that Jarrell had walked into the room. "Is it Beverly? Did something happen?"

Shayna snorted. "Beverly's fine."

Jarrell walked over to the light switch and turned the dimmer to its first position. He continued across the room and sat next to Shayna on the couch. "Doesn't look like you're fine."

"I've been better."

"What happened, Shay? Something with you and your dude?"

Shayna slowly shook her head. She hadn't even thought of what this news might mean to her career, and to her relationship with Michael. With information available at the tip of one's finger about all of the world and everybody in it, there were a thousand ways that this news could get out. *How will Michael feel knowing that the father of the woman he's dating is a felon? How will my sponsors feel? Will the Triple S brand be affected and if so, how?* And then Shayna realized that in this moment she didn't give a damn about how the public, her supporters, or her boyfriend would feel. This was an "all about her" moment right about now.

Jarrell inched closer. "What happened, Shay? You're scaring me."

Shayna's eyes were wide and fearful as she turned them on her childhood friend and ex-lover. "My father isn't dead, Jay. I found out tonight that he's in prison. He's been alive all of these years, Jay, all of this time." With that simply delivered truth, something burst inside Shayna's chest and one lone tear gathered at the corner of her eye. It felt so good falling that another one joined the party and soon she was letting out the anger and frustration and surprise. And she was doing so wrapped in Jarrell's arms.

50

Michael sat in the coolness of his shaded patio, watching the ripples of water cascade over the edge of his infinity pool. It looked so peaceful, that blue liquid ribbon, totally unlike the tumultuous fire burning in his heart. It had been thirty minutes since he'd gotten off the phone with Shayna. And still, he hadn't moved. Of course he'd been shocked to hear the news of Shayna's father. But that wasn't what had bothered him the most. What had him now fuming was how many times in the retelling of the last two days' chain of events Jarrell's name had been mentioned.

"The next day we all talked about it," Shayna had told him. "Me, Mom, Larsen, and Jay."

"Why would you want to discuss something so personal with them?" he'd asked. *And not me first,* he'd also wondered but had not voiced.

"Because," Shayna had continued after a patience-inducing sigh, "Larsen and Jay grew up in the same neighborhood as us, and their dads (because each of them had a different one) knew some of the same people as my father. Jay called his father and it turns out that his dad knows my father's cousin, the one with whom Mom lost contact so long ago. He's going to try and help us find him, the cousin. So that I can get in touch with my father."

Then Michael had heard Jarrell's voice, low and muffled. "Thank you," had been Shayna's reply. Michael was still trying to figure out what it was he'd heard in her voice. Gratitude? Affection? He couldn't tell.

Michael's phone rang again. At least a dozen calls had been ignored since talking with Shayna, and that was just from the BlackBerry on the patio table. He'd also heard his landline and God only knew how many calls he'd missed on his phone, the one he used mostly for office and clients. The others he'd not wanted to talk to, but after glancing at the ID, picked up the phone. "Hi, Mama."

"Hello, Michael. You must be at the office."

"No, I'm at home."

"Then why aren't you answering your home phone?"

"I'm out back, on the patio."

A pause and then, "What's wrong, son?"

Michael told her. About the news of Shayna's father and about Jarrell's role in helping her contact him. "He supposedly has this girl in Vegas, and no interest in Shayna. But that's not what my gut says, Mama. I don't trust him around my girl."

"It's not him you have to trust, son. It's Shayna. Does she know how you feel? Have you even told her you love her?"

"I did, and she didn't say it back." Michael realized his voice was precariously close to sounding like that of a two-year-old, but that was the least of his worries at the moment.

"Sounds like you need to step up your game."

"You think I should go to Vegas?"

"I think you should do more than that. I think you should find a piece of jewelry to go along with those earrings you bought her."

Michael ended the call, thinking about what his mother had said. He tried to look at the situation from Shayna's perspective and realized that when he did, some of his anger faded. Here she'd found out the kind of news that was earth shattering and life changing, and all he'd been consumed with was the fact that her ex and not him had heard the news from her first. *How must she be feeling now? What was she going to do?* Thinking of Shayna and the surprising news about her father turned his thoughts toward Sam Morgan. So many memories, such a large part his father had played in his life, from the very beginning. Their activities had been varied and many: hunting, fishing, trips to the beach. But more than anything, sports had been the constant that had made him and his dad so close. All of the boys loved sports and played sports. But Michael was the only one for whom sports was a passion bordering on obsession. He remembered staying up nights, talking stats with his father, never tiring of hearing his dad tell stories about how he'd been a great football player and had almost turned pro.

Tears came to Michael's eyes and fell as he remembered those good times, those heartfelt conversations, the wisdom and lessons his father had imparted to him. As he wiped his eyes, he realized that it had been a long time since he'd cried for his father. And in that moment he realized something else. He also cried for Shayna.

51

"Happy Valentine's Day, baby." Michael leaned over and brushed his lips over Shayna's.

"Thank you, Michael. This is so wonderful. Happy Valentine's Day."

This lover's holiday had fallen on a weeknight, but that had done nothing to dampen the mood of the diners in the exclusive Foundation Room. A mostly members-only area atop of Mandalay Bay, the plushly designed interior was a paradise of East-meets-West, understated and elegant, with a sweeping view of the colorful Strip. Conversation had been hushed, and glances telling, as those fortunate enough to get a coveted reservation on this, the most popular of nights for the award-winning restaurant, had not been disappointed. Amid the teal heavy velvet curtains, priceless Oriental rugs, stark white linens, and silver changed after every course, came some of the best food Shayna had ever eaten: jumbo lump crab cakes, "street" tacos filled with Maine lobster, Angus beef tenderloin, creamed Swiss chard, sherry-braised mushrooms, truffle macaroni and cheese, and now, the pièce de résistance, a molten chocolate cake oozing with don't-even-think-about-the-calories goodness. Michael had arrived in town just before seven. Since the start of their dating, this was the longest the two had been apart, just over two weeks. He'd picked her up at Beverly's house, taken her to a showroom for the custom-designed dress and shoes she now wore, and continued on to this fancy restaurant—its ambiance as luxurious as the wine that Michael drank and Shayna sipped. Conversation had been easy, mostly about the Super Bowl and his time spent in New Orleans, a new client he'd picked up and another who, after a seventh arrest, he'd finally dropped. Shortly before the dessert course, conversation wound back around to Shayna, Vegas, her mother, and Jarrell.

"Your mother must be climbing the walls, having to stay in bed all day."

"It's driving her crazy, especially not being able to come and go"—*run after her husband*—"as much as she'd like. Larsen lost a couple drivers and his business hasn't slowed since the holidays. It makes for long work hours, which Mom doesn't like at all. Thank God that Jay has been there. He's helped me keep her calm about the situation and focused on staying positive until she has this baby."

"Why, what is there to be negative about?"

Shayna hesitated for a moment before taking Michael into her confidence. "Mom has been suspecting Larsen of cheating for a long time. That's one of the reasons she got pregnant, as a way to keep him." Michael shook his head. "I know, it's the age-old go-to that women have used since the beginning of time."

"And one that hasn't worked since then."

"Exactly. But it is what it is, and for now, Larsen seems to be focused on work and his family. Jay has been honest with her, admitting that Larsen hasn't been above a booty call here and there, but assuring that my mother is where his heart is. For now, she believes him."

"When is the baby due?"

"In April."

"I miss you, baby. Please tell me that you don't plan on staying until then."

"No. I talked to Coach and he needs me back there. The next Classic series meet is in Colorado Springs. Because of the altitude, we've got to train differently. I have to be back at work next week. But I'm worried about my mother. We're closer now than we've ever been. It's going to be hard to leave her. I'm thinking about doing the Classic and a couple other events and then taking a leave for two or three months after the summer meets are done."

"To live here? In Vegas?"

"It's not that far from LA. Just a forty-five minute plane ride. Maybe you could come down here when your schedule permits and I could visit you like every other weekend."

"Every other weekend? Let me ask you something, and no, I'm not trying to be upset or upset you. I just want to know something."

"What?"

"Does Jarrell know that you're planning to do this?"

"Yes, but only because Larsen is his brother and they've talked about my mom."

"Did your mom ask you to come down, or did Jarrell?"

"Jarrell did, but that's only because he knew it was what my mom wanted."

"Baby, it's what he wants."

"Remember when I found out about all the women

and the phone numbers and you asked me to trust you? Well, now that's what I'm asking you to do for me. This is something that I want to do as well. It will help me get closer with my mother, and to bond with my little brother."

"So she knows it's a boy?"

Shayna nodded. "I know you might not be one hundred percent in agreement with it, but since losing my grandmother, strengthening my relationship with my mother—and now that I've found him, my father—is very important to me."

Michael reached across the table. "That's why I'm here, baby. So that you don't have to face situations like this alone. Even before you told me this, I had talked to Mama about it and she had an idea."

"You talked to your mother about my mom's pregnancy?"

Michael nodded. "More specifically, the bed rest. Mom suggested I hire a nurse to stay with your mom until she's had the baby. I've already talked to Gregory and he's putting out some feelers at the hospital. How does that sound to you?"

"Baby!" Shayna rushed over to hug him. "That's such a wonderful idea!" When she pulled back there were tears in her eyes and as she sat back down, her joy had been replaced with worry. "But a full-time nurse is going to be expensive. I can't believe you'd do all of that for me."

"I'd do that and much more," Michael said. "I told you, baby. I love you."

This time it was Shayna who grabbed Michael's hand. "And I love you, Michael Morgan. I really do. I love you." She kissed him and then asked, "Would you be okay with me staying a little while in Vegas?"

"We'd have to look for a house or a condo," he said with a sigh. "And I'd have to coordinate it with my schedule."

"Why?" Shayna asked, truly perplexed.

"What do you mean, why? Because I'd be living down here with you, of course."

"Is that so?"

"Yes, that's so. Do you have a problem with that?"

"No, Mr. Morgan," Shayna said, kissing him again. "No problem at all."

52

A week later, Shayna left practice and headed to her mailbox on National Avenue. Since most of her bills were paid online and the utilities came directly to the apartment, this trip was a rare occurrence. But Shayna had gotten the box while still in college and because she'd had the address for so long and the rent was so inexpensive, she kept it. It had been her most stable address to date. She walked inside, unlocked the box, and retrieved her mail. As expected, most of it was junk this and "to occupant" that. But there were a couple items from USC, including that year's alumni gathering, and also a note reminding her that her latest dental checkup was way past due. She stopped at the large trash receptacle near the boxes, discarding the sale fliers and letters to the current resident. She was just about to toss two such addressed envelopes when she noticed a smaller, thinner envelope between them. She pulled it out, curious as to who would be writing her using something as archaic as a ballpoint pen. She turned over the envelope and read: *This correspondence is being sent from an inmate at California State Prison,*

Solano. Shayna's heart slammed against her chest. In the ongoing concern for her mother's health, she'd almost forgotten about the letter (more of a note actually) she'd written to her father—and then mailed before she could lose her nerve. It was simple, to the point, containing only five lines:

> *Dear Antonio:*
> *My name is Shayna and I am Beverly*
> *Washington's daughter. Until a few days ago, I*
> *thought you were dead. I am twenty-five now,*
> *and would like to meet you. I have so many*
> *questions. If possible, please contact me.*
>
> *Shayna*

It was possible, evidently. He'd written her back. Her hand began shaking as she turned the envelope back over and read the front, upper left side:

> *Antonio Bell, #91437*
> *PO Box 4000*
> *Vacaville, CA 95696-4000*

She noted that he'd spelled her name correctly, not changed it to *Shana,* the way some people did. His handwriting was strong, the strokes bold and slanted to the right. The pen he used held black ink. To Shayna the way he wrote his numbers hinted at his need for individuality. His number four was closed at the top, the way she made hers, and his seven had a line through it, British style. There were no loops or curlicues to his penmanship. She imagined him to be a straightforward, cut-to-the-chase kind of guy. The *i* in *Antonio* wasn't dotted. Did that mean anything? Should Shayna stop

dotting her *i*'s? she wondered. Hadn't even met him yet
and already she was trying to find ways to be like him.
Was that a good thing? She wondered about that, too.
One thing that didn't need to remain a mystery was the
contents of this letter. She hurried to her car, took extra
care in opening the envelope so as to preserve it for all
time, and reached inside. She carefully unfolded the
paper. A picture fell out. She picked it up and saw eyes
like hers, and a nose like hers, and a smile. The dark-
hued man sat on what looked to be a picnic table. He
had on a light-blue shirt, a white T-shirt, and blue jeans.
After staring at the picture for untold minutes, she
placed it on her dash and picked up the paper. The letter
had been written on a piece of paper torn from a note-
book. It filled every line on one side of the page.

Dear Shayna:

*I can't tell you what it meant for me to get
your letter. I've thought about you every day of
my life, wondering how you were, who you were,
hoping that you were okay. I don't know what
your mother told you about me, but from the time
I learned of your existence I tried to become a
part of your life. After your mother's second
marriage—WTH???—when she moved to
Louisiana, my cousin lost contact with her. And
after many years of trying to find her and you,
I'm sorry to say that I gave up. But I never lost
the hope that I would meet you. That's why
receiving your letter brought tears to my eyes.*

*Your letter stated that you have many
questions. That's understandable. So do I. I hope
that one day soon we can meet, and have a
chance to sit down and get to know each other.*

I know it's a long time in coming, but I feel it's never too late to start something new. Wow, I'm finally connecting to my daughter. Today is an answered prayer.

For now, I'll say this. My full name is William Antonio Bell. I was born in North Carolina, but my family moved to Los Angeles when I was two. I don't remember the South at all and have never been there. I went to Crenshaw High School. I loved sports and excelled in football. I was a running back and when I hit the straightaway, no one could beat me. I could run the forty in under 4.5!

I could have gone on to college ball, maybe even pro, but I got caught up in hanging with the wrong crowd, and trying to live too much life too soon. But I want you to know something, Shayna. Your father is not a bad man. Your father is a good man who made some bad choices. Maybe one day we'll meet face to face and I can share my story. If I am blessed to ever have that time come, I'll tell you everything.

Thank you so much for writing me. Please write again.

Your dad, Antonio.

P.S. Your brother, Antonio Jr., is six months older than you and lives in Atlanta.

Shayna read and reread the letter at least half a dozen times. Her emotions were as jumbled as sticky spaghetti, her mind swirling like water down a drain. Her mother had been married twice? She'd lived in Louisiana—which meant that Shayna had lived there as well? Or was that one of the times she'd stayed with Big Mama? Shayna wasn't an only child, but had a brother? And for her the most amazing fact . . . her father was a runner! Big Mama had always assumed that Shayna's talent came from her father's side of the family. And she'd been right.

Wiping tears away, Shayna reached for her phone. Her first thought was to call Jarrell, the man responsible for finding the cousin who helped put her in touch with her dad. She touched the screen and tapped the name of the most important person in her life, the person for whom this news would matter most.

"Baby," she said when he answered, "I just got a letter from my father."

"That's great news," Michael exclaimed, "really great news." Shayna could hear the smile in his voice, telling her how much he cared.

53

The next day, Shayna phoned Beverly from Michael's home, where she'd gone directly after leaving the mail center. She told her about receiving the letter and of learning that she had a brother living in the Southeast.

"Are you going to go meet your father?" Beverly asked.

"Yes," Shayna replied with no hesitation. "He's in California State at Solano, which is near Sacramento. It will be a few months before there is a break in the schedule, but we're going up at the first opportunity."

"You and Michael?"

"Yes."

"He supports this?"

"Yes," Michael replied, having heard everything because the call was on speaker. "I do."

Michael and Shayna listened as someone entered the room where Beverly was talking. A mumbled conversation ensued, with Beverly obviously holding her hand over the microphone. "Hold on a minute," she said, once she'd returned to the phone. "Jarrell wants to talk to *you,* Shayna." The implied message was to take the phone off speaker. Shayna did not oblige.

"I hear you've got good news, baby girl!"

"Yes, Jarrell. And I owe you a big thank you for helping to make it happen. I got a letter from my father."

"Word?"

"Yes." She relayed the same information that she'd given Beverly.

"Remember, baby. I'm right here. He probably knows my cousins; hell, some of them might even be in the same joint. When you get ready to go and visit him for the first time, I want to be right there. I've got you, baby. We'll get through this, I promise."

The male response was not the one that Jarrell expected. "Jarrell, this is Michael. We appreciate what you've done. Along with Shayna's gratitude, I'll add mine. But there's nowhere for you to stand by Shayna's side. I'm taking up that space."

"Jarrell," Shayna added, hoping to prevent a verbal showdown, "we had some fun moments while I was there helping to take care of Mom. But I told you then, and I'll tell you now. Nothing has changed. I love Michael. And I hope that in time you can find love, too." Shayna and Michael exchanged a glance during the long pause that followed. "Hello?"

"He left," Beverly replied. Her voice lowered as she continued. "Y'all, don't worry about Jarrell, or me either for that matter. I know I haven't always shown my support, but at the end of the day, Shayna, you need to live your life. Mama always said I was selfish and self-centered and she was right. For a long time I've used the drama I endured as an excuse for my behavior. But that's got to stop. You're your own person, Shayna. Most of the time when you thought I was mad at you, I was really jealous of you."

"But why—"

"Let me say this. I wanted the carefree childhood that you received. I wanted Big Mama to feel about me the way she seemed to feel about you. I'm just now realizing that the bed I slept in as a child and especially as a teenager was one that I'd made. It wasn't your father's fault that I got pregnant. I lied and told him that I was on the pill.

"I wanted to be the woman that you are, with something going for herself besides her looks. You've become who you are in spite of a mother like me. I just hope that one day, you can find it in your heart to forgive me."

"Don't worry about it, Mom. I already have. That started as soon as I got the letter from my father. But the healing will take a lot longer. Hopefully we'll do that together."

"I hope so. Listen, guys, the nurse just got back from her dinner break. Shayna, when do you think you'll be down again?"

"Not until after the baby arrives. We've got meets and promotional obligations back to back. But call me if you need me, Mom. I always check my cell."

"I'm proud of you, Shayna."

"Thank you, Mom."

"I love you."

"Me, too." Shayna hung up the phone, and for the life of her couldn't remember the last time she'd heard her mother say those words.

54

Today was a big day: the official launch of Triple S, Shayna's sportswear line that through 2017 would be sold exclusively in XMVP stores. Her line included running outfits, a cologne called Sprint, and the shoe idea that Shayna had conceived. It was all happening in the Big Apple at XMVP's Times Square location. Michael and the PR company he'd hired had done a bang-up job. In the week before this Saturday launch, Shayna had appeared on the *Today* show, *ESPN, Live! with Kelly,* and the popular hip-hop show, *106 & Park*. In addition she'd been interviewed by the *New York Times, USA Today,* the *Washington Post,* and the *Huffington Post*. In the coming months she was scheduled to do a spread in *Essence* magazine and also to appear on OWN. As her manager, Michael had done everything he'd promised. As her man, he'd done so much more.

"You ready, baby?" Michael reached across the limo seat and took Shayna's hand.

"I think so." She looked down at her vibrating phone. "Ah," she said once she'd tapped the message icon. "Coach and his wife send me their wishes." Always

proud and supportive of his team, John had assured her
if not for the any-day-now baby on the way, he would
have been there.

"Good man right there."

"Yes, he is." At times, Coach had felt like the father
Shayna had never known. "Wish he were here to calm
my nerves!"

"Just be yourself. You'll do fine."

"I kinda wish Mom were here."

"You know she'd be here if she could travel."

"I know." Shayna also realized that the phrase her
grandmother often spouted—"God may be working in
mysterious ways"—was particularly fitting right this
moment. Because had Beverly made the trip, Larsen
would have accompanied her and Jarrell more than
likely would have come along for the ride. Much too
much drama. As it were the entire event was being
videoed. She'd make sure that her mother got a copy of
the DVD.

They turned the corner and Shayna's eyes widened.
Is all of that crowd here for me? The answer came as
soon as the driver opened her door and she stepped out
of the car. Photographers began screaming her name
and girls with gold-medal dreams in their eyes began
pushing pieces of paper in her direction.

"Baby," Michael said, reaching into his pocket and
handing her a pen, "sign a few on your way in."

Unexpected tears came to Shayna's eyes as she
reached for the first piece of paper. Never in her wildest
dreams did she ever imagine herself a celebrity or role
model, someone from whom anyone would want her
signature. She remembered being a child and watching
other athletes sign autographs for their fans, something
that always appeared so cool. And now, here she was,

looking into the eyes of a little cocoa cutie with long braids and braces who appeared to be about ten years old, thinking, Shayna imagined, that someday she too could bring home the gold.

After smiling and waving to the crowd, Shayna continued into the store, flanked by Michael, Michael's assistant, Keith, the PR rep, Choice McKinley-Scott from Chai Fashions and the designer behind the running gear and jogging outfits bearing the Triple S logo: Shayna's Sprint Sensations. It was a good thing Michael had warned her, otherwise she would have been stopped in her tracks by the larger than life picture of herself running along the back wall. The day wasn't totally without surprises, however, as she found out when she rounded the corner and saw several of her teammates and her BFFs!

"Tee! Britt!" Shayna made quick work of the distance between her and her friends. "Why didn't you tell me y'all were coming?"

"Because it was a surprise, silly," Tee said, giving Shayna a hug.

"Girl, you are doing the damn thing," Britt whispered with a squeeze.

"She's right, Shay. This is crazy, girl." Talisha looked beyond Shayna and smiled. "'Bout time y'all got here!"

Shayna turned around and saw Kim and Patrick heading in her direction. "Wow! This is amazing!" She hugged them both. "Thanks so much for coming, guys. This means a lot."

"Thank Michael," Kim replied. "He's the one who rounded us all up and set us up with the travel agent that gave us group rates."

Shayna turned to thank Michael only to find that he'd gone across the room and was talking to the store manager with whom they'd had dinner last night. She turned back to Talisha. "Cameron couldn't come?"

"No, he couldn't get off work. He's happy for you, though; wanted me to tell you that dinner was on him when we get back home."

"Ah."

"You'd better take him up on it, too, 'cause you know he's tighter than a fat lady's girdle."

"Ha!"

A pair of arms wrapped around her. Shayna would know that scent anywhere, and even though the move had surprised her, there was a smile on her face as she turned around. "What's with the PDA?"

"Can't I give my baby a hug and tell her how proud I am of her?"

"I thought we were keeping the fact that we're dating on the down low." While this hadn't been the official position, more than once Michael had alluded to not giving off the appearance of mixing business with pleasure. Yet here he was nuzzling her neck in full view of the cameras as if it were the most natural thing to do.

"Maybe it's time we change that."

Further conversation was interrupted as Dina and her team mounted the temporarily erected stage. "If I can have your attention," Dina began, after she'd signaled the DJ to lower the volume of the hip-hop music pouring through the speakers. "On behalf of XMVP Shoes and Sportswear, I'd like to welcome you to the launch of Triple S from the triple threat, Shayna Washington!" Applause and whistles sounded out, while those around Shayna high-fived. "We are absolutely thrilled to be represented not only by an athlete of her talent but also a person of her caliber. In the short time I've known her, I've found Shayna to be a person of integrity and compassion, with a keen understanding of the world's events. Which is why at her request fifty percent of the proceeds from today's sales will go to benefit those still recovering in earthquake-ravaged Haiti." More whistles. More applause. "We'd also like to recognize Chai from Chai Fashions, whose talent is behind the stylish yet comfortable looks that make up the Triple S line. Shayna will be up to speak later, but right now please enjoy the buffet, drink from the champagne fountain, and most importantly . . . buy, buy, buy!"

With that admonishment, the music revved up, the crowd around the stage disbursed to shop, and for the next hour, Shayna was pulled here and tugged there: photographed, interviewed, and complimented on the successful launch. Heady stuff for a once shy girl from Inglewood who'd been told by her mom it was more important to get a man than get a job. The hug from Michael hadn't gone unnoticed and more than one reporter had inquired of their relationship. "We're very good friends and business partners," had been her pat and coy reply.

At the end of the successful evening that included a fashion show, Dina once again graced the stage along with Michael, the Times Square store manager, and other company brass. After she'd gotten their attention, she spoke into the mike. "Ladies and gentlemen, without further ado, the star of the evening, Shayna Washington."

Shayna nodded, smiled, and gave little waves as she mounted the stage and walked to the podium. Laughing out loud, she gave a look to her "crew," who were whistling and hollering like the fools that they were and the ones whom she loved. "Wow, thank you," she said sincerely when the noise had quieted. "I normally do my talking on the track so . . . this will be quick."

"Just like you, Shayna!" someone yelled.

"Thank you. Um, I'd like to thank Dina DeVore and all the people at XMVP for allowing me to represent you and to introduce my line through your popular establishment. I'm especially proud that part of the proceeds will benefit the children in Haiti, providing shoes to those who don't have them and food and clothes for those in need. Thank you so much. My coach isn't here, but I want to shout out to him, John Joyner; my California Angels teammates, especially Brittney, Talisha, Kim, and Chantelle; and also my mom, Beverly Powell. Lastly, I'd like to thank my manager, Michael Morgan, for making this all possible." She looked at Michael. "Thank you." And then to the crowd. "Thank you all for coming. Thanks so much."

As the audience applauded, Michael came to the stage. He gave Shayna a light hug before approaching the mike. "As you all know, the foundation for the Triple S line is the lightweight running shoe that hopefully all of you will be purchasing tonight. Shayna's expertise as a runner was invaluable in the designing of this footwear, which is lightweight yet durable, with an innovative tread and nonintrusive heel and toe support. She was a part of the process from start to finish. What she doesn't know, however, is that there is one part of the design that, until now, we've kept hidden from her. Dina . . ." He turned to the marketing VP who in turn nodded to an assistant holding a shoe box. The assistant brought the box to the stage. "How many of you remember the famous gold shoes worn by track star Michael Johnson?" A few hands went up. "Well, after tonight, there's another pair of famous shoes you'll instantly recognize on the racetrack." He turned with box outstretched. "Shayna."

Shayna frowned slightly as she took the box. *Didn't we discuss this? And didn't I tell you that I didn't want any sparkly shoes?* Cautiously lifting the lid, she looked down on the coolest pair of shoes she'd ever seen. Michael had catered to her wishes. The shoes weren't gold, silver, or even iridescent. They were see-through, made of a thin yet sturdy mesh-like material with a solid toe and heel! The only nod to pizzazz was found in the shoelaces, which were white and covered with small Swarovski crystals. "Wow," she quietly exclaimed, holding up a shoe for the crowd's observance. Reactions ranged from oohs and aahs to claps and cheers. Again, Shayna felt teary. Such a classy gesture, these shoes. She looked at Michael. *I really love that man.*

"Try them on!" someone shouted.

The crowd cheered her on. Someone brought a chair up on the stage. Shayna sat in it and reached for the first shoe to try on. She was just about to pull the lace when she noticed one sparkly stone that was quite a bit bigger than the ones covering the lace. *Oh, maybe that's like a tassel. Cool!* She pulled at the "tassel." A band prevented the string from coming loose. Shayna's eyes widened. *No. Can't be.*

Before she could wrap her mind around what she thought she saw, Michael was before her. On his knees. *What?*

"Shayna Washington. I've been running away from marriage for a long time. And the journey has led me straight to you. I'm through running. Will you marry me?"

55

"Umm . . . you taste good." Michael lifted his head from between Shayna's legs, where he'd just licked creamy caramel icing from her mound. "I think I want some more." He reached over to where the now melting sundae sat on the nightstand, scooped up a spoonful of ice cream, chocolate, caramel, and nuts and placed it on her heat.

"Ah!" Shayna shuddered as the cold cream hit her nub.

Michael chuckled as he reached for one of the cherries languishing in the ice cream bowl, used it to swirl the ice cream around her love button, dragging the cherry between her folds, enjoying the quick intakes of breath as his love tried to hang on to the remaining shreds of her sanity. They'd been at it for well over two hours, ever since they'd left the sports store, declined late dinner invitations from retail execs, Dina DeVore, and Shayna's besties, so that they could order room service instead. The meal had started out innocently enough: steak, potatoes, broccoli, rolls. Assuaging Michael's sweet tooth is where things had gotten naughty. He ate the cherry, spread Shayna's legs farther apart, and licked the melting ice cream away before it could hit the sheets.

"Ooh, baby, wait." Shayna pushed Michael's head away from her, believing that otherwise she'd die from pleasure without having traveled to Brazil to run in the 2016 Olympics. But it wasn't only that. It was the fact that she'd had a thing or two in mind herself when that ice cream was ordered, things she wanted to implement before the delicious dairy melted or ran out. "Lay back."

A lazy smile graced Michael's face as he followed his new fiancée's instruction. His engorged flagpole twitched and fluctuated as it rested against strong, hard abs. Shayna wrapped one hand around Master P, reached for the spoon and scooped up some of the sundae ingredients with the other, and ladled them on the massive tip with the precision of a sculptor. Then tossing the spoon onto the covers, she bent down her head and traced the tempting tip with her tongue before pulling his prize inside her mouth and licking it clean. Michael hissed long and low; his hips rose and fell of their own accord. Shayna enjoyed the feel of power as she ran her tongue from base to tip, outlining the thick vein that throbbed, sucking the mushroom into her mouth, massaging the length of him with her hands. Over and again she took in his piece, bobbing her head up and down to a rhythm that only she could hear, running her nails across Michael's skin: his thighs, stomach, and up to his chest.

She would have gone on forever but this alpha male could only be dominated for so long. He gently eased her head away from him, motioning for Shayna to move up, slide down, and then hang on for the ride. She did and he did: bouncing, grinding, moaning, moving, each trying to give the other all of themselves, to communicate a lifelong message in an age-old language. Skin-to-skin slapping was the only sound, aside from Michael's low moans and Shayna's quick intakes of breath. She would have done a Bill Pickett rodeo proud, so expertly did she ride his pony. He held her hips, thrusting himself off the mattress, trying to push through to her very core, to brand every part of her body with his own, to show her love in ways that words could not. Many women he'd been with, hundreds of them, he imagined. But never before had he felt the intensity of feelings that he had for this one, the desire to provide for, protect, and preserve their love.

After several long, arduous moments during which a thin sheen of sweat broke out on each lover, Michael once again changed the dance. He sat up, giving Shayna a slow, wet kiss as he twirled her nipples with one hand and scorched her heat with the other. She shivered as he ran a fingernail between her dripping folds, tweaking her love nub, and pressing his thick middle finger inside her. His forefinger joined the middle one as he set up a rhythm that was matched with his tongue. Shayna cried out with a release that had come on so quickly she had no time to brace herself. Instead she found herself face first into the pillows, her body experiencing one spasm after another. But Michael wasn't done; the night was far from over.

He lifted her to her knees and with one long, continuous thrust, buried himself inside her. Grinding himself against her body, he kissed her back, licking the salty wetness. With an unobstructed view of her glorious ass, he placed a hand on each cheek, threw back his head, closed his eyes, and concentrated as if he were creating a cure for cancer. In. Out. Up. Down. Thrusting, grinding, loving with every fiber of his being. And later, when both had given up every ounce of strength within them, they rode one last wave of ecstasy together before floating back down to earth into a cloud of sleep.

56

Several months later

It was winter in many parts of the world, but on the beaches of Riviera Maya, Mexico, it was sunny and seventy-five with clear blue skies, turquoise water, and soft white sand. The intimate crowd of thirty people was seated at the water's edge, where a white gazebo trimmed in lilacs had been erected. The dark pink color scheme was continued in the form of bows securing the stark white draping over each chair, in the color of the bridesmaid dresses and in the groomsmen's ties. A soft murmur existed among the attendees, their voices floating across the summer breeze gathering on the wings of dusk. A red-orange sun throbbed in the distance, suspended between earth and sky, waiting to bear witness to yet another couple's promise to "remain true to each other as long as you both shall live."

Shayna stood at the back of the gathering, with her mother, waiting to make the life-changing walk down the aisle. It had been well less than a year since her mother had brought Larsen Jr. into the world, but one looking on would have never guessed that Beverly had just had a baby. Just like how people scoffed when told she was Shayna's mother. After the engagement, Shayna had gone to Vegas and shared her desire to have a better relationship with Beverly in the future than she'd had in the past. She'd conveyed how with the engagement, she hoped all thoughts, desires, and attempts at a reconciliation between her and Jarrell would end and that if not possible, she was ready to throw in the towel and love her mother from a distance. Fortunately for both of them, Beverly agreed. The birth of his son had brought about a change in Larsen Sr. He'd become more focused in his business and more attentive at home. This was great news for Beverly, but what had made Shayna want to do the happy dance was the fact that Jarrell had fallen in love with an exotic dancer turned real estate broker. They were now expecting their first child. So both Larsen and Jarrell were in Vegas, Beverly was here, and Shayna couldn't be happier.

"Your friends look nice," Beverly said, nodding toward the altar.

Shayna nodded her agreement. Talisha, Brittney, and Kim looked positively radiant in uniquely styled dresses sewn from deep-pink satin. "So do the guys."

Beverly gave Shayna a sistah-girl look. "Girl, those men are fine." And they were. Michael wore a casual, white linen suit, while the groomsmen—Gregory, Troy, and Michael's assistant, Keith—wore the same suit in black. The guests were dressed casually as well, with pink, yellow, light blue, and purple abounding.

Reaching over and clasping Shayna's hand, Beverly spoke. "Shay, I know I wasn't always the best mother to you. There were lots of mistakes made along the way. But I want you to know that I am so very happy for you, so proud to be able to share this day." She nodded toward Michael. "You got you a good one."

Shayna reached over and hugged her mother. "I did, huh?"

The ceremony was short, less than fifteen minutes, and afterward the wedding party feasted on a sit-down dinner of lobster, chateaubriand, wild rice, winter vegetables, and—as a private joke to one of the newlyweds' favorite pastime aids—an ice cream sundae cake. They danced to jazz, R & B, hip-hop, and salsa music well into the night. One of the highlights of the evening had been when Shayna threw the garter, and her crazy friends pulled the thing apart, each trying to grab it for themselves. She didn't know what she'd do without her wonderful friends, and just as Michael whispered that he was ready to leave, she knew that she had to let them know just how special they were in her life.

"Hang on, baby, I'll be right back, okay?" She walked over to where Talisha and Brittney were in deep conversation. She'd just seen Kim and Patrick getting down on the dance floor. "Okay, do I have to even ask what you two are talking about?"

"You sure don't," Talisha replied a tad too loudly. It was obvious that someone had helped themselves to the bubbly. "We're talking about those fine brothers over there, and which one of us is going to walk which one of them down the aisle."

"Uh, isn't someone forgetting about a certain man named Cameron, a man who even now is taking his real estate license test to secure your future, the only reason that he isn't down here right now?"

"You say his name is Cameron?" Talisha asked, watching as Troy twirled one of the guests around on the dance floor, laughing as his mother danced with a man named Robert. "What did you say his last name is?"

"You're crazy," Brittney said. "But she's right. Shayna, you were holding out on your friends all this time."

"I told you guys that Michael had brothers."

"Yes, but you didn't say that he had *brothers*." Brittney's eyes danced as she watched Gregory head to the bar for a drink. "You say he works at UCLA. I think a sister is getting ready to have an emergency just as soon as I get home!"

Shayna looked over and saw Michael's almost imperceptive nod. It was time for them to leave. After saying their good-byes, they boarded a yacht for a honeymoon night at sea. There, in the privacy of the spacious bedroom, they continued to make their own music, melodiously, harmoniously . . . in perfect key. They danced under the moonlight while the sounds of jazz bounced off the waves. Michael wanted to make love on deck, but the sea breeze was a little too brisk for Shayna. They went below and within minutes were naked and lying beside each other, tracing every inch of each other's skin as if it were the first time. Shayna nestled her head in the crook of Michael's arm and ran a lazy hand over his chest.

"Are you happy, Mrs. Morgan?"

"Deliciously so. Everything was wonderful; all the guests seemed to have such a great time. I only wish—"

"That your dad could be here? I know, baby."

Shayna still felt it was a miracle really, that in such a short time she'd not only established a relationship but had come to love the man who was her father. From the first visit, the first time she looked into his face and saw her own, the connection was established. They came together on the subject of track and now, without a doubt, her father was one of her biggest fans. He knew about every race she ever ran and whenever he was able to catch her on television he'd have a step-by-step replay of what she should or should not have done. At first, Shayna had to work not to get bitter at the years lost, when she thought him dead. Interestingly enough, Jackie Morgan had helped her come around. "Life's too short for any more regrets," she'd said simply when Shayna shared her pain. "Best to enjoy the days God has given you now."

"Are you happy, Mr. Morgan?" Shayna said, coming back from her thoughts to the hand now stroking her thigh.

"Deliciously so," he said, mimicking her earlier answer to him. "And I'm getting ready to be even happier in just"—he slid a finger along her wet folds, her legs already parting in welcome—"in just about two seconds." He kissed her deeply as his finger said hello to her heat and she moaned her approval.

"I didn't think it was possible to be this happy," Shayna murmured after Michael had again stroked her body like a maestro into a crescendo.

"Me either," Michael said behind a yawn. "Or this tired. You're insatiable, woman!"

"You've got your nerve!" She playfully swatted him with a pillow.

"I've got you, too, don't I? Even though it was you chasing me from the very start."

Shayna rolled over and straddled Michael's lean frame. "Oh, yeah? If I recall it was you who introduced yourself to me after the London Olympics. Not the other way around."

"You kept swinging this"—Michael grabbed her butt cheeks—"in my face. You knew I was a butt man."

"Oh, so I get it. I chased and chased you until you caught me?"

"Something like that." Michael hoisted Shayna's body and then thrust himself inside her before gently settling her onto his thigh. Shayna closed her eyes against his slow rhythm, wondering if she'd ever get enough of this man. "But don't worry, baby. I wanted you to win this event. And believe me . . . I'm not going anywhere."

1

"Mom, we've got a new coach!"

"Uh-huh," Dominique Clark absentmindedly replied, barely hearing her eleven-year-old son. Her mind was on a zillion other things: the upcoming model shoot, the rapidly approaching magazine deadline, her lovable gay assistant who'd just lost his man and therefore his mind, and right now the fact that there was nothing in the refrigerator to cook her son for dinner. Moments like these made this thirty-eight-year-old magazine executive feel that she was a much better career woman than she was a mom. It also made her value Tessa, her nanny/housekeeper who was out sick, all the more.

"Justin, you want McDonald's?"

"Yes!"

"Okay, let's go." As Dominique walked to the car, she texted one of the editors to ask about the article on being fat, fit, and fabulous. *I wonder if we've heard back from Sean Combs's people about buying the back page.* She sent off a quick text to the advertising manager as well.

All the while Dominique clicked BlackBerry keys, her son continued to prattle. "Did you hear me, Mom? We got a new coach! And he is *so* cool. He's big and tall and can run really fast, and he used to be a professional football player like for real though, Mom, like in the NFL. He played for the Oakland Raiders, Mom. The Raiders . . . my favorite team! Mom!"

"Justin! What?" Dominique buckled her seatbelt, put the car in drive, and headed for the fast-food-lined boulevard less than ten minutes from her comfortable San Fernando Valley home.

"We got a new coach!"

"That's good, baby," Dominique said, reaching to click the hands-free and answer her ringing cell phone. "Hello?"

"He hasn't called! I waited all day, just knowing that he would have left a baby-I-made-a-big-mistake message on my home phone. And that bastard didn't call, Miss Dom." Reggie fairly screeched the nickname he almost always used to address his boss. "He didn't call!"

"Reggie, you have got to calm down!" Dominique ordered in a quiet but firm voice. It was clear that her assistant, Reginald Williams, was no better now than before what she thought had been a successfully calming talk. "If a man can walk away from you, let him leave," she'd admonished. Now, here was Reggie in a Boyz II Men moment making it so hard to say goodbye to yesterday.

"You're only upsetting yourself while the man who can't see your value and is therefore unworthy is off playing kissy face with some new dude." Reggie's cries began in earnest. *Okay, that probably wasn't the best thing to say.*

"Mom, you passed the McDonald's!" Justin cried.

I don't have time for two kids right now! Yet many times that's how Dominique felt when it came to her and

Reggie's relationship, that she was the mother he never really had. She made a right, did a quick U-turn, and headed back to the Golden Arches.

"Reggie, look, I'm sorry that you're feeling so badly and I know you need to talk, but I have to go. Why don't you take a nice, long soak and try and take your mind off what's his name. We'll talk tomorrow, okay?" Silence. Dominique remembered Reggie's last breakup and how some designer suits became cloth confetti thanks to his skill with sewing scissors. "Reggie, don't even think about doing anything crazy like going over to that man's house or out with your instigating friends. I need you bright and early tomorrow and the day's going to be a beast. We'll both need to be on top of our game."

"I don't know if I'll be in tomorrow," Reggie lamented between sniffles.

"Don't start with me, Reggie!"

"I can barely breathe, boss." His voice had now dropped to a raspy whisper.

Dominique pulled into the drive-through and rolled down her window.

"I want the number three, Mommy!"

"Welcome to McDonald's. May I take your order?"

"I gave that man everything. Every part of me," Reggie emoted, and then began crying again.

"I'm sorry you're hurting," Dominique replied.

"Hello, are you ready to order?" The question crackled through the drive-through speaker.

"Mom, I want the number three with a strawberry shake instead of soda."

"Just two weeks ago he sang 'I'll Always Love You' and said I was his soul mate!" Reggie held out the word like he was Don Cornelius in a *Soul Train* flashback.

Reggie's lost his mind and now I'm getting ready to lose mine!

"Welcome to McDonald's. May I—"

"Hold on a minute," Dominique barked into the speaker.

"Mommy, I want a—"

"I heard you, Justin." Dominique threw the words over her shoulder. "Reggie, I'll call you back."

Three hours later, Dominique sat back against the headboard of her king-size four-poster, canopied bed—the one she'd had shipped from Europe after seeing it in a magazine. Her home definitely was her castle, a fact that had been very important to this former South Central projects-dweller when she'd become able to afford a place of her own. This abode was understated elegance with a little opulence sprinkled throughout. Her bed wasn't simply a place to sleep, it was a masterpiece—a place to be seen sleeping. It was made from rare pommelle sapele lumber, shrouded in silk, and draped with a politically incorrect chinchilla spread. Dominique had purchased this bed to celebrate her release from what she vowed would be the last nonproductive relationship of her life. She'd further vowed that no man would sleep in this bed unless he was "the one."

She sat there surrounded by photos slated to be included in a future *Capricious* edition, with several articles to read and approve. In this age of technology, Dominique still preferred to read the work in paper form, feel its weight in her hands, and use a red marker to highlight and comment. Glancing at the clock, she eased reading glasses away from her face and rubbed her eyes. Then she reached her hands to the heavens and gave her five-foot-nine, 175-pound frame a good stretch. She'd been up since six and now it was almost eleven. The long day had held few dull moments. She chuckled, recalling how her son had gone on and on about his new coach at school. *What was his name? Jack? Jason?* Whatever they called him, Dominique was glad that her son liked this new guy. Justin was an intuitive judge of character and didn't take to just anybody. Good male role models were just what her son needed. Dominique often felt guilty at the lack of such men in her son's life. She kept planning to get him involved in some type of mentor program, or a Boys & Girls Club, somewhere where he could be around strong men who looked like him. She wished his uncle could be more of an example, but her brother had not handled life well and had seen his nephew less than a dozen times in the last five years. Thankfully, her sister's husband, Aaron, was a good man and an example to Justin, who spent time in their Inglewood household every weekend.

And then there was her other son, Reggie. *What am I going to do with that drama queen?* After returning home from the drive-through she'd called him, refused to let him wallow in his own misery, and threatened him to within an inch of his life if he wasn't gracing the desk in front of her office by nine AM. Dominique couldn't remember when her and Reggie's five-year relationship had gone from boss-employee to friends (or mother-son depending on the day or circumstance). But at various times he'd been the girlfriend she needed to talk to or the brother she never really had. Dominique remembered how heartbroken she'd been to find out that her last lover had dipped his hands where they didn't belong. Reggie had been a comforting presence throughout that fiasco and Iyanla Vanzant, yoga, white wine, and buffalo wings had helped her heal. *I was probably too hard on him,* she belatedly thought regarding Reggie's predicament. *He was crazy about that man.* But the publishing industry was relentless, giving no quarter to breakdowns and broken hearts. Reggie Williams would just have to put on his big-girl panties. They had a deadline.

Dominique finished her work, turned off the lamp on the stand next to her bed, and slid down between luscious Egyptian cotton sheets. She adjusted the pillow under her head and snuggled the body pillow against her stomach. For a moment, more like a split second, she wished that there was someone there to wrap his arms around her, to knead her tight shoulders, or to hug her spoon-style. Dominique quickly replaced thoughts of a man with plans to have Reggie schedule a massage. Better to pay somebody to put their hands on her body, she figured, than take chances with a man who could grab ahold of her heart again and break it.

2

Jake McDonald cut a commanding presence as he walked out of the back door of Middleton Prep, crossed a lined asphalt racetrack, and stepped onto the grassy football field behind the school. At six five and 275, he stood out everywhere. Even without the height and solid build, his well-groomed head, smoldering brown eyes, luscious lips, and sparkling dimples would ensure that he got noticed. Jake McDonald was a triple threat—looks, talent, and personality. He'd been special his whole life.

"Coach Mac! I'm ready to play!"

Jake laughed and playfully slapped the shoulder of the energetic boy who'd become his shadow since the first day of practice a week ago. When he'd been hired as athletic director, boys like the one standing before him were the reason he'd also stipulated he be the football coach as well. So that he could change lives. He'd liked Justin Clark right away, had seen a bit of himself in the child's eager, searching eyes. Just as Jake stood out in life, Justin stood out on the elementary school football field. Tall and big for his age, he was also one of the few boys of color at this award-winning suburban private school, where the annual tuition was more than some folks made in a year. He'd heard from other teachers that Justin was academically sound, but it was his talent on the football field that made him popular. Jake had gleaned from school records that Justin had brought home the gold in that region's punt, pass, and kick competition and that kind of talent, along with his smarts and ready, infectious laugh, would help Justin Clark go a long way.

Jake blew his whistle, rounding up the team from various parts of the field. The assistant coach, who was also the offensive coordinator, ambled over as well. Twenty-five boys dressed in a mixture of shorts, sweats, gym trunks, and T-shirts made a sloppy circle around Jake, giving him their undivided attention.

"All right, team. These first practices are going to be all about conditioning, so get ready to run—sprints, routes, Oklahomas. And that's after you drop and give us 100 push-ups, 250 crunches, and 100 squats." Jake ignored the chorus of moans and groans, and continued. "And, since your verbal reaction tells me that what we've planned is not enough, we're going to divide up into offense and defense to work on a few basic techniques." Jake put his hand to his ear and listened. You could hear a mouse pee on cotton. "That's more like it. Guys, if we want to be number one then we've got to put in the work! Practice, heart, and attitude is what it takes to rise head and shoulders above the competition. We've got to come hard or go home. Are you with me?"

Twenty-five heads nodded and for the next two hours tried to give Jake McDonald and the other coaches everything they had and then some. Jake was impressed and let the players know how much he appreciated their hard work, which, of course, only made them want to work harder.

"How does it feel?" The assistant coach, Shawn Gallagher, moved the folders from a chair in front of Jake's desk and plopped down.

"How does what feel?" Jake asked, handing Shawn a bottled water from the mini-fridge before sitting behind the desk.

"Being a god."

Jake snorted.

"Coach, Coach!" Shawn mimicked, his green eyes sparkling. "The boys love you, man, especially that Clark kid."

"Aw, well, what can I say?" Jake drawled, straightening invisible lapels. "I'm the man."

Actually, it had been a difficult time of adjustment when Jake retired from the NFL eight years ago at the ripe old age of thirty-two. He'd experienced an unexpected bout of fame- and team-withdrawal—one moment he was part of a family whom thousands adored every Sunday, and the next moment he was sitting in his home gym minus the cheerleaders and the roar.

Shawn took a swig of water. "I noticed somebody else who wants to play on your team."

Jake raised an eyebrow. "I hope it's that Burnett kid. I know his mind is set on basketball, and his father is pushing him to just concentrate on that and track, but I think that he'd make one heck of a running back."

"It's not just his dad; Alvin isn't interested in football. But I'm not talking about him."

Jake looked up from the player chart he'd been studying. "Then who?"

Shawn's smile widened. "The new fourth-grade teacher."

"The tall brunette with those long, sexy legs?"

Shawn nodded.

"She's gorgeous, but I don't think she's interested in me. I saw y'all hanging out before the meeting started, and her looking at you goo-goo-eyed."

Shawn was a red-haired, green-eyed heartthrob with an infectious smile and charming personality everyone loved. "I wish, man," he said. "Our conversation before the meeting was friendly chitchat. But *during* the meeting she was looking at you. Which is just as well, since I think Taylor might throw a few penalty flags if she caught me flirting with a colleague."

Jake laughed. "Your wife might have a problem with that? You think?" A reminder pinged on Jake's computer. He clicked on his calendar. "Damn."

Shawn stood. "Forget about a hot date?"

"Hardly. It's this Hollywood educational benefit where I'll rub shoulders with celebrities and influential movers and shakers . . . maybe rustle up a few deep-pocketed sponsors for our program."

"That's definitely your arena, man. I'm not the black-tie type."

"Me either," Jake said, putting away the folder and reaching for his duffel bag and keys. "But duty calls."

3

Dominique ran her hand discreetly over her abdomen as she stepped into Hollywood's W Hotel's great room. Having grown confident in and comfortable with her plus-size figure years ago, she still thanked God for the body shaper that smoothed, toned, and highlighted the curves that flowed in all the right places. Her freshly done twists accented the high cheekbones in her otherwise round face and her auburn hair with gold tones sparkled under the light of the chandeliers. In this room of size twos, Dominique felt good about how she looked. She went to black-tie events all the time.

So why is my stomach fluttering?

Was it because of the stress of a deadline a week away, Reggie's continued depression, or the fried catfish with jalapeño cornbread she'd had for lunch? No matter, *Capricious* rarely missed a PR opportunity and tonight's event benefiting education was one that would get major press. When solicited last year, Dominique and the board had immediately agreed to be one of the night's sponsors and she'd also agreed to provide complementary subscriptions to one hundred lucky student winners. In an

age when girls under sixteen were having plastic surgery
and a size 10 was considered big, the magazine's brass
felt it more important than ever to tout their message:
beauty comes in all shapes and sizes, and in every
Capricious magazine! So even with a looming deadline and the knowledge that she shouldn't stay long,
Dominique had braved an hour of LA traffic to show her
support.

Secure that she was a walking ad for "fat, fit, and fabulous," she looked around, recognized the organizer
whom she'd lunched with last month, and headed in her
direction.

Someone tapped Jake's shoulder. He turned and saw a
TV host he'd known for years, a beautiful blonde who
was the ex-wife of one of his NFL buddies. They'd just
started to chat when he saw someone else—a statuesque
African American woman gliding across the room, her
chin slightly tilted as she scanned the crowd. Her formfitting copper dress showed *pow* out to here and *bang* out
to there and as if that wasn't enough to make a brothah's
mouth water, those thick, shapely calves would definitely do the job. *Dayum! Who is that?*

"Jake, did you hear me?"

"I'm sorry, Madison, what did you say?"

"I was asking if you'd seen my ex lately. I heard he got
divorced again, and quite frankly I'm worried about him."

Jake answered Madison's question but later that night
if someone had offered him a million dollars to do so, he
couldn't have repeated what he said. Big and natural
wasn't normally his type, but there was something about
the woman who commanded the room, as she'd walked

through, it that touched his soul in a deep, almost primal way. Maybe Shawn was right. Not about the fourth-grade teacher but about what he'd suggested the previous week—that Jake get back into the dating game. Jake hadn't dated seriously since relocating to LA a year ago. So maybe he did need to pull out the Big Mac skills and make a play. And maybe he needed to do so tonight.

Later, Dominique sat chatting with those on each side of her, enjoying the delicious second course of lobster bisque. The president of the foundation hosting the benefit had just done the welcome and an award-winning actor had delivered a succinct and humorous speech, and then underscored his belief in the importance of education with a check for $100,000. Several honor roll students from various districts—both privileged and at-risk—gave short speeches on what education meant to them, followed by a pop singer's rousing performance of her latest hit single. Other well-known speakers graced the stage and awards were given. By the time a short, fifteen-minute film had ended, Dominique had finished her main course. She looked at her watch and decided to skip dessert. Having made an appearance and secured a few cards for future interviews and ad campaigns, she felt it was time to go.

She said good-bye to her tablemates, including the event's organizer, and during a lull in the program Dominique stood to make her move. Walking alongside the wall and trying to be as inconspicuous as a woman who stood six foot two in heels could be, she kept her eyes downcast as she made her way to the double doors leading out of the room.

"Next on the program," she heard as she was midway to her destination, "is one of the NFL's shining stars, a man who knows firsthand how getting an education can change a life. Ladies and gentlemen . . . Jake McDonald."

The audience applauded and, thankful for the noise and distraction, Dominique quickened her pace. She was almost to the doors when she heard his voice.

"Thank you, and good evening."

The voice was deep like still waters and sweet like molasses. She'd reached the door, but turned to see the being from whom this captivating voice had emanated. The flutter that she'd felt earlier that evening returned full force and a little squiggle went from navel to nana in nothing flat. She was a sistah from the streets who could play it as cool as an ice cream float, but *Oh. My. Goodness!* The man's very presence seemed to touch her even though he was on the other side of the room. He easily filled the tall, *really tall,* dark, *really dark,* and handsome, *really handsome,* bill . . .

But it was more than that.

Dominant. That's the word that came to mind when she looked at him. And then, in a heartbeat, a few other words filtered in as did remnants from the ain't-had-none-since-dog-was-a-pup conversation she'd had with Reggie the other night, when both had had probably one too many glasses of wine. But if she was going to do what she and Reggie had discussed, it would be with someone like the chocolate candy now commanding the room. For an instant their eyes locked, and held. The squiggle became a throb that caused Dominique to clench muscles that hadn't felt action in months. She exited the room on shaky legs, walked across the lobby, and handed her ticket to the valet.

She thought of him. On the forty-minute drive home, while wrapping up work with returned phone calls and e-mails, and while taking a shower. Oh, especially then. Afterwards she performed her nightly ritual of getting in just the right position to welcome slumber—head pillow positioned just right, body pillow snuggled against her stomach. Eventually, finally, Dominique went to sleep. And dreamed of still water and sweet, sticky molasses.

The Hottest African American Fiction from
Dafina Books